Assault
on a Queen

‒‒‒‒‒‒‒‒‒‒‒‒‒‒‒‒‒‒‒‒‒‒‒‒‒‒‒‒‒

by Jack Finney

SIMON AND SCHUSTER
NEW YORK

For Margie and Kenny

During the writing of this book I was given countless and fascinating hours of help by Commander John B. Cooke, USN, Retired. His long career, which began in the early days of American submarining, and throughout which he both served in and commanded U.S. submarines with great distinction, would make a far better book than this. And if I have been able to give any feeling of reality and authenticity to those portions of this book dealing with submarining, I am completely indebted to my friend John Cooke.

I also acknowledge gratefully the hours of invaluable help which Lieutenant E. L. Rairdon, USN, Retired, who served with Commander Cooke for many years, so generously gave me.

J. F.

Prologue

FROM THE LOBBY of the little resort hotel on Fire Island, New York, a man in blue swimming trunks walked out onto the big veranda. Under one arm he carried a large, cylindrical metal tank wrapped in a tangle of canvas webbing and rubber tubes; dangling from his fingers by their straps was a pair of green froglike flippers. In his other hand, held by the heavy cord which bound it, was a bundle of rubber, a small deflated one-man raft, wrapped around a short paddle. Strapped to his strong hairless wrist, like a watch, was a pressure gauge. For a moment he stood at the head of the brief flight of stairs leading down to the sand, looking out over the wide beach at the green-white Atlantic ahead; then he glanced up at the sun, narrowing his eyes. It was nearly noon, the sun almost overhead in a clear sky, and he welcomed the warmth of it on his untanned white skin. He was a short man in vigorous middle age, his straight brown hair thick and ungrayed. His body was thin and paunchless; his calf muscles bulged strong, though corded with varicose veins; his feet, on the sand-gritted wood floor of the porch, were very flat.

"Nice day for it, Mr. Lauffnauer." Behind him the hotel clerk had appeared in the doorway, and as Frank Lauffnauer turned, the clerk nodded at the diving equipment under his arms.

"Yes, very good visibility." Lauffnauer smiled and instantly the clerk's polite friendliness became genuine, for Lauffnauer smiled with his eyes, pleasurably and responsively; all his life people had liked him for it. In repose his face seemed stern, the cheeks hollowed to flatness, the nose large and beaked; and from the base of his nose two deep, absolutely straight lines ran down past the corners of his thin mouth. Unlike his pale body, his face and neck were tanned, the skin rough and masculine. A forbidding man, people usually thought—until he smiled.

He smiled again, his long white teeth flashing, then he walked down the steps, and began to plod through the fine ankle-deep sand toward the beach ahead. It was a magnificent beach, extending for miles in either direction, and very wide; here where the sand was dry it was nearly white; ahead, where the receding tide had flattened and dampened the sand, it was a dark rich brown. The beach was almost deserted; several hundred yards to Lauffnauer's right, a young woman in a yellow bathing suit sat reading, a small child in a sun suit digging in the sand beside her. Far to the left, well back of high-tide line, an old man wearing a tan suit, a necktie and a black felt hat sat on a blanket. There was no one else in sight; this was a Monday early in April, all weekend guests gone late yesterday or early this morning.

Reaching the water's edge now, he turned to look back, studying the shore through several long seconds. Then he walked on beside the water, to the north, moving briskly on the firm, packed sand. From time to time he searched the shoreline again; once he walked backward for a dozen yards, watching the gabled roof of the hotel slowly recede. Back of the sparsely weeded dunes into which the beach rose stood an irregular line of summer cottages, all more or less alike, and typical of Fire Island in their drab, gray-shingled, weathered exteriors. He was counting these as he passed them, all of them, that is, which seemed old. The newer ones, however—and it wasn't always easy to tell which were comparatively new, they were so much alike—he omitted from his count.

When he had counted twenty-six houses to the north of the hotel he stopped at the water's edge, more than a mile from the hotel, and lowered his equipment to the sand. For a few moments he stood looking out at the ocean, flexing his arms and fingers, ridding them of strain from the weight they had carried. The water was very placid today, waveless and undisturbed except for a slow gentle swell which broke in less than foot-high waves into a thin froth running up to his feet. He had expected calm today; he was a weatherwise man, always aware of it even in the heart of the city, Manhattan Island, in which he lived.

Kneeling in the sand, he inflated the little raft from a tube of compressed gas which had been wrapped in it, and it quickly popped into shape—a sausage-sided, flat-bottomed, wedge-nosed little raft just big enough for one man. In addition to the short paddle and the gas bottle, there had been wrapped in it a weight belt, two coils of rope, one of them attached to a ten-pound concrete anchor, and a square red flag on a thin wood standard. The flag he fitted into a socket at the nose of the raft; then he loaded in his other gear, dragged the raft out into the surf, and began walking through the water, pushing it ahead of him.

The bottom slanted very shallowly here, and he walked out into the ocean for a considerable distance; several hundred yards out he was only waist deep. From time to time he glanced over his shoulder at the shore behind him; sometimes, then, he moved to the left or right, keeping the twenty-sixth house directly behind him. Finally, the water chest high, he climbed carefully into the little raft and began to paddle, again glancing regularly back at the shore to the house which was his landmark. It was hard work; the tiny keelless raft tended to revolve, and he had to switch paddle sides often. But he kept at it, stopping only once to rest. Then, finally, a mile out from shore, he lowered the concrete weight and began sounding the bottom.

He sounded, the first time, at just over seventy feet—the line was knotted at ten-foot intervals—then snubbed the line to a ring at the prow, and paddled ahead. He sounded again at over eighty feet, and the third time at ninety. Once again he glanced back over his shoulder, then shrugged and tied his line, tightly this time, with a double square knot. Anchored in just ninety feet of water, he began to put on his diving equipment, kneeling in the raft and working carefully, adjusting the straps to a nicety. He knew it would be cold in the water; it was only April, and not far below the sun-warmed surface the ocean would retain its winter chill. He would have liked to have a rubber suit, but he had rented this equipment, and the expense of this together with the cost of his room at the hotel was all he could afford.

As always, he was afraid of what he was about to do. He was an experienced diver, but he was going under in a hundred feet of water or more; in the ocean, and alone. His equipment on, the lead-weighted canvas belt around his waist, he lowered his mask over his eyes and gripped the rubber mouthpiece of the breathing apparatus in his teeth. Then he stood, his back to the water, and allowed himself to fall backward into the water, the tank on his back splashing and cushioning the fall. Face down in the water, holding onto the anchor rope, the other coil of rope in his hand, he lay just under the surface and tested his aqua-lung. For half a dozen slow breaths the chains of bubbles purred smoothly from the valve at the back of his neck, bursting to the surface a few inches above.

He raised his masked head for a last look at the far-off shore, orienting himself, then began to descend down the anchor rope through the sunlit green water toward the blackness below, his hands moving slowly and regularly down the thin white line. Eight or ten feet below the surface, the water suddenly lost its warmth, and as the chill enveloped him, he was afraid again.

Always, not far below him, was the blackness, but he never reached it. As he descended, his arms moving regularly like slow-moving pistons, the light seemed to move with him. It had changed in color to a hazed deeper green, and now he swallowed to clear his ears of pressure. Presently—he had counted the knots and was eighty feet down—the water's color changed to a yellow-green; and then he saw the bottom, of clean yellow sand, six or seven feet below the rubber-encased glass plate strapped to his face, and he grinned. He could see, he estimated, for eighty or a hundred feet in a circle around him, and now he tied the end of the rope coil in his hand to the anchor line. Then, paying out the rope as he moved, he swam just over the bottom until the rope was taut in his hand. Now, guided and oriented by the rope, he began to swim in a great circle around the anchor line of his little raft, searching with his eyes as far as he could see, glancing from time to time at his depth gauge. He saw, at first, only sand and occasional waterlogged wood fragments lying on the shimmering bottom. He was afraid, but ignored the fear and even took pleasure in the effortlessness of his motion and the strange, exhilarating absence of weight. A cluster of smooth-worn rocks slid beneath him; snug against them lay a heavy beam studded with rust-eaten spikes, and in the bar of shade alongside it, fins barely moving, he saw the speckled black body of a large fish. These things moved under and then behind him, and he stroked with one hand to curve like a seal around a tall sea-growing plant, its black-green fronds undulating in the gentle watery breeze of his passing. This was the closest to flying, he felt, to riding the wind like a hawk, that a man could achieve, and now his fear was forgotten.

For ten minutes he swam, soaring dreamlike and effortlessly over the undersea landscape, the lifelong weight of his body gone. He had seen, so far, fish of many sizes and kinds, crabs, shells, rotting logs, squat black kelplike plants or tall green ones, rusting cans, a crimson bathing cap, and he knew that presently he must ascend, taking minutes to do so, through the slowly decreasing pressures above him.

But now, on the opposite side of his circle, he moved into deeper water. The sun strong and nearly vertically overhead, the ocean's surface almost completely calm, the light came down clearly. The circle of his vision had contracted with the greater depths into which he had moved, its edges a dead black curtain. But still it was large, and the sand bottom just under his mask was still bright with green sun. He paused, swallowing to break the pressure from his eardrums, his hands and feet moving only enough to maintain his position. Then once again he thrust out with his flippered feet, eyes never shifting from the far boundary of his vision, and almost instantly he stopped, braking himself hard with his arms. For this time, finally, on the ninth day of his search, a portion of the blackness ahead had failed to retreat with the rest.

Hanging motionless just over the bottom, he stared at it, a narrow swatch of blackness protruding into the yellow-green circle of light of which he was the center. Through four or five slow breaths, the little chains of bubbles climbing over his head, he watched; it did not move nor did he. With a slow thrust of his feet, he edged closer; and the section of blackness did not retreat. As always, the remainder of the formless darkness moved ahead as he did but the narrow black strip remained behind, increasingly solid, beginning to take shape, and protruding well into the cone of shimmering green-yellow light. And now he was certain; he was staring at a sunken ship, and his breathing deepened and became more rapid, the silvery bubbles purring furiously from their vent.

Suddenly, recklessly, he thrust himself powerfully forward, dropping his rope. As fast as he could move, he flashed over the sand toward the sunken ship, then had to reach out quickly to fend himself off from the sharp prow that shot toward him through the sun-slashed green haze. His hand closed on slimed steel, and through the circle of his mask he saw the ship's bowed side curving off into the blackness beyond. He could not move; his emotions overwhelmed and confused him, and through several moments, the ascending bubble-chains thick and gurgling, he clung to the prow. Then he released his hold and began to swim slowly and cautiously along the ship's side, keeping a yard or more from it, following its bulge into the darkness ahead. Greenly but clearly, in the cone of his vision, he saw the ship's side, not rust-reddened, for no reds were visible at this depth, but evenly coated with slime and a whitish moss from which hung long tendrils swaying in the disturbed water as he moved. He swam clear around the little ship—it was no longer than a hundred feet—inspecting its sides, his excitement and certainty growing. Then, with a downward thrust of his flippered feet, he shot his body vertically upward through the green water, his masked face lifted. And now, his mask rising level with the cable-railed deck, he saw it: the tiny moss-crusted conning tower of this sunken submarine.

He knew he had to be careful; his heart was pounding, his breathing harsh, and the bubbles flashed from his air vent in a furious high-pitched and tinny purr. Both hands gripping the slimed deck-rail cable, his body parallel with the ocean floor, Frank Lauffnauer lay motionless in the water, staring at the ghostly conning tower before him, waiting for his heart to slow, keeping out of trouble until his excitement should subside.

Then, hands shoving at the deck-rail cable, he glided over the little deck and, his arms outthrust, caught one of the welded steps on the side of the tiny conning tower. Then he lowered his legs to stand on the slimed and pulpy deck grating. With the palm of one hand, he began sweeping the tendriled moss from the side of the little tower. His hand swinging rhythmically like the windshield wiper of a car, he cleared a yard-wide space from the steel surface before him and continued downward. An edge of flaked white paint appeared under his hand, and continuing to sweep aside the furry slime, he worked on down, increasing the arc of his swing, until he could read a portion of what had once been painted there. It was a *U,* followed by a dash. Then he cleared the numbers following it and stared at the whole legend. *U-19,* it read. This ancient ship was, or had been, a German submarine; and Frank Lauffnauer closed his eyes, and stood, a hundred and ten feet under the surface of the ocean, his body encased in water, blue with cold, forgetting where he was in remembering the last time he had stood on this deck.

He pictured it, he remembered it clearly in a sense; but he could not really recapture it. He remembered it, but could not recover the feeling of it—the dread and sick excitement. He could not even picture the face of the boy—the smooth unlined face of a fifteen-year-old Frank Lauffnauer—who had slammed this hatch cover shut over forty years before. Then he opened his eyes and smiled a little, shaking his head, watching in memory the vague figure of the boy who had been himself in a world in which Kaiser Wilhelm seemed supreme. Like a man watching an old and silent motion-picture film, he saw this ancient submarine, new then, floating on the surface a mile off the coast of America, off Fire Island, though he did not know that then. It was night, and on this deck stood two sailors—one of them himself, wearing a broad flat cap with long ribbons dangling from its back. They could no longer sail or fight her—there were too few of them now; he and the other man on deck—Biehler, his name was—and a waiting third man in an inflated life raft were the only able-bodied crewmen left. He slammed the conning-tower hatch closed, climbed with Biehler into the raft, and they paddled a dozen yards off. Sea water gushed into the tanks then, the air vents roaring—he remembered the sound of it—and they sat watching the deck come quickly awash, the water creeping up the sides of the tower.

The sea closed over it then, and they were paddling, so long ago now, toward the black unknown coast of *Amerika*—Lauffnauer was thinking in German—as their submarine had touched bottom, scraping the sand, under the water, far below them. He had pictured it then, and he pictured it now, slowly coating through the years of his life ever since, with silt, sea moss, and slime. He wondered what had happened to Biehler and Strang—Strang, Willi Strang, the third man in the raft had been. Whatever had happened to them, they must surely be dead now; Biehler would be over eighty, Strang nearly ninety—it seemed impossible.

He had to leave, but he did not want to. His eyes widening behind the glass of his face mask, the past dismissed, he stood for some moments in the grip of a tremendous exaltation. He had thought of the *U-19* occasionally through the years, wondering about her curiously. He had thought idly of searching for her, as he had today and for more than a week past; but the trouble and expense of doing so to no purpose but old curiosity had never been worth it. Now, forty years later, there was a purpose, a tremendous one, and he had found her, and he stood exulting, his hand almost unconsciously stroking the slimed side of the primitive conning tower. For the ancient submarine seemed in good condition—as far as he could tell, he reminded himself cautiously and superstitiously. But this was a clean bottom, swept by currents with every tide; she should be all right if her valves had held. If they had—and they might have, they just might—her interior not flooded, it was at least possible, he told himself, and grinned, that the little sub could be made operable again; no one could say. But if so— there under the ocean, he clenched his fist—it was *his* submarine, and he thanked the innate caution that had made him keep the secret of her for forty years. No one else in the world, undoubtedly, even dreamed that the *U-19* existed.

He began to climb finally, with regular slow strokes of his flippered feet, toward the surface far above. He rose slowly through the decreasing pressures toward the growing brightness overhead, occasionally slowing the speed of his ascent. Behind his mask his eyes moved regularly from side to side, watching, making sure that his body did not rise faster than the strings of silvered bubbles which rose in short bursts over his head. Presently, his masked head broke the smooth surface of the water, and he shoved the mask back, glancing around him, and saw the red flag of his raft. But he did not immediately swim to it. Staring at the shore, he estimated its distance, and by triangulation, using the big roof of the hotel to the south as one point, and a new aluminum roof glinting in the sun to the north as another, he fixed his position as well as he could. Then, knowing he could find the *U-19* again, this time more easily and quickly, he began to swim slowly toward his raft.

On the beach he lay face down in the sand, head cradled on his forearms, resting. He was very tired, ravenously hungry, and cold to his bones, his skin waxy white. But he allowed himself only fifteen minutes or so of rest, the spring sun—almost hot at midday—gradually warming his body. Then he made himself stand, deflated his raft, packed his equipment, and began to walk back along the empty beach toward the hotel. There was no more time to rest, there would be no more leisure for many days. Beginning immediately—he grinned at the thought, feeling alive again for the first time in years—Frank Lauffnauer had a crew to enlist.

Book One

One

I suppose there are unrecognized moments in everyone's life when enormous events begin with no least hint or indication of it. A man believes he is doing no more than speaking a casual sentence or two; words he might just as well not have spoken. But though he does not know it, he has taken the first irrevocable step on a road which leads to fame or disaster, misery or happiness, even death. I thought I was doing no more than walking slowly, at the end of one of the first days of last spring, toward Lexington Avenue in New York City, on Forty-seventh Street. A girl I'd met at work, Alice Muir, was with me; I'd been seeing her for the past few months.

We had met in the building lobby at five-thirty; now, a few minutes later, we were on our way to have a drink and then dinner someplace, we didn't much care where, and we took our time—it was Friday night—enjoying the walk and the day. After a month of rain and gray drizzle, this last week had been bright and sunny, almost warm; once again my hair was beginning to streak yellow from the sun, and for the first time this year I was wearing a lightweight suit of tan gabardine. This was the last date I'd have with this girl, almost the last time I'd see her, but I didn't know that, and strolling toward Lexington just ahead, I kept glancing down at her, enjoying what I saw. I'm six feet one, and she's five feet six at most; through the open-work top of her white spring hat, I could see her blond hair, and below the wide brim of her hat, the slow swing of her red-striped white skirt. She glanced up, saw me looking at her, and smiled, and her intelligent eyes softened. Then she slipped her arm under mine, and it was a nice moment to be alive in.

I suppose that sooner or later I'd have broken off with Alice, or rather she with me; in another week or so, another month. But it needn't have happened that night; we might have reached Lexington a few seconds earlier or later, when the light was green. But as it was, half a dozen yards ahead, the traffic light clicked to red, and three or four people who'd been about to cross stopped at the curb to wait.

One of them, a woman of about thirty-five, had actually stepped down off the curb, then waited, standing just on the street. An enormous amplified voice boomed suddenly from a loud-speaker somewhere. "Will the lady in the gray suit step back on the curb," the voice drawled very loudly and clearly over the traffic noise, "or she may be attending a funeral soon; her own." Then I saw the cop across the street, microphone in hand, sitting in a squad car parked on the cross street, and facing Lexington; a pygmy with a giant's voice. As we stopped beside the little cluster of people waiting for the light, I watched the woman in gray step back onto the curb again, and her face was flushed and she stood staring straight ahead, a set embarrassed smile on her lips. Just behind her, the citizens who had stayed obediently on the curb had the same smug little smiles I remembered on the faces of the good boys in grade school.

I got mad. I've been getting a little tired lately of unctuous warnings from every disc jockey and television comedian, and of printed admonitions on everything from bread wrappers to license plates, that the life I save may be my own; as though there were an assumption somewhere that most of us are idiots who couldn't survive a day without help. If my life still is my own, I'll claim the right to do as I please with it, within reason; including, certainly, risking the dangers of crossing the street without a hand on my elbow. I looked both ways, the street was perfectly clear at the moment, not a car within more than a block; and while I suppose that cop may have been doing his duty, I didn't agree that he'd been given the right to be a comedian about it. And on impulse, I gripped Alice's arm, stepped deliberately out onto the street, and began leading her across it.

Instantly, on the roof of the squad car, the loud-speaker crackled into life. "If the young couple crossing the street," the giant voice said with the slow expert timing of a Jack Benny, "wants to live to be an *old* couple—" he paused as though for laughs or applause—"they'll get back on the curb where they belong."

There was no least possibility of our being struck in those particular moments; the sun was down, but it was still clear daylight; and I continued, my hand on Alice's arm, leading her across the street. Then

I walked on a few steps, to the open window of the cop's car. My hands gripping the window sill, I leaned in and spoke to him, my mouth an inch from the stick microphone in his hand. "We've each been crossing streets by ourselves for over twenty years now, without help from the cops or the Boy Scouts," I said, my voice sounding loud and strange through the streets for a block or more in every direction. "And if we want to risk our necks, they're our own necks to lose, and nobody else's."

And so I got a summons, and a fifteen-dollar fine; the summons written out on the spot for jaywalking; the fine mailed in without protest or demanding a jury trial. I could have handled that big cop— I weigh a hundred and ninety pounds, and I'm thin—and I'd have loved to try. But of course I didn't; I stood by the car giving my name and address, signed the summons, accepted my copy, then walked on with Alice.

"Well?" she said after a few steps, smiling up at me wryly. "You satisfied, now? Had your little rebellion for the week?"

"I guess so." Then I smiled, too. "I know," I said, "it was foolish; childish."

"Honestly—" she shook her head, still smiling a little—"the things you do every once in a while. Is it really worth it, Hugh—being the perpetual rebel? You don't seem to win."

I glanced at the folded summons in my hand, then shoved it into a pocket and shrugged. "I suppose not," I said. "But it seems I have to try."

"Yes." She looked up at me strangely, her smile fading. "I guess you do."

I said, "Look, you know the head of my department retired this week?"

"Yes, I heard."

"Well, he's sailing tomorrow on the *Queen Mary;* most of the department's going down to see him off. How about coming along?"

But she shook her head. "No; I don't know him, Hugh."

"That's all right; come along with me. Might be fun, if the weather holds; I've never seen a big ship like that, have you?"

"No, but—I don't think so."

I shrugged. "Okay; but why not?"

"Well—" she hesitated a moment, then said it. "Hugh, I'm not going out with you any more after tonight."

I didn't reply for a few steps, then I said, "Why? The cop?"

"No, not really. But—in a way, yes."

"I embarrassed you, didn't I?"

She shook her head firmly. "No, you didn't; and I understand why you did what you did." She stopped on the walk, and put a hand on my arm. "But most people don't react that way, Hugh! They learn to accept things like that and shrug them off."

"There's a little too much casual interference with people's liberties these days. And a little too much casual acceptance of it."

"But not by you," she said quietly, turning to walk on. "Not by you. And to me it proves something I've been thinking about a lot lately; tonight is just one more example of it." I waited, walking slowly along beside her toward Third Avenue ahead, and she glanced up at my face, and said, "I've had a good time with you this winter, and I'd like to continue. But I don't think I can afford you any more. I'm twenty-three years old, and I'll be twenty-four soon; I want to be married and begin having children before too much longer. And you'll never marry me; you won't let yourself fall in love with me or anyone else just now."

"That's reading a lot into nothing more than talking back to a cop," I said. We reached Third Avenue, and turned uptown toward a little restaurant I liked.

"No, it isn't." She was shaking her head, and she smiled a little sadly. "Women are supposed to be more romantic than men, but they're a lot more realistic, actually. And I know that a man doesn't fall in love and get married till he's ready for it. And you're not. You aren't ready or willing to settle down and accept life as it is. There's something important still unresolved for you, I don't know what. But something's eating at you, Hugh; you live in a state of rebellion, and against a lot more than that cop."

"You seem to know more about me than I do."

"Well, that's not impossible. Tell me; how do you like your job?" I actually paused for a step, grinning down at her incredulously at this abrupt change of subject. I still didn't believe she was going to quit seeing me. But she wouldn't smile back. "Go ahead," she said. "Answer me."

"Why, fine." I walked on with her. "I like it fine; you know I do." We both worked on the same floor, for one of the big broadcasting networks; Alice in the record library, and I in the publicity department, writing publicity of various kinds, and even being allowed to originate some of it during the past three or four months.

"And when are you going to quit?"

"Quit?" I said after a moment. "What do you m—"

"Hugh, stop it!" She swung toward me angrily. "Answer me honestly, Hugh; *think* about it. Right now. And then tell me truthfully; how much longer, at the very most, do you think you'll still be working at this job?" She stared up at me for a moment, her pert good-looking little face angry and set, her eyes snapping; then she turned away.

For four or five slow steps I was silent, thinking about what she'd said, and we crossed Forty-eighth Street. Then I smiled and answered her question. "I don't suppose I'll last out the summer."

She nodded, turning to glance at the darkened window of an antique shop. "And that's been your history for quite a while, Hugh. You were in the Navy, and you left it."

"I never planned to stay in; I had my time to serve in the military, that's all."

She just glanced at me, shaking her head. "You were in the forestry service, and liked it, but you left that, too. And every other job! You quit them all, after a while! As you will this one. *Why,* Hugh?" She clutched my arm momentarily.

"Well, last year I wanted to sail, Al; really learn how to sail a boat. And I did; spent the whole summer at it. I was broke toward the end; actually hungry part of the time. But I learned how to sail a boat." She sniffed angrily, turning her face away from me toward the shop windows, and I said softly, "That sounds trivial to you, doesn't it, Alice? You think it isn't important. But it is; there's nothing *more* important."

"More important than a job you could have had a *career* at?" She glared at me. "And what about this job; are you going to quit because you want to learn to play the trombone?"

"No, but if I did, that could be important, too. Come on; we're here." I took her arm and we turned into the restaurant.

It's a small place with half a dozen leather-padded booths along each wall, and a tiny bar at the front. We took a table, ordered drinks, then sat awkwardly silent till they came. I tasted mine, then set the glass down, and leaned forward toward Alice across from me. I'd never put this into words before, even for myself, but now I tried; it seemed necessary, even vital. "Look, Al," I said gently, "what's important, and what isn't? How long does a man live? Except for the lucky ones, seventy-odd years maybe, a terribly short time. And a third of it is already gone for me. And how many of those years are you young? Far fewer; so few, it's pitiful. So what's eating me, you say? What am I rebelling against and fighting for? My own life, Al; the freedom to live it—as much of it, anyway, as I possibly can. Haven't you ever thought of this? You have to *sell your life*—most of it, the best part of it!—simply in order to stay alive!"

She was staring at me, her glass in hand. "What do you mean?"

"Well, what have I done with the last five days, for example? Warm, sunny, beautiful days—the first we've had in months, and a part of the little handful like them I'll ever have to be alive in. I *sold* them—" I was leaning toward her, staring into her eyes, trying to make her understand—"each of them for less than a twenty-dollar bill! I spent them sitting at a desk, all six feet and a hundred and ninety pounds of me. And when they were nearly over, I got the last bits of them, the tag ends, for myself. Once a week I get a couple of days, or a day and a half, or not even that much often as not. And once a year, a two-week vacation. Is that all I get—of my own life?" I nodded. "Almost! If I give in and accept that, if I keep *on* selling off my own life—*all* of it, by God; all my youth and middle age!—why, I'll finally be given the last few years of it that are left as a sort of refund. Retire on a pension at sixty-five not even knowing any more what else there is to do with a man's life except work it away."

I sat back against the leather padding, picked up a spoon, and began fiddling with it on the tablecloth, staring down at it. "You could make me out a sort of bum, Al, or shiftless or lazy; but it wouldn't be true. I'll work, hard!" I glanced up at her. "And you know that I do. More than once in this job I've worked till midnight and later, when it was necessary. And on this job and others, I've worked through whole weekends, and actually enjoyed it. I *like* work; it's an important part of life, too, and I like it—ask my boss what he thinks of me."

She nodded. "I know what they think of you at work; that's what makes me furious with you."

"All right, then! I'll give good value for every meal I eat, the clothes on my back, and the roof over my head; I'll work like a stevedore." I took a swallow of my drink, then my lips compressed, and I shook my head. "But I want some of my own life for myself, too; I won't sell it all! I'll work, but in between—" again I leaned forward over the table toward her—"in between, Al, I want to walk across Europe with a knapsack on my back, I don't care how trite or juvenile that sounds. And I want to live in Venice for a year, and learn Italian." I sat back. "For no reason, Al, no practical dollars-and-cents reason, anyway. For no more or no less purpose than learning how to sail that boat; I just want to *do* it, that's all. Those are a couple of the ways I'm going to spend part of the only life I'll ever have. And there's nothing more important."

She sat staring at me, eyes large and wondering; I didn't know what she was thinking. "And there'll be other things, too," I said after a moment. "And for a long, long time, I hope; people don't grow old as early as they used to. I want a whole summer, for example, in the West somewhere—this summer, maybe; I've been saving money all winter. In Arizona, say; just to find out what it's like; whether it's greatly different from here. And whether it might not be where I want to live, maybe; most people live where they do almost by chance, just because they never have time to choose any other. Is that all so crazy, Al? Is it *really* too much for a man to ask out of life? To take a little of it for himself now and then?"

"No," she said slowly, but she wasn't sure. "Not the way you put it, anyway." She took a little sip of her drink, then added, "But still; most people don't seem to feel that way. At least they don't do it."

My mouth quirked. "Most people accept whatever's put before them; never really questioning it or even wondering whether it could or should be any different. Our office is full of them; young guys, and girls like you, spending their whole lives at desks! Oh, they rush out on weekends for a little tennis, swimming, or whatever; trying to salvage a little of their own lives for themselves." I laughed shortly. "Some of the guys in my office go to gyms during the week, for a workout! To keep fit, they say. But what the hell for—sitting at a desk? All they're really doing is draining off useless strength and energy as though it were simply something to be gotten rid of, as I guess it is. Stick with them; is that what I should do?" I shook my head. "No, ma'am; some of my life isn't for sale."

For a little time Alice didn't answer. She finished her drink, and I raised my arm, signaling the waiter for two more. Then Alice said slowly, "You could be right. And maybe you are, Hugh, but it doesn't matter; because you can't get away with it. For a while, still in your twenties, you might; at least it'll seem like it. But in only a few years you'll be in your thirties, less experienced in whatever work you're doing than far younger men all around you; and then you'll be an object of suspicion. What's wrong with you, they'll wonder; what happened? A few more years, and you'll begin having trouble even finding jobs."

I nodded, shrugging angrily. "You think I haven't thought of that, Al? I have an older cousin who fought in the last war, and when it was over he finally finished college, at twenty-seven. And he's never really caught up in the race since. Because that's what it is, apparently —a race. And you can't sit out a lap now and then." The waiter brought our drinks, and I tasted mine, then set it down. "I don't think it was always that way," I said softly. "Only a hundred years ago, men could drop everything and go off to California to join the gold rush. Or cross the country in a covered wagon; most of them, if the truth were known, just to see what the hell was out there, the best of reasons. But people don't seem to do those things now; maybe they aren't here to do any more. All we do now is sit and watch them acted out for us in the movies. Today, time out for even a walking trip across Europe sounds absurd; for a man of twenty-six, anyway. Almost something to sneer at. All right for an occasional college boy, maybe, but certainly no one else. It doesn't even sound sensible; yet somehow sitting at a desk *does*. You're right; the twentieth century won't give you any important part of your own life now and then, to spend as you please." I took a swallow of my drink, then sat back in the booth, shoving my hands into my pockets. "But I'm going to take it anyway, Al. And if I have to pay for it, I'll pay."

She nodded. "You're paying already. I'm a nice girl, Hugh. I'd be a wonderful wife, and you'd fall in love with me if you'd let yourself. And you *will* fall in love with someone eventually; you can't help it. And you'll marry and have children; there's nothing more important, and you can't do without that!"

"I don't intend to."

She leaned toward me, eyes flashing. "Then *they're* the ones who'll pay for what you're doing now."

I actually brought my clenched fists up and struck them against the sides of my head. "I don't want to argue with you about it any more!" I said. "I know, I know! You're right!" Then I brought my hands down and looked at her, slowly shaking my head. "But there must be *some* way to beat it, Al; there's got to be." I sighed, then my mouth twisted angrily. "You better find yourself a guy who can accept things as they are. Because I won't; I can't. I'm damned if I will."

"All right." She nodded. "I can, and I will; I'll forget all about you, Hugh. It won't be easy, and I won't even try at first; I'll just get through the time somehow. Monday I'll ask for my vacation; just as soon as I can get it. And maybe when I get back, you'll already be gone."

After a moment or so I smiled at her. "Let's order dinner now, then have a little fun," I said; and she smiled a little, too, and nodded.

I'd never before put into words what I'd just tried to explain to Alice, but now I had. It was clear and defined in my mind now, and I was ready—ripe—for what happened on Saturday morning.

Two

IN A CAB Saturday morning—a bright sun-filled day—I sat watching the between-buildings glimpses of the Hudson River as we moved down the west side of Manhattan Island. I saw a couple of tugs on the oil-splotched gray water, some ferries, a red-bottomed tanker anchored far out in midstream, a bargeload of freight cars. Then we reached the dock area on the lower West Side, and presently the cab drew in to the curb. As it slowed and stopped, the space between two of the docks slid into view, and I saw a wonderful sight. Her prow not twenty-five feet from the open cab window, there lay an enormous ship towering over the street and dock beside her, so big it was hard to take in.

In the two years I'd lived in New York, I'd never before seen a great liner, and now I sat for a moment staring out and up at that tremendous ship. This close to the street, she dwarfed everything around her. Docks, people on the sidewalk, the waiting cars, even the building fronts across the street, all seemed reduced and out of proportion. Just above the dirty-gray water, a few feet of her red-leaded bottom showed; then the black-painted sides began, soaring up out of the water to the invisible decks high above. Far up on the ship's bow, my eyes lifting to see it, hung one of her anchors, small with distance; and above it and to the right, on a band of white, I saw her name in great golden letters, *Queen Mary*. Then my eyes dropped to the endless length of the black side of the ship, extending far out into the Hudson, gradually swelling with increasing width, and dotted with row after row of portholes glittering in the sun. Above it all rose the ship's white-painted superstructure, the complexity of her yellow-painted masts and cargo booms, and finally her three red-painted, black-banded stacks, each obviously the size of a small apartment building. It was quite a sight, that ship towering over the city street, and I wanted to talk about it, and wished Alice were along.

I stepped out to pay the driver then, onto a sidewalk thronged with people standing in little groups, milling around, calling to each other over people's heads, pulling luggage out of cabs and car trunks; and I grinned at the driver, feeling suddenly excited. Nodding at the crowd around me as he handed me my change, I said, "It's an ordinary day everywhere else in New York, but hell—this is like a carnival!"

"Yeah," he said as I handed him a tip. "For them, not for me." Then I turned into the crowd, making my way toward the line of swinging doors leading into the great shed-like enclosure of the Cunard Line pier.

I had far less trouble boarding the *Queen Mary* than the passengers did. They had to line up at a booth on the floor of the vast covered pier beside the ship, waiting their turns to have their tickets, passports, and inoculation certificates examined, and their names checked off on the passenger lists. But as a visitor, I simply walked aboard, up a canopy-covered gangplank to one of the enclosed decks of the ship. At the head of the gangplank as I climbed it, several ship's officers in blue uniforms and white caps stood waiting, each wearing his war ribbons, and they smiled pleasantly as I stepped aboard.

A steward directed me to my boss's cabin, and I found it easily enough, and had a drink with my boss and his wife. Then I chatted with some of the people from the office, glancing around me, admiring the room I was in. It was one of two rooms of a suite, a bedroom and a sort of living room, both large and handsomely furnished. But I didn't stay long; I was anxious to see as much of the rest of this ship as I could, and I finished my drink and left.

Out in the corridor, I walked back the way I'd come, then stepped out onto the deck, busy with people just now, their steps sounding incessantly on the scrubbed white planking. I walked to the rail, and stood wondering where to go and what to see first. For half a minute or so I stood there leaning on one elbow, facing forward. Just back of my left shoulder a voice said, "How about taking my watch for me tonight, Hugh? I've got a date in port." I turned, and Vic DeRossier —I'd served in the Navy with him—stood grinning at me.

"You dead beat," I said, "you owe me three watches already." Then I grinned at him. "How are you, Vic?"

"Good, good," he said exuberantly as we shook hands, and I was sure he was. Vic's a little man with thick, straight, coal-black hair; handsome in a dapper way, and full of life and energy. He was holding a pencil and a booklet in his hand, the booklet opened to a printed diagram of the ship, labeled *Main Deck,* the deck we were on.

"What're you doing here, Vic?" I said, and he grinned.

"Come aboard the *Mary* any time she's in New York these days, and you're a cinch to run into me. I'm studying the ship." Gesturing with the booklet, he grinned again. "I got this from the Cunard Line office, along with every other scrap of literature they have on the *Mary*. She's an old hobby of mine; I'm in love with her, and I come aboard every chance I get. You seeing someone off?"

"Yeah; I just did. Now, I'm looking around."

"Well, come on then—" he grabbed my arm—"I'll show you the ship; I know her better, now, than half the crew."

"Okay, swell," I said, and we walked forward into the ship.

"Where you been keeping yourself?" Vic said. "I tried to phone you not long ago, but you're not in the book."

"No, I live in a hotel; a little apartment hotel on Fiftieth, the Cliff."

He nodded, and walking along with him, I had time to wonder why Vic had wanted to phone me. It had been nearly three years since we'd finished a hitch in the Navy together, and while Vic DeRossier and I served on the same ship—we were in submarines—and I knew him well and liked him, we'd never been close friends. He'd been the dashing young naval officer when I'd known him last, twenty-two years old and busy every minute of every leave; a handy man with the women, most of them spectacularly good-looking, and all of them, even when they were two or three inches taller than Vic, seeming to like him very well indeed. He wasn't the type to hunt up acquaintances just to sit around chewing over old times.

I was glad I'd run into him now, though, and I glanced down at him—a dark, graceful little man walking briskly along beside me. He hadn't changed, I thought. In a white shirt, dark blue suit and tie, he looked—except for the absence of gold braid on his sleeves— precisely as he had when I'd seen him last. He touched my elbow now —I'd been letting him lead the way—and turning into a short passageway, he led me through a set of paneled swinging doors, each inset with an oval pane of glass, and we walked into an enormous room.

The ceiling soared over us for I don't know how many feet, and it was supported by pillars of polished marble. The entire vast floor was carpeted, so thick our feet made not a sound. And throughout the whole great room were scores and scores of upholstered chairs and great davenports. They were arranged around delicately carved tables of polished wood, grouped for two, three, four, five, or half a dozen or more people. "The first-class lounge," Vic murmured. "Come on," he said then, "there's a lot more to see," and we walked forward, on through the lounge, and out through a set of leather-padded doors beside the stage.

I'll cut it short, though it was an interesting tour. I remember a long room, bright from the sun on the deck alongside, its floors covered with oriental rugs, and there were two grand pianos in it. We stood in a complete movie theater, and we passed miniature kitchens used to prepare hot bouillon and tea for passengers sitting on deck. Vic pointed out the radio room, and a set of phone booths for making and receiving calls to Europe and the States during a voyage. We saw a barber shop, a beauty parlor, a wonderful children's playroom, a huge paneled smoking and card room. We saw a library, its shelves enclosed by doors with leaded glass panes, a great polished table in its center covered with American and English magazines in leather covers. We saw at least four or five bars and cocktail lounges, and Vic said there were still others. We walked through one of them, at the forepart of the ship, a gorgeously decorated lounge with great plate-glass windows, so that you could sit with your drink watching the ship plow through the Atlantic. We looked into a restaurant that stayed open all night, a sort of ship's night club; and we saw a swimming pool, a gymnasium, an enormous and beautiful dining room, and still there were places we never did get to.

"You're right," I said; we were leaning on a rail looking down at the unbroken green surface of the swimming pool. "You know your way around the ship."

"Yeah." Vic nodded. "I've read all the literature, studied the photographs, the deck plans, and been aboard her as often as I could. Every once in a while I've dropped into a travel agency and discussed sailing dates and cabins as though I were thinking of sailing on her." He smiled. "As I was; thinking about it, that is. And some day I will; actually sail on a ship like this." He glanced at his watch. "Right now though," he said, pushing himself erect from the rail, "we've got to get the hell off her."

Leaving the *Mary,* walking down the gangplank into New York again, Vic said quietly, "Hugh, I want to be on a ship like that—not looking, but *having;* sailing on her!—more than anything else I've ever wanted in the world." For a moment or so he stared up at the ship, then he smiled at me suddenly, charmingly. "Silly, isn't it?" he said, and I shrugged, and we walked on out toward the street, down the length of the great dock.

"What are you doing these days, Hugh?" Vic said pleasantly, as we approached the street doors, and I told him, and he nodded. "Not married, are you?" he said, and I had the sudden feeling that this was more than casual conversation, that my answer was somehow important to Vic, and I glanced at him curiously as I shook my head no. For several steps, then, we walked along in silence, and I was aware that Vic was eyeing me speculatively. Then, his voice very casual, he said, "What are you doing right now; got time for a little lunch?"

"Yeah, if you're not too hungry; I had a late breakfast."

He nodded. "A sandwich will do me fine."

We had lunch at a big Owl drugstore on West Forty-second Street; the lunch rush hour was just ending, most of the tables still uncleared, and we sat down beside the window in a booth whose table was littered with crumbs, empty plates, half-filled glasses, and several lipstick-smeared napkins. "Quite a contrast," I said, grinning at Vic; I was needling him a little, I don't know why, but he simply nodded, his face abstracted and thoughtful. Glancing around the store, his eye was caught by a big floor display half a dozen yards away—a table piled with packaged airplane- and ship-model kits, the kind you put together yourself. Vic got up, walked over to it, and I watched him then, looking through the kits. Presently he came back, a package in his hand, and he smiled and shrugged as he sat down again. "I kind of like these things," he said. "I get a kick out of putting them together," and I didn't believe him.

I was certain, somehow, that it was a lie, and I looked at the colored illustration on the package in his hands; it showed a surfaced submarine, one of the later S-types, her decks awash, plowing through a very blue sea. "Look good to you, Hugh?" Vic said, and I didn't answer, wondering what he was getting at, and he pulled open a flap at one end of the package. "Let's see what it looks like," he said, sliding the plastic parts out onto the table. Then he picked up two long sections of gray plastic, and fitted them together to form the slim tapering hull of a miniature submarine. "Beautifully made little thing," he murmured, holding it up, and I nodded.

Like a lot of these model kits, this was perfectly to scale and fully

[34]

detailed; you could even see the tiny seam overlaps of the welded hull. Reaching out, I found the two fat plastic bulges of the main ballast tanks, and with Vic holding the hull together, I fitted them to the sides. Then Vic slid the sugar bowl and the chromed napkin box over the table, and wedged the little hull between them, propping it upright. He picked up two curved shells of gray plastic and fitted them into an oval groove on the little deck to form the sub's conning tower. There was a full set of deck gratings of black plastic, and hunching over the table top, Vic and I laid them carefully on the decks, fore and aft; I was interested now, and could see the appeal of putting these things together. I tore open a cellophane envelope and spilled out a little coil of thin wire and a dozen or so toothpick-sized stanchions. While Vic wedged on the twin brass-colored screws, I strung the stanchions on the wire, then we fitted them into their sockets around the perimeter of the deck. There were two periscope assemblies and a radar mast, but we could see the parts wouldn't hold together without gluing, and Vic and I sat back in the booth, grinning and looking down at the miniature ship sitting upright on the table before us. "Looks like a little sub in drydock," I said.

"Yeah," Vic answered, "stripped down for repairs and refitting in a main yard." He glanced up at me shrewdly. "Like to be sailing on her, Hugh?"

"Oh—" I smiled—"I wouldn't mind; but for two or three days, not a three-year hitch."

The waitress brought menus then, smiling down at the little sub as she cleared the table and swabbed it off, and while we studied the menus I was wondering what Vic was up to. He was staging something, I felt; I was sure that if I hadn't been with him, he'd never have given the model display a second glance, let alone hunted out a submarine kit. Again I wondered why Vic DeRossier had tried to phone me, and after I gave the waitress my order, I sat back in the booth waiting for whatever he had to say.

He lounged back and spoke idly, conversationally. "Be fun, wouldn't it, if half a dozen guys, say, all ex-submarine men, got hold of an old sub?" He smiled thoughtfully. "I think I'd be tempted to take a little cruise some night. When there was no moon, and no Coast Guard in sight. Just for old times' sake, and not far; nice and slow, and taking it easy." He took a sip of water, glancing up at me over the rim of the glass as he swallowed. "And if that worked out—" he set the glass down—"I could even see us taking her down a little way." My face must have shown something, because Vic said softly, "I thought that might get you; and it does, doesn't it, Hughie-boy?"

I smiled a little, and didn't deny it. No one serves in a United States submarine unless that's where he wants to be. Some men are there simply because they don't mind the service, and like belonging to an elite group; the extra pay is no objection either. But others are there because they love submarines. Most civilians, and plenty of Navy men, can see nothing pleasant, nothing that isn't at least a little horrifying, about a handful of men deliberately submerging a ship under the surface of the ocean, and continuing on down into the dark silent cold. But I loved it when I was in the Service, and I smiled and said, "Beats weekend sailing, all right."

"Yeah," he said softly, leaning forward over the table top toward me, "it will."

"Will?" I said, after a moment.

He nodded slowly—grinning, enjoying this—his narrowed eyes exuberant and alive. "Yeah, Hugh," he said gently, "we've got a sub; five of us. A little one; less than five hundred tons, and the oldest you ever saw. But we think it's just possible we might get her operating again; and then six men could man her, hands down."

For several seconds I sat studying his face and eyes, but I knew he was serious. "All right, Vic," I said quietly, "cut out the build-up; I don't need it. What the hell are you talking about?"

He leaned still further toward me, and spoke almost in a whisper. "About money, Hugh; hundreds of thousands of dollars. More money than you'll ever get your hands on in any other way."

Again I watched him, studying his eyes; then I sat back in the booth, thumbs hooked into my belt. "And what way is that?"

He shook his head, sitting back too. "I can't tell you now; not till we know you're pretty well interested."

"Then we've run out of conversation, Vic; because I'm not."

"Why?"

"Hundreds of thousands of dollars—" I smiled—"that you need a submarine to get, and it's all a big secret. Whatever you're doing, Vic, it's illegal, isn't it? A crime." It was as much a statement as a question.

"Sure." He nodded. "I don't think it's really too much of a crime, and I don't think you would, either. But still—get caught, and you'll sure as hell go to prison, and for a long, long time. You might even get killed; it's dangerous, too."

I smiled. "You still selling me, Vic, or you talking me out of it now?"

"Still selling you, Hugh." He smiled back. "We've got four or five possible guys on our list for the sixth man, but you're the one we want. I'm glad I ran into you today, but I'd have located you one way or another; I'm pretty sure you're the guy we want, and I'll tell you why." For several moments he was silent, staring at me, then he said quietly, "There's a word you don't hear much any more, Hugh; not spoken seriously, anyway. It's out of style, and you're supposed to smile when you say it. You know what the word is?" His eyes went somber, and again he leaned forward, his voice dropping. "It's *adventure,* and you hardly hear or see it any more, except in the titles of books for boys. But myself, I still like the word; I still like what it means. Why, hell—" he threw himself back in the booth—"today even college boys talk security! Fresh out of school, they want jobs with guaranteed pensions. Pensions, Hugh, for college boys!" He laughed shortly. "Plus hospitalization, sure-fire promotions, and clockwork raises; everything except risks. *Protection*'s what they want; against everything you can think of. And when you get it, the idea is, you start paying on a house, have kids, and drift serenely into middle age. Kids talk like that! Nineteen-and twenty-year-olds, with the hot blood of youth supposedly in their veins!" His hands flat on the table top, Vic leaned closer to me, his voice a murmur. "But you're not like that, Hugh, and that's why I'm talking to you now. I don't think you're willing to grow up into a man, and then settle for life in the suburbs. I'm sure as hell not!" He glared at me. "I always wished a war would start when we were in the Service. You're not supposed to think that way, but I did." His eyes holding mine, he was almost whispering now. "Adventure, Hugh; it's still possible, even in today's world, and it's not to be jeered at by men without the life in them to take it seriously."

For several moments, his nostrils flaring, his eyes bright, Vic sat staring at me. Then he sat back, and said quietly, "And that's all I can tell you now, Hugh. And all I can promise you, now or ever, is this: decide to come in with us, and you'll be scared to death, and with damn good reason. And you may end up dead, or regretting it forever." His eyes wide, he was staring past me. "But you'll have a good time," he murmured, "the kind you were made for." His hand suddenly clenched to a fist, and his eyes focused on me again. "You'll have a good time," he repeated more loudly, "the best there is. With a chance of making a fortune to boot!" He brought his fist down hard, banging the table top, and the sugar bowl bounced, and the little submarine split down the center and collapsed, its parts spilling loose on the table, and we both sat staring at it.

If a man were superstitious, he might have made something of that. A few centuries earlier any man would have, and even now a flicker of dread shot through me, staring at that broken little submarine. Then I looked up at Vic again, and he said softly, "What do you say, Hugh; are you interested?"

I smiled at him. "No," I said, and leaned toward him. "Because you know what this sounds like to me? Whatever it is? Like something four or five guys sitting around over a few drinks might have dreamed up, and gotten all excited about. Sunken treasure, maybe, or something of that sort, which sounds like fun; adventure, maybe, but it sounds unreal, even childish, and if you say different, you've got to convince me."

"And if we did, what then?" I didn't answer immediately, and Vic said softly, "You'd be interested then, wouldn't you, Hugh? You like money, don't you? You'd like a lot of it, wouldn't you? How'd you like to sail on the *Queen Mary* first-class? With the clothes to match? How'd you like to be able to buy a car, *any* car, the kind you really want? And *all* the things, the wonderful things, money can buy."

I was irritated. I don't like to be sold anything; I don't like being handled or managed, the way Vic had been trying to; and I spoke the truth besides. "I wouldn't give a damn for them," I said. "I don't care if I never sail on the *Mary* or any other ship; first-class or tenth. But it eats you up, doesn't it, Vic?"

He nodded. "Yes. It does. There's a little handful of people out of all the millions alive, who always get the best of everything. I want to be one of them."

I shrugged. "But it means nothing to me. A car, you say. I don't need one in New York, and if I did, any car would do; I'm not trying to prove anything. And I get my shirts at J. C. Penney's, my suits cost forty to fifty dollars, and I've got plenty of ties. The wonderful things money can buy bore me to death, Vic; I don't need them or want them." For the first time Vic looked defeated, puzzled; he'd shot his wad, and this was the answer, and I sat grinning at him. He had this coming for being a salesman and trying to manipulate me. Then I leaned forward, still grinning. "But I'd like a lot of money," I said gently. "Lord, how I'd like it. And do you know what I'd do with it, Vic?" He sat staring at me, and shook his head. "Nothing," I said. "I wouldn't spend a lousy dime of it."

The waitress brought our sandwiches and coffee then, and we each sat back, watching her set them, with the silverware, on the table. Then I picked up my sandwich, and leaned toward Vic again. "A lot of people think this, and say this, Vic, but they wouldn't really do it. I would, though; I wouldn't spend that money. I'd buy government bonds with it, at banks and post offices here and there. And at only three per cent interest, it would give me a pretty fair little income every year for the rest of my life, and my family'd have it after me—I wouldn't even need life insurance. For that, Vic, I'd do almost anything; not for the lousy money itself, but for the little annual income it would bring me each year. You could live on it, maybe, and raise a family! And if not, then a man could always pick up a job that'd bring in a few thousand extra." I took a bite of my sandwich, then said, "That's what money can *really* buy, Vic, something really worth while; *you could buy back your own life!* You could do what you want to; what *I* want to, anyway. You'd work, and work hard, but in between you could spend some of your *own life;* take a year off now and then, a whole summer every once in a while, and still be able to have a family in the security you'd want to give them." I was silent for a moment, then I took a sip of coffee, and said, "That's all I want, Vic; that's all money means to me. But I'd give plenty for that; I'd do a lot. Now, what's it all about? What kind of crime isn't really much of a crime at all?"

"Well—" Vic answered slowly, smiling faintly—"there are a lot of things you wouldn't do; even if you were broke and hungry, I don't think you'd take a dollar from someone who needed it. But think about this: it's an example I dreamed up that might explain something to you. Picture a house party, let's say—" he leaned toward me, forearms on the table—"at a very wealthy estate somewhere. It's filled with guests, and every last person there is either out-and-out wealthy, very well off, or making a slug of money. Every one of them, Hugh, or they wouldn't be there. Would you take a few hundred dollars from each of them, if you could? It'd be illegal, all right; a crime, and yet—every single one of them could easily afford it. It'd mean no more to them than losing fifty cents to you; nobody'd miss a meal or a Cadillac. They wouldn't like it, of course; but a few hundred, even a thousand from each of them, and they wouldn't really be hurt at all. To you, though, it would make all the difference in the world; you'd be closer to rich, to having the kind of life you want, than you ever will be otherwise." He grinned and sat back. "That's not our plan, of course. We don't know of any house parties where everyone's rich, and wouldn't know how in hell to rob it anyway." Vic's smile faded. "But it's a fair example, Hugh; enough for you to make up your mind on. Don't decide now, though; don't decide anything. Come and meet the others; size them up, and let them size you up, those who don't already know you. And if they suit you, and you suit them, you'll hear what we have in mind." He sat waiting, grinning and exuberant again.

"And when would that be?" I said, not sure what I thought at the moment.

"Tomorrow; we're ready to start, Hugh, and we're pressed for time."

I took another sip of coffee, then said, "If I do come, Vic, I'll decide for myself just how much of a crime this is, and how much sense your whole scheme makes. And if I don't like the sound of it, I'm out."

"Sure."—Vic tossed his napkin onto the table and dusted his palms. "One thing, though; if you didn't come in with us, we'd have to trust you to keep your mouth shut. We could do that, couldn't we, Hugh? You'd better be sure we could." After a moment I nodded, and Vic said, "Well, then. Tomorrow's Sunday; can you meet me in Penn Station around ten o'clock, at the main information booth?"

I answered in only a moment or so, after only the barest pause. But I'd had time to think, in the lightning-like way people sometimes do, of a lot of things. If someone had asked me an instant ago, it suddenly occurred to me, why I was going to answer as I knew I was, I'd have said that I knew. Because I hoped there was at least a chance that this would turn out to be something I could permit myself to go along with. Because I loved submarines and submarining. And because Vic's promise of adventure excited me deeply, whether I'd showed it or not. But we seldom do anything important for only the reasons that show. There was something else still, I was realizing, staring at Vic, something that may sound trivial but is not. I don't think we often realize, in fact, what an enormously powerful influence it is in human affairs of all kinds, from the very smallest to launching a rocket for the moon. It was nothing more or less than simple curiosity. *What in hell,* I was wondering back of everything else we said, *are they going to do with a beat-up old sub?* And as I nodded and replied to Vic, it wasn't money, or adventure, or danger, death, crime, or prison I was thinking of; it was the sudden excitement of knowing that tomorrow I could learn the answer to that question. I *had* to go along, to find out that much; whether I intended ever to do anything more about it or not. "Sure," I said, nodding at Vic. "I'll be there."

Three

WE WALKED IN SILENCE for a quarter of a mile along the beach at Fire Island, after a three-hour train and ferry trip from Penn Station. We hadn't said much on the way, either; just read the Sunday paper, occasionally exchanging sections of it. It was another fine day, the magnificent beach here as crowded as it ever gets, a few dozen people lying in the sun or fooling around in the water. Then I looked down at Vic beside me; he was wearing blue denims and work shirt; I wore a white shirt and gray wash pants. "You haven't said anything about who I'm going to meet here, Vic."

He looked up at me. "No."

"You want to watch my reactions when I meet them cold."

He nodded. "We thought it might be a good idea; I was on the phone with them last night, to say you were coming."

"All right." I nodded. "That's all right with me; but you'd have found out what I think, anyway. I don't consider this a social call, Vic; no occasion for politeness or pretense. Several hundred thousand bucks with a damn good chance of death or prison instead is serious. You'll find out what I think, all of you; precisely and in clear detail."

"Okay, Hugh." He smiled up at me. "Don't get huffy."

"Sure," I said. "But don't treat me like a kid, either. Now, just exactly where are we going?"

He pointed to a gray-shingled cottage some two hundred yards ahead, one of an endless row of almost identical houses just back of the low dunes. "That one; we've rented the place for a month."

I stared at the open porch of the little cottage ahead. A man sat on the railing, and as we walked along the smooth damp sand toward him, I narrowed my eyes, and within a few dozen more steps I could begin

[41]

to make out his features. He was about fifty, I thought, though I learned later he was older, and his face was thin, the cheeks cutting in very sharply under the cheekbones, and grooved with two straight lines angling down from the base of his nose. His nose was large, bone-thin, and beaked; and he had straight brown hair combed back from the forehead.

Now we were closer, turning in from the beach to climb the low dune toward the house, and I could see that, thin though he was, he wore a rather tight-fitting brown suit with unusually small lapels. His white shirt collar seemed small, too, as though the manufacturer had skimped on the material. But his tie was extra-wide and very short, hanging outside his buttoned coat. His pants were baggy and unpressed; he didn't seem like a man much interested in clothes, but he had presence. There was a stern dignity about the man, and I felt he was, or had once been, somebody.

Now—we were a dozen yards from the steps—he stood up from the railing and smiled at us very pleasantly, his eyes friendly and pleased, and I suddenly felt that I was going to like him. From the corner of my eye I saw Vic smile; he'd been watching my face, and when he spoke I could tell from his voice that he was relieved at my reaction.

"Come on down, will you, Frank?" he called to the man on the porch. "And bring the others." Turning to me, he said, "Let's sit out here in the sun; okay?" and I nodded.

We sat down on the sand in front of the house, and a moment or so later a woman in a black bathing suit, and a man in maroon trunks carrying a folded beach umbrella, walked out of the house and came down the porch steps toward us. The man's face was hidden by the orange folds of the umbrella, but I could see the woman clearly; she was young, olive-skinned, and had a magnificent wide-hipped figure. Her face wasn't pretty, but it was striking, memorable; the nose small and delicately hooked with a perfectly even curve, the brows wide and arched and dead-black, as was her hair coiled in two tight braids on top of her head. Her eyes, as she stared at my face, studying me frankly, were big and black. In her black bathing suit she was a stunning sight, and Vic was grinning as I got to my feet.

"Rosa," he said as the girl stopped before us, looking up at my face without smiling, "this is Hugh Brittain. This is Mrs. Lucchesi, Hugh," and I spoke and smiled, and held out my hand.

"Hello, sucker," she said in a soft, surprisingly low-pitched voice; then she smiled suddenly, a flashing, wonderfully friendly smile, taking

[42]

the sting out of what she'd said, and took my hand. "You are crazy, like the rest of us?" she said, and I realized she had a faint foreign accent—Italian, I supposed.

"Not yet," I said, smiling down at her. "I haven't joined the club; so far I'm just looking, not buying."

She smiled and sat down then, arms clasped around her knees, looking out at the water, and I turned toward the man with the umbrella. He was planting it in the sand beside us, tugging it down deep and firm, his arm muscles bulging. Then he unfurled it, raising it till the catch snapped, and now I saw his face, and knew I'd seen it somewhere before. For a moment he stood looking at me, a corner of his mouth curling in a wry little smile. Then, drawling it slowly, his voice and eyes amused at my inability to identify him, he said, "Hi, Lieutenant," and I stared at him, and could not think who he was.

He was probably thirty-two years old; short, quite dark, his chest very thick, and black with hair; a strong, heavily muscled but very lithe man. His face, though, was beginning to round a little with fat, and I knew he was heavier, thicker in the middle, than when I'd seen him last. And his hair was thinner on top; still thick and black at the sides, but sparse on top and combed back in what looked like a streaking of suspended black crayon lines over the olive-toned scalp underneath them. "Moreno," he said then, his voice deliberately contemptuous of my failure to remember his name, but amused, too, as though it wasn't worth his trouble to be annoyed about it. As he spoke, he pushed a hand forward with an easy roll of one shoulder, and the way he did it supplemented the manner in which he spoke.

"Yeah." I shook his hand perfunctorily and dropped it. "I remember now; Torpedoman, First Class, weren't you? And not on my ship at all; no particular reason why I should remember you, is there?" And I smiled at him. It was perfectly true; he'd been on a sister ship of the squadron, and I'd had only two or three unimportant encounters with him before in my life.

"No, no reason," he said, still smiling at me a little mockingly as he sat down on the sand beside the girl. "But I remember you, Lieutenant."

I didn't answer—I wasn't here to bicker and act the kid—and I sat down on the sand, smiling at the girl across from me because I had the sudden feeling it would annoy Moreno. She smiled back, but

[43]

faintly, her eyes amused, knowing exactly what I was doing, and I grinned.

"Rosa is a relative of Ed's," Vic said, nodding at Moreno, which didn't explain anything to me, but I didn't question him because the man I'd first seen on the porch was coming out of the house and walking down the steps toward us.

He smiled, plodding through the dry sand, and I started to get to my feet again, but he wagged a hand at me. "Stay where you are," he said pleasantly, and sat down on the sand a yard from Moreno. We were more or less in a half circle now, seated or lounging back on the sand under or near the orange umbrella. Vic was beside me to the right, lying back on one elbow in his denims and blue work shirt, idly scooping up sand and letting it trickle from his cupped palm. He seemed to have withdrawn and become a spectator, no longer participating, letting the rest of us get acquainted. Moreno sat opposite him, crosslegged on the sand, hands resting on his heavy thighs, his thick bare upper body held straight and upright—to hide the beginning bulge of a paunch from Rosa, I suspected. Rosa, beside him, lay back on the sand on an elbow, one good-looking knee raised, watching us all with amused interest.

"This is Hugh Brittain," Vic said to the new man; then he turned to me. "Frank Lauffnauer," he said, and scooped up another handful of sand, letting it trickle from his palm, waiting idly for whatever we wanted to say to each other.

"Glad to know you," Lauffnauer said, smiling and leaning forward from the waist to extend his hand.

"Glad to know you," I said as we shook hands, and in that instant I decided it would be me who'd open the meeting, and that whatever I said would be abrupt and challenging. For while I was here to be presented, judged, and sized up by this group, I was also here to do the same thing myself, and I decided I'd demonstrate which came first. Lauffnauer and I shook hands, leaning across the sand toward each other, and I spoke immediately, taking the floor before anyone else could begin. "You a Navy man, Frank?" I said.

"Highest ranking man here," Moreno said casually but instantly, lounging back on the sand watching me, still with that amused look in his eyes. He was trying to take the initiative away from me, I knew, but I didn't give him the chance. I simply nodded in response, keeping my eyes on Lauffnauer's face, so that when I spoke it was again directed to him.

"What rank?" I said, and Lauffnauer folded his arms across his chest, regarding me pleasantly.

"Commander," he answered, and something in the way he pronounced the word struck a spark of recognition in my mind, and I realized something else that had been simmering in some part of my brain. *I'm glad to know you,* he'd said a few moments ago, and now I realized that he'd pronounced *glad* almost, though not quite, as though the *d* had been followed by a *t*. And now the *C* in *Commander* had been slightly stressed, as though in his mind the word were spelled with a *K*.

"What Navy was that, Frank?" I said, and the man across from me in the European-made clothes, still smiling affably, nodded in recognition of the fact that I already knew the answer.

"German," he answered, his tone confirming that he understood I knew he would say this; and the *G* in *German* came out a *Ch*.

Moreno said, "You know, Lieutenant, we might have a question or two ourselves. If you don't mind."

"Yeah, Hugh," Vic said easily and conciliatingly, "we'll brief you thoroughly on everyone here; and there's still a fifth man in the house. But first—"

I cut them off, not even glancing at them. "Were you in submarines, Frank?" I said gently.

"I commanded one. For over three years of the war, I trained others. But I commanded a U-boat for five months, just before the war ended."

"Sink many ships?"

"Four. And hit two others."

"Were any of them American?" I said softly.

"No; none. As it happened," he added, shrugging. Then he leaned toward me. "I sank four merchant ships, three of them British, one of them Greek. I torpedoed an English grain vessel, completely disabling but not sinking it; it was my last torpedo, and I returned to base. Later we learned that the grain ship was towed into an English port."

I sat there in the sand thinking, or trying to. Watching me, waiting for any more questions I might ask, smiling a little, sat a former German U-boat commander. It seemed incredible. I didn't quite know what to think or do, and I temporized, stalling for time to think. "Well," I said, glancing around at the others, "any more navies represented?"

"One," Moreno said shortly. He was sitting up now, and I could see he'd had enough of my taking over, and he muttered something I couldn't make out, which was probably a good thing. Glancing up at the house, he called, "Linc!" and we all turned and sat staring at the door. A tall, thin Negro in gray wash slacks, black sweater, and a white shirt open at the collar, came strolling out onto the porch, eating an apple. His skin was a milk-chocolate brown, his mouth quite wide, his hair a snug-fitting cap of short wiry hair. As he came down the steps, smiling, and walked toward us across the sand, I saw that his brown eyes, deepset under his brows, were wise and intelligent; just now they looked a little amused. I got to my feet, as he stopped beside us, and Vic said, "This is Lincoln Langley, Hugh; usually called Linc. Hugh Brittain, Linc," and we each said something and shook hands.

"Sit down, Hugh," Linc said then, "I'll be going right back to the house." He grinned. "It won't quite do for me to hobnob with the rest of you out here in broad daylight."

"Yeah—" Vic grinned back at him—"we're strictly an ordinary little group no different from anyone else on the island today; out sunning ourselves on the beach. I guess Linc must be the cook or chauffeur or something. What do you want to be, Linc?"

"Butler," he answered, smiling down at us.

"Let's get on with it," Moreno said shortly. "Linc's an Englishman, and he served on a Limey sub."

I was astonished, and I'm sure my face showed it, because Linc smiled. "Quite right," he said. "I'm of Jamaican descent; my father was a merchant seaman, he was often in England, and he and my mother emigrated there just before I was born; they bought a small farm. We were the only Negroes in a hundred square miles; most people around there had never even seen a Negro before, and we were well received, made welcome. So I was born in England, an English citizen, and I served four years in British submarines; Wireless Operator First Class, later a Chief." His speech—well, I don't suppose I really know what an Oxford accent is, but the way Lincoln Langley talked was my idea of it. Close your eyes, and it could have been Anthony Eden speaking.

"Well—" I grinned up at Linc, then glanced around at the others— "there's a phrase I've seen in print a thousand times. You're always reading about 'a motley crew,' but this is the first time I've ever seen one. We're a motley crew, all right."

"We sure as hell are," Vic said, "and a good one." Then he glanced up at Langley. "Any questions about Hugh here, Linc? Want us to move on up to the house so you can sit in on this?"

"No." Langley shook his head. "He's qualified; you've told us that. And he looks fine to me. Whatever the rest of you decide is okay. See you later, Hugh," he said pleasantly, and I nodded, and he walked on back to the house, working on the apple again.

"All right, Lieutenant," Moreno said then, "you ready to listen? Or you got more questions?"

"Yeah," I said, "one more, anyway," and I nodded at Rosa Lucchesi. She was sitting now, arms around her legs, one cheek resting on her knees, and she just smiled, and Moreno grinned, too.

"Why, sure," he said, "I can tell you why Rosa is here." He paused momentarily, enjoying this. "She's part of the crew; any objections?"

"Objections? No." I shook my head. "You can recruit Shirley Temple, if you want to. But before you recruit me, I have to know why."

"We've got to have Rosa, Hugh," Vic said quickly. "There's a reason, a good one, and you'll hear all about it."

"In any case," Lauffnauer said gently, "we are not sailing around the world; we may not even need to dive. A few simple duties, that is all, which she can perform quite as well as a man. I say it, and you can believe me; I commanded a submarine."

"I will make as good a man as you, Mr. Brittain," Rosa said, and I nodded.

"Sure," I said, "and a lot better girl."

"That's right," Vic said with a grin. "The Navy was never like this, was it, Hugh?" He looked over at Rosa appreciatively, and she stopped smiling, shrugging a shoulder disdainfully, and turned to stare off at the water.

"Well, if we're sure the Lieutenant hasn't any more questions about us," Moreno said, "maybe it's all right if we ask a few about him?"

Again Vic spoke quickly, intervening. "Sure. I haven't any; I served in the Navy with Hugh, and I'm the reason he's here now. I think he's all right with you, too, isn't he, Frank?"

Lauffnauer nodded. "So far as I can tell, I am sure he is. If he walked onto a ship of mine to join the crew, I'd expect him to do well. If he didn't—" he smiled at me—"I would shoot him."

I nodded at Lauffnauer, then turned to Moreno. "What's on your mind?" I said.

He didn't answer or glance at me. Speaking to Vic and Lauffnauer, he began talking, slowly, choosing his words and thoughts carefully. "He's qualified to serve on a submarine. Just as well as anyone here. No question about that. And I'm sure he has guts. Of a certain kind. In a war I'm sure he'd be noble and heroic, an inspiration to his men . . ." He grinned slightly with one corner of his mouth. "But this takes nerve of a different kind. And you all know that or ought to. Every one of us has to be ready to do anything necessary; *anything that's necessary.*"

"And you think he won't?" Vic said.

Moreno shrugged. "I don't say that; I just don't know. Do you? How good is he? How tough? *Really* tough?"

"As tough as you are, Moreno," I said, lounging back on the sand on one elbow. "Any day at all."

He nodded slowly. "Maybe," he said. "Maybe you are. I hope so anyway, Lieutenant." He smiled.

"And now's as good a time as any," I said, "to knock off that 'Lieutenant' crap. You want trouble, Moreno, you want to find out how tough I am, just say it again. I'm not in the Navy now, and neither are you."

He smiled again. "That's right," he said. "Now you're in my crew."

"*Your* crew?" I stared at him for a moment, then sat upright again, swinging to Vic.

"That's right, Hugh," he said, nodding. "Moreno is captain."

"*Moreno?*" I said angrily. "Why?"

Vic shrugged, and Moreno lounged back on the sand, grinning. "Hugh, any of us could captain the sub," Vic said. "Somebody has to, and any of us could do it; Frank's *commanded* a sub! In wartime. Moreno's like a lot of chiefs in the U.S. or any other Navy; as good as many a man I've known with stripes on his sleeve, and in some ways, for what we're planning, even better. This takes a special kind of nerve, and for that kind of nerve he's the best choice among us. Not snobbish about taking orders from an ex-seaman, are you, Hugh? We've got a full Commander who isn't."

"No, of course not," I said instantly, though I wasn't sure. I shrugged. "Anyway, it's up to you people; it's your plan. Which brings us to the big question: just what the hell *are* you planning?"

Vic's eyes came to life, glowing with sudden excitement, and he opened his mouth, but before he could speak, Moreno interrupted. "Hold it!" he ordered peremptorily, and I swung my head to glare at him; I'd suddenly had as much of Moreno in one dose as I wanted.

Then he smiled at me, and this time it was with complete friendliness, his eyes warm and with no least trace of irritation; and after a moment I smiled and nodded at him in recognition of something I was suddenly sure he understood. A man who could assume complete control over his own emotions as Moreno just had—I knew he didn't feel friendly at all—was at least something more than just a thug. It was perfectly possible, I realized in that moment, that Moreno was qualified for command. And knowing it, I was ready to admit it, and Moreno understood that, too. "I think everything we want to tell Hugh," he said quietly to Vic, "will make more sense if he sees what we're talking about first."

Vic nodded. "I guess it would. Ever do any skin-diving, Hugh?"

I nodded, and Lauffnauer said, "Well, we have equipment to lend you, and one of us will take you down; to see something I am sure will surprise you."

"I'll do it," Moreno said, getting to his feet. "Right now. I need to attach a buoy, anyway."

And so, for the first time, I saw the *U-19*. In the house I changed into a pair of trunks Vic loaned me, and we carried our diving equipment to the beach. Moreno brought along a short pine board wrapped with line. We dragged a battered boat out from under the porch down to the water, then rowed a mile out into the ocean, Moreno in the stern watching landmarks on the shore to position us.

We didn't talk much on the way, but the atmosphere between us was—almost, anyway—one of wary friendliness. I didn't try to tell myself I liked him; I didn't know, and it didn't matter. I had the feeling that there were a lot of things I wouldn't like about him if I knew him better; he'd implied that he'd do anything he had to, to get what he wanted—morally, he might be an untouchable. But it isn't true, unfortunately, that admirable qualities are possessed only by the virtuous. Whatever else he was, this Moreno was a good man, I knew, in whatever way it is you can sense things like that; and I acknowledged in myself a kind of grudging recognition of it.

We anchored, fitted on our equipment, and I followed Moreno down the anchor rope to the ocean floor; he carried his rope-wrapped board shoved in his weight belt. At the bottom, actually standing on the clean white sand for a moment, the light a hazed yellow-green, visibility maybe eighty feet, I watched Moreno begin to swim slowly into deeper water, and I followed. Within minutes—it was hard to judge time here—we reached the ancient sunken submarine; I learned later that he'd been out to her twice before.

Of course Lauffnauer was right; when I saw that black bulk looming just ahead in the yellow-green-lit depths of the water, and then, swimming closer, understood what I was seeing, I was astounded. I was utterly absorbed, fascinated, and reaching the little conning tower, I clung to it, staring around me. Beside me, Moreno had released his pine-board buoy, paying out the line attached to it as it floated to the surface; then he tied the end of the line to the conning tower. But I simply hung there under the ocean staring down at the incredible sight just below me in the silent green-yellow haze. Frank must have some reason, I knew, for thinking or at least hoping that we might raise and operate this tiny sub. She must have been put down here undamaged, her ballast tanks filled, whoever had done it leaving through the escape hatch. But what chance there was, after all these years, that she was anything but a ruin I simply didn't know; no one could say with certainty until we'd raised her, if we could, and found out for ourselves. She was probably full of sea water long since—and yet, I thought, her valves might have held; they just possibly might have. Certainly there was no harm, anyway, in finding out. Moreno touched my shoulder then, pointing upward, and I nodded, and we started up.

Four

FRANK LAUFFNAUER told me, then, what they proposed to do with the *U-19* if we could possibly raise and operate her again. The girl, Rosa Lucchesi, had a lunch ready when we got back: sandwiches and potato chips set out on a big round old-fashioned wooden table in the center of the dining room; she was still in the kitchen now, making coffee. The rest of us wandered around the little cottage eating, or sat down here and there.

I couldn't stand still. Pacing between the living room and dining room, still in my trunks, I was too excited over what I'd just seen to sit down; I'd even forgotten for the moment why we were all here. All I could think or talk about was the astonishing sight I had seen a mile or so out in the water, and a hundred feet under. Sitting on an old kitchen chair tipped back against the dining-room wall, Lauffnauer watched me pace, his face amused at my excitement, and told me something of how the *U-19* came to be where she was, and why he thought there was at least a chance that we could get her operating again. I listened, nodding, utterly astounded by what he was telling me and what I had seen. Vic and Linc were standing in the living room, their backs to the front windows. Moreno, in his trunks, was sitting at the dining-room table, all of them eating, as was Frank. But I was too excited to eat just then, though I held a sandwich in my hand.

Finishing what he'd told me, Lauffnauer turned to Moreno at the dining-room table, and said, "What do you think, Ed? Have you changed your mind about getting her out?"

"No—" Moreno shook his head calmly, chewing—"I don't see any big problem. Water's calm. The weather report's good for tonight. With a little ordinary luck, and no bad breaks, it shouldn't be too tough."

Turning to me, Lauffnauer said, "I brought Moreno into this for two reasons. He was the first man I asked, in fact."

"How'd you two get together, by the way?" I said.

"We met at the Brooklyn Navy Yard. Your government—mine, too, now—brought me over from Germany in 1946, after the war. The Navy was interested, as you may remember if you weren't too young, in the German schnorkel. I was hired as an expert on them, which I was, and brought to America as a civilian employee of the Navy, with the opportunity to become a citizen. Here I met very many submarine men, among them Moreno, and I remembered him later. I was impressed by his abilities—"

Moreno laughed, and leaned toward me over the table top; I was standing facing him. "He was impressed by the fact that I had larceny in my heart; just like he does. Birds of a kind, and we both knew it on sight, and made a little money." Moreno grinned. "Loading supplies on a ship, a sub especially, things can fall in the drink now and then; or so your reports say. A case of cigarettes once in a while, other supplies. I was in charge of loadings, Frank was a civilian with an old car, in and out of the Yard, so—" he shrugged.

Lauffnauer smiled deprecatingly. "My pay was small. Your Navy saves money, sometimes, in odd ways," he said, shrugging, "and Europeans who survive a war must understand how to get along. In any case, it was fortunate that I knew Moreno; he is a good submarine man, and he and his cousin were commercial fishermen. Tell Hugh about that."

Moreno popped a potato chip into his mouth, then put his heavy forearms on the table, his hairy shoulders hunched over them, and looked up at me. "It's what I've done since I left the Navy, commercial fishing with Aldo's boat, and a lousy way to make a living. But I've been in the Navy since I was eighteen, and don't know much else. Aldo was my cousin, Rosa's husband. Aldo got drowned four months ago, right after I got out of the Navy—" Moreno glanced toward the kitchen—"and I been fishing the boat with Rosa ever since. The boat belongs to her now, and she owns the dock where we keep it. The dock's roofed and enclosed; you know the kind. It's typical: plank flooring on each side, and you run the boat in between. The boat's a good four or five feet longer than the sub, and a lot wider; the dock'll take the sub easy. It's roofed, enclosed, and the door padlocks; a big fishing boat's valuable, and so is its cargo sometimes. And the dock's isolated; nobody around there for a couple of miles. Sits on cheap Jersey swampland, all Aldo could afford. You couldn't want a better place to work on the sub. So now you know why Rosa is in this. Lauffnauer recruited me and Linc, I looked up DeRossier, and he found you."

After a moment I nodded. "Okay," I said. "We've got a sub, a place to work on her, and a crew of sorts. Now say we get the sub operating; what then? Let's have it now."

And then Lauffnauer told me. "Don't interrupt," Moreno said first. "Just listen, and save questions till later." Then, for twenty minutes, maybe longer, Lauffnauer talked. After a time I walked over to the davenport, just inside the living room, and sat down, forearms on my bare knees, hands clasped, staring down at the floor and listening. Presently Rosa brought in coffee in paper cups, and handed it around; Lauffnauer took his, glancing up to smile his thanks but without pause, continuing to talk. I took mine, but forgot to drink or even taste it. It grew cold in my hands as I listened to Frank, and even the others who'd heard all this before sat or stood staring at him like children listening to a story. I listened, Frank's quiet voice the only sound in the room; and if I'd been astonished at the submarine I'd seen under the ocean, now I was astounded at what the men around me proposed to do with it. It was incredible, it was beyond belief, and I couldn't seem to think or form any real opinion about what I was hearing. Once I glanced up at Vic standing near the front windows, and he grinned at me over the edge of his paper cup. But I just shook my head, not smiling back, and Lauffnauer's quiet deep voice droned on, slowly, steadily, and methodically explaining everything in full and complete detail.

Finally his voice stopped and the room was silent; outside on the beach I heard the surf crash. I looked up at Lauffnauer then. "Are you serious?" I said, though I knew he was, and he simply nodded. "Vic," I said, "you told me nothing like this had ever been done before; you were sure as hell right."

"Wasn't fooling, was I, Hugh?" he said, smiling, and I nodded shortly. My decision had been made for me; I was having no part of this. It no longer mattered whether this was a crime, or how much of a one; I was out of it, and now I looked up, glancing around at all of them. In the kitchen doorway Rosa stood watching me.

"Look," I said quietly, as though speaking to a bunch of bright but unruly children, "this is fantastic. It's worse than that; it's completely impossible." I was irritated, almost angry, and I let my face show it, though I kept my voice calm.

"You may be right," Moreno said surprisingly; he was sitting at the dining-room table in his trunks. "Maybe you've spotted something we've all missed; let's go over it and see. Now, we can either raise the sub and get it operating again, or we can't. If we can't, that's that; we've all had a little fun, we shake hands, and forget it. Okay?" I nodded, because there wasn't anything else to do, and he said, "All right; say we get it operating. Once we do, you know we'll test it; from bow to stern, over and again, and damn carefully, believe me. Then we'll trial dive it; probably right in the dock at high tide. A stationary dive at less than conning-tower depth before we ever think of taking her under. And we'll fill and blow all ballast and trim tanks dozens of times before we even go out. We'll have the engines and motor apart; they'll be simple enough, you know that. And we'll see whether there's any prayer of charging the batteries, and there better be, or damned if I know what we'll do. We'll repair and test the rudder, the bow and stern diving planes, and go over every single square inch of the hull. We'll replace all gaskets, and test, repair, or replace every part in the damn boat. We'll surface cruise at night, a dozen times if we have to, and we'll—but hell, I don't have to tell you what we'll do before we ever go down in her. And when and if we ever do go down for the first time, it'll be at easy periscope depth, with the ballasts ready to blow, you can bet on that. Next, we'll each take an ordinary skin-diving outfit along, an aqua-lung like the one you wore today. We'll trial dive at a hundred feet, on a clean bottom, and if for any reason the main ballasts won't blow under pressure, we'll go out the escape hatch. We'll really test the boat out; you know that."

"All right." I nodded impatiently. "That part's all right."

"Okay, then." Moreno got up, walked into a bedroom that opened off the dining room, and came out a moment later with a thick folded paper. He spread it open on the dining-room table—I saw that it was a marine chart—then hooked his chair leg with a foot, dragging it up to the table behind him, and beckoned me over. Vic, Linc, and Lauffnauer came over, and sat down around the table across from Moreno. Stopping beside Moreno's chair, I looked back over one shoulder to see Rosa in the kitchen, and she grinned at me and shrugged, I don't know why.

"Our submarine operating, do you doubt that we can reach exactly this point?" Moreno said, his thick forefinger touching the chart just under a tiny, neatly penciled cross on the blue-tinted area representing a portion of the Atlantic Ocean. "There's nothing to the navigating," he said. "We'll use a gyrocompass, if we can install one; Frank doesn't remember if the old boat's got one. Or we can do it by stars and by sun; if the chronometer's rusted out, we'll buy our own. We'll leave the dock at first dark, and travel surfaced at just above negative buoyancy, only the tower out. We'll ride the main vents, everyone at dive stations, so long as we sight no ship. If we do, it's under, periscope out, till their running lights are over the horizon. Same thing after dawn, and by four o'clock on the afternoon of May 17—" his finger tapped the little cross several times—"there's where I guarantee we'll be. That okay with you?" he added softly, glancing up at me.

"Sure," I said just as quietly. "If we get the sub operating, a Naval Reserve crew could do it on a weekend training cruise. Everything's fine up to there." I nodded toward the little penciled cross, glancing around at the others. "Because up to there—" I tapped the little cross—"we're depending on ourselves, and no one else. And we can do everything you say, assuming we don't founder the damn boat. The worst that can happen is maybe a Coast Guard cutter spots us, and runs us in. Then we hang our heads, scrape our feet, and explain that we found the old sub by accident, and that we just couldn't resist a little trip, old submariners that we are. We've been bad boys, and we're sorry; they can't hang us for that.

"But after this point—" again I reached down to tap the penciled cross—"they can. And will. Because after that point everything depends, not on us any more, but on what an absolute stranger is going to do! Success or failure, and maybe our lives, depend on *guessing precisely* how some stranger is going to behave! Now, what kind of damn fool scheme is that?" I glanced angrily around at the others.

Vic and Linc were frowning now, and I knew the same thought had occurred to each of them, more than once, and long since. But Lauffnauer and Moreno sat watching us, their eyes amused. Then Moreno said quietly, "It's not a guess," and Lauffnauer nodded in agreement.

Hooking his thumbs in the band of his trunks, Moreno slouched back in his chair, tilting it up on its rear legs. "What *is* a submarine?" he said, glancing from one to another of us. No one said anything. "It's a gun," he said softly. "A submarine is nothing but a damn big pistol, big enough to hold men, food, fuel, and tons of machinery.

And it'll move and shoot on the surface or below it. But still—all it is is a big pistol. Loaded with blanks in this case, but still loaded. And in this case it's pointed, actually, at only one man, and that man a stranger, as you said, with everything depending on how he will act. You make good sense."

He dropped his chair suddenly down onto its front legs with a bang, staring up at me now, standing beside him. "But maybe you'll believe me when I tell you this: I'd have no part of any scheme that depended on *guessing* what some damn-fool stranger would do with a gun pointed at him. Against all odds and common sense—a lead-pipe cinch to fail—the guy might put up a fight just the same, tell you to go ahead and pull the trigger; you're absolutely right." Again he shoved his chair back, thumbs hooking in his trunks, looking up at me, and smiling sardonically. "Except about one thing," he said softly. "This ain't no ordinary stranger, mister." For a moment he stared at me, then suddenly barked out, "Think about it! I don't know who he is, what he looks like, or even what his name is. But I don't have to. All I have to know is that there aren't any more than twenty-five people in the whole world like him. He's one of a damned special group. And that means there's *only one possible way he can act*—I don't care what he's like personally! Maybe he's the kind of guy who'd charge a machine gun to keep you from stealing two bits from his pocket; it don't matter. In this setup there's only one thing he can possibly let himself do. *I* know that. Frank knows it." Very quietly he added, "And you ought to know it, too. All of you! Let yourself think about it. Figure out every other choice he's got. And then tell me the answer." For a moment, glancing around the table, he stared at us; then he grinned suddenly. "I'm going for a swim," he said pleasantly, and swung around on his chair, got up, and walked toward the front door. Over his shoulder, he called, "Think about it, Brittain; take your time. We've got all the rest of the afternoon."

For a while Vic and I lay on the beach, facing the ocean, chins on our folded forearms, watching Moreno swim awkwardly but powerfully, far out in the water; Vic in his denims and blue shirt, while I still wore my trunks. We talked, casually and idly, mostly speculating about surf fishing here. Vic thought it might be good, and wished he could try it. Lauffnauer sat up on the porch, and Linc, I knew, was lying inside on the davenport, reading a paperback book. Presently Rosa came out and walked to the water, moving very gracefully and prettily, pulling a white rubber cap over her hair. She waded right in, then struck out, swimming on a course that took her away from Moreno. Five or six hundred yards out, she turned on her back and lay floating on the swell.

I stood up then, walked to the water, and swam out to her; I wanted to find out about this girl. I reached her, then floating on the slow swell beside her, our feet and hands moving occasionally to keep afloat, I made a little conversation—about the weather, the beach, and what a nice day it was. She responded politely enough for a time, her English accented but good, and quite fluent. Then she said abruptly, "All right; now what do you want to know?"

"About you," I said. "Why are you in this?"

She shrugged, lying there floating in the water. Then she gestured with her chin toward Moreno, several hundred yards away; he was swimming toward us, I saw. "He told you," she said.

"Yeah; your boat. And the dock. But why? I still want to know."

"What is there to explain?" She was laughing at me for some reason, mockingly, with her eyes. "Isn't money enough reason?"

"Maybe; maybe it is. What do you want it for?"

"Oh—" again she shrugged—"fur coats. Diamond rings, jewelry; don't you think I will look nice in them?"

"Sure," I said, nodding, and—I couldn't help it—I glanced at her fine full figure awash in the swell. "Though you don't need them."

"No!" she said angrily, and her arms and legs thrashed as she lifted her head and shoulders from the water to glare at me. "I do not! Now or ever! Listen, you. You have never lived—and survived—in a poor country! You do not know what it is like; you don't! You send CARE packages, and you are sorry, but you don't know." Her arms moving slowly, keeping her afloat, she stared at me for a moment, then said quietly, "But I lived in Italy; as a child in a war, and afterward. I saw small children roaming in packs like animals, hunting for food. It is better now, but still worse than anything you ever knew. So what will I do—with money?" Her eyes widened, and she shook her head slowly several times. "I will take it, and I will spend it. Where it will do more good than you have ever thought of. You and the greedy rest of them up there." She nodded toward the shore and the little house; I could see Vic, a small blue figure on the sand, and Lauffnauer sitting on the porch rail.

"Okay." I nodded. "So now I know."

"Maybe." She smiled, her mood swiftly and utterly changed again, the mocking amusement back in her eyes, and I was suddenly annoyed, my face showing it, which only increased her amusement. I'd known her less than an hour, and she'd done this several times as though I were a child, my understanding limited, though she was certainly four or five years younger than I was. "You could not keep me out of this," she murmured. "Moreno tried. I was to stay home, and wait; knitting perhaps." She laughed. "Am I not a nice girl, Mr. Brittain? Perhaps you would like to kiss me."

I was staring at her; nothing occurred to me to say in answer. Then I heard a little splash, and looked up past Rosa. Moreno was swimming toward us, no more than a dozen yards away, and Rosa smiled, and turned to him. "What took you so long?" she called sweetly. "There is no telling what might have happened with Hugh and me—out here in the ocean," and Moreno's face flushed. He glanced at me, a look of pure hostility and warning, then gestured savagely at Rosa with his chin.

"Come on," he said roughly, angrily, and she nodded, her face blandly obedient, and began to swim with him toward the shore. Yet I knew she was humoring him only to amuse herself; and that Moreno knew it, was helpless against it, and that in that moment at least, he hated me for knowing it, too.

I gave them a start of a hundred yards or so—I didn't know what was between Moreno and his widowed relative—then swam slowly to shore after them.

When I got back, taking my time, Rosa was in the house, and Moreno was on the porch, dressed for the city, wearing tan slacks, and a short-sleeved white knit shirt, open at the collar. It was time for him to go back, and a few moments later Rosa came out, too, carrying a small bag, and wearing a good-looking summer print dress, sheer stockings, and high-heeled shoes. They came down the porch steps, and called goodbye to us, Vic and Lauffnauer answering. Then I stood up from the sand. "Moreno!" I called, and walked toward them.

You do your important thinking, I've noticed—or at least I do— when you're not consciously thinking at all. Your mind goes off somewhere by itself, in a manner of speaking, and then presently returns to let your conscious self know that it has reached a decision. I'm not making excuses, but—the French have a phrase, *fait accompli,* which means, as I understand it, an accomplished fact. And the power of the *fait accompli* is enormous. If Vic had told me on Saturday what I'd learned today, I wouldn't have bothered to even laugh in his face.

With no need for thought or debate, I'd have said no automatically; I'd never in my life done anything more seriously illegal than parking overtime.

But somehow it was different today, here on the spot, seeing the submarine, seeing the others; and I hadn't instantly said no—I'd waited. Don't blame me too fast. You can't brag about your virtue because you haven't robbed the local bank, and don't intend to; not if you're stopped by simple fear of the consequences, or haven't the faintest idea of how to go about it. It's easy enough to resist temptation when no temptation exists, and most of us live out our lives and die in the conviction that we're honest—because no real test of it ever occurred. Wait till you're tested before you condemn me too much for what I did now.

As Rosa and Moreno came down the porch steps, a tiny excitement rose up in me, physically felt in the pit of my stomach. It began and grew instantly, coursing through my nerves, tangibly, like a shot of whisky. For now I knew, without any conscious previous thought, that astonishing as this fantastic scheme was, it could work; it might—it was just possible. And I knew, too, that I was going into it. As I stood and called to Moreno, he stopped and stood waiting for me on the sand, his eyes and face expressionless.

I walked up to him and nodded shortly. "All right," I said, "I'm in."

He looked me up and down, face still expressionless, then nodded. "Okay," he said, "we've got a crew. See you later." Then he gestured to Rosa with his chin, and they walked on, down the beach toward the ferry.

Five

AT SIX-THIRTY, during the last hour of full daylight, Frank Lauffnauer changed to trunks in the bedroom off the living room, while I got dressed again. He finished changing, then carefully wrapped his clothes in a big striped beach towel. "Mind taking these out for me, Hugh?" he said, and I took the bundle.

"Listen," I said, "take it easy out there. The light won't be so good."

"It'll do," he said, and grinned at me.

We left the house, the four of us, Vic locking the door behind us, and walked down to the beached boat carrying Frank's diving equipment, including a fresh tank of air and a good powerful underwater light. The surface was breaking a little harder than it had been earlier, but the swell beyond it was still smooth; it was still bright daylight, too, though it wouldn't last long.

We rowed out toward the sub, Vic in the stern watching his particular set of landmarks to get us there. Linc was rowing, and I began sounding with the anchor presently; when it showed ninety feet, I snubbed the anchor rope, and we all began watching for the white-pine buoy Moreno had attached to the sub. Frank spotted it first, and we rowed over, and I anchored beside it. All this time no one had talked very much, and no one said anything now; Frank Lauffnauer was about to do a dangerous and frightening thing. He was going into the sub through her escape hatch if he could, and none of us had any particular comment to make to him about that right now.

Helping him on with his equipment—tank, lung, weight belt, flippers —none of us made the meaningless gesture of offering to take Frank's place; Frank was the man to do this. He'd been instructed and trained in using this very hatch; though not to enter but to leave the sub by, and in 1918 when the sub was new and he was a very young man. Now, years later, to try entering that sub, alone and far under the ocean, not knowing what he'd find even if he succeeded—I didn't envy him, and was willing to admit that to myself.

He stood up in the boat now, fastening the underwater light to his weight belt; then he grinned at us, nodding a goodbye, and let himself fall over the side. Then the rest of us, kneeling at the prow of the boat, watched him sink steadily down in the water, following the anchor line, till he faded from sight.

The escape hatch of the *U-19*—Frank had described it—was a simple device: a steel tube set into the topside of the submarine, just big enough to hold a man, crouched. At the top side of the tube was a watertight hatch cover. Inside the submarine at the tube's bottom end was another round watertight door. To escape from the submarine, the idea was, a man crawled into the escape tube from the bottom, inside the sub. Clinging to a riveted hand and foothold inside it, he pulled the hatch closed underneath his feet, or someone inside did it for him. Then he turned a valve which admitted sea water into the tiny space he was crouched in. The water came in, compressing the air into the top of the escape tube. Presently the inside and outside pressures on the hatch cover just over his head were equalized; and the man in the tube could push open the hatch, and leave the submarine, a spring on the hatch cover closing it behind him. Whether he ever reached the top, or if he did, whether he reached it alive, was another question; it depended on a lot of things, any of which could go wrong.

Frank must be at that hatch right now, I knew; he was about to pull open the cover of that escape hatch, might be doing it this moment. If he got it open, he would climb inside it, and crouching there in the tube in the water, he would pull the lid closed over him; the thought of it made me actually shiver, sitting up on the surface with Linc and Vic in the boat. When the upper hatch cover closed over Frank as he clung to the brackets inside the tube, he would unfasten and shove open the round metal door at his feet, if he could. And then he would see one of two things. Frank would see and feel the water in which he crouched drop away from him, out the bottom of the tube down into the submarine. Or the water would simply stay where it was, unmoving—because the submarine, long since undoubtedly, was filled with sea water already. Frank would open the hatch just over his head then, and leave the little sub behind him forever.

If that's what happened, if Frank reappeared climbing up our anchor rope in the next few minutes, our adventure was over before it had really begun. For with the sub full of sea water, we couldn't possibly raise her, and there'd be no reason to do so anyway; she'd undoubtedly be ruined in that case.

But there was hope of raising her if Frank—and it might be happening underneath us right now!—felt the water in the escape hatch drain away from him. There'd be hope then, and fearful danger for Frank. For in that case he'd climb down into the submarine. He would keep his lung on; he would not try to breathe the dead air through which he moved. All oxygen would be gone from it, we believed; used up long since in corrosion. This was why we hoped to find not too much corrosion throughout the submarine if we raised her; for no new air, no additional oxygen could have entered the little sub since the day she went under. Once corrosion had used up the original oxygen, it would virtually stop, we believed and hoped. Moving through that dead air, his light on, breathing from the tank on his back, Frank would blow the sub's ballast tanks if he could. For that was the final *if;* had the valves of the air flasks held, too? Was there pressure enough still to blow the water from the ballast tanks, and allow the *U-19* to rise to the top once again? Almost superstitiously I said yes; if one set of valves had held and the sub wasn't flooded, then our luck would be good and these valves, too—the valves of the air flasks—would also have held. It wasn't true—it didn't follow at least; but I believed it.

It occurred to me suddenly that the first question was already answered. We sat staring down into the water along the white slanting line of our anchor rope—and Frank hadn't reappeared, climbing up through the water toward us. Vic said it aloud. "He's inside the sub now," he muttered excitedly. "Unless he's trapped in the escape hatch—can't get in or out."

"Don't talk that way," I said. Vic shrugged. "Linc," I said, just to be saying something, "what're you doing in the States?"

"Well—" he smiled—"perhaps you've read how very many men have migrated from England—young men, at least; it's been going on quite steadily ever since the war. There's not a great deal of opportunity left in England any more. At times one can actually see long queues of men waiting on the sidewalks before various consulates, getting visas for Australia, Canada, the States. I left two years ago."

"Hasn't worked out for you, though," I said questioningly.

"No, I wouldn't say so."

"Why not?"

"Well, where would you say I'd been living since the day I got off the boat?" He smiled again.

"Harlem?"

"Certainly; where else? In a single room, with a bathroom on the floor which I share with nine others. But the rent is sixty-five dollars a month; that's a third of what I make, because the jobs I've been able to get—night elevator man, janitor, dishwasher, shoeshine boy in a barber shop—don't pay very much. I'm afraid I leaped from the frying pan into the fire."

"Like to go back?"

"With my share of the loot, I would. Otherwise it doesn't matter."

"What would you do?"

He smiled pleasurably, sitting there in the bottom of the boat, his teeth flashing white, his dark skin almost invisible in the near-darkness. "I'd open an inn," he said softly. "There's quite an old one, not a dozen miles from where I was born. Three hundred years old, a fine old place, but in rather bad repair. But if that place were modernized—skillfully, I mean, so that one couldn't see it, and was hardly aware of it—that place would do well, I'm sure." The quality of his voice changed, and I knew he was talking to himself now, speaking an old daydream aloud, and I wondered if it could ever possibly come true. "A new slate and lead roof," he said lovingly, "walls insulated, central heating, bathrooms that work, old rotten beams duplicated with sound lumber, new floors—a million things. Keep all the charm of the old place, but make it quite comfortable, run a good restaurant, and you'd be in business, as you say, and a good one. I should think we'd have waitresses in Elizabethan costume," he went on, "and a hand-painted signboard hanging out front, the way it was when the place was new. Restore not only the inn but its atmosphere. But out of sight of the front is an asphalt parking space, and out of sight of the guests is a stainless-steel kitchen; do you see what I mean?" I nodded, and Linc said, "That will take money." His teeth flashed in a smile again. "So I'm trying to get it. If the world won't give me a chance to get it any other way, then with no hard feelings on my part, I'm going to take it if I can."

I nodded; several minutes had passed and now we heard the sound of Moreno's diesel, and looked up to see the big fishing boat slowly approaching through the last of the daylight, perhaps a quarter mile away. This was the worst moment of all. I knew, I suddenly *knew* that

Frank was inside the submarine he'd left so many years before. Sitting there in the boat a hundred feet above him, Moreno's big boat chugging steadily toward us, I could see Frank in my mind, moving through the pitch-blackness of that ancient little sub by the beam of his light— a strange weird figure, peering through his mask, flippers still on his feet, glancing around him, glancing occasionally at the watch on his wrist, waiting till it was time to blow the ballast tanks if he could. This was the worst time of all, for if the tanks didn't blow, I wondered if Frank could escape. Would the escape hatch work properly; would it fill with sea water as it should; or if it did not, could Frank nevertheless force open the hatch cover just over his head against the pressure of a hundred feet of water lying on top of it? Suppose he were trapped forever in the little sub he'd left forty years before, waiting for the air in the tank on his back to be exhausted? Suppose Fate had never intended that he should really escape her? I simply made myself quit thinking about it, and waited.

We sat in the boat smoking, watching Moreno bring the big fishing boat steadily closer, listening to the low steady growl of his big diesel. I dropped my cigarette over the side, and heard it hiss as the water doused it. Then I stared down the anchor rope again, wondering what Frank was doing at this instant. Suddenly I pictured him trapped between the two metal doors of the escape hatch, shouting and screaming for help there under the water; and I lighted another cigarette, then realized what I'd done, and threw it after the first. Moreno's boat swelled in size, growing fast, heading directly toward us, and I muttered angrily, "Be ready to jump if the damn fool runs us down."

He passed us close, deliberately, I knew, rocking our boat; and slowly continued on till he was perhaps a hundred yards to the west of us, and between us and the shore. He reversed his engine then, the propeller thrashing, and I heard the splash of his anchor. The engine died, and in the new silence I turned to look at the sun, low over the dunes behind us. We were timing this, or trying to, to avoid attracting any more attention than we had to; none at all with reasonable luck, for there weren't many people on the island this time of year. We couldn't wait for full dark, but we were cutting it as close as we could.

The big boat was in position now, anchored well clear of the sub, and Linc hauled up our anchor, and we rowed clear too, and lay drifting on the gentle swell, a dozen yards from the side of Moreno's boat. Moreno had turned on his running lights, and he stood watching us, leaning on the rail, his face green in the reflected rays of the light on the side. "Think I was going to run you down?" he said, grinning.

"Sure," I said, "give you half a chance. Lauffnauer's down." I nodded over my shoulder. I heard a step behind Moreno then, and turned to see Rosa appear from the little cabin. She walked to the rail, glancing casually down at us; she was wearing dark slacks and a dark turtle-necked sweater. Then, without speaking—she wasn't interested in us now—she turned to stare out over the water toward the floating white board under which lay the submarine.

Now we waited in absolute silence, no one saying even a word. The edge of the sun was below the horizon, and dropping surprisingly fast, as it always does when you actually watch it set. It was dusk on the slow swell of the ocean, the air suddenly chill, and I was fearfully glad that I wasn't Frank Lauffnauer.

Suddenly, loudly, Moreno said, "It's time, damn it, it's *time!* What the hell's the matter with him!" No one answered, and we waited for I don't know how long then; it might have been a minute, a half minute, or it might have been four or five. The sun was down completely now, and though it was still daylight in the sky, the first star was suddenly visible, and here on the face of the ocean it was more night than day. I must have looked away for a moment without realizing it, for it was the sound that I heard first; the sound, not loud yet enormous and strangely prolonged, of a vast object gently breaking the surface of the water a hundred yards away; the sound, it must be, of a whale emerging on the surface. It was a sort of enormous gentle plop, and as I jerked my head up to stare I was grinning; for I had already heard the familiar sound of water draining from the docks of a submarine. And then, there she lay, out on the water. Her deck was nearly awash; but the fuzzed silhouette of the conning tower of the *U-19* lay above the surface, black against the darkening horizon, in the center of a widening ring on the smooth surface of the ocean.

We yelled; the exultant sounds tore at the linings of our throats, and we thumped each other's backs till the boat rocked. Then Vic was at the oars, grinning wildly, heading for the sub. Moreno shouted angrily then, and Vic braked, shoving on the oars. Then he rowed toward the big boat instead. As we passed under her stern, Moreno dropped a great coil of line, new inch-and-a-half manila hawser, into our boat. I heard a dull metallic clank out on the water, and swung around in my seat to see Frank Lauffnauer standing in the conning tower of the sub. There was another clank as he quickly closed the hatch cover at his feet again, then he pulled off his mask and mouthpiece. He yelled at us exultantly. *"Gott sei dank!"* he shouted over the smooth water, and Vic began to row then, heaving hard on the oars, through the new darkness toward the *U-19*.

Behind us I heard the whine of the electric anchor motor on Moreno's boat, then the big diesel rumbled to life again, and now Moreno was ready to maneuver if the sub drifted too close. His lights could be seen from shore, of course, but Rosa had made a point of mentioning to those few neighbors who were on the island that she and her husband—that was Moreno—had just bought a cabin cruiser. They were bringing it over tonight to take the rest of us home. Anyone seeing Moreno's lights now would figure that that was what was happening out here, I felt sure. I doubted that anyone could see the sub's dark tower from shore, and the bulk of Moreno's boat lay between it and shore anyway.

At the side of the sub, Linc and I helped Frank—he was shivering, his teeth chattering, but grinning—down into the boat, clapping him gently on the back, murmuring our congratulations. Linc began helping him out of his gear then, and he gave him a pint bottle of whisky to nip at. Vic rowed to the prow of the wet moss-coated little sub, and I slipped an end of the big hawser through her towing eye, and pulled about fifty feet of the heavy line on through it.

We rowed back to the boat then, Frank and the rest climbed up on deck, and I handed up Frank's clothes. There was a moment then—I in the rowboat staring up at the others, lined up at the rail looking down at me—when we just grinned at each other, almost foolishly, like a bunch of kids. What the odds had been against us up to this point; what the chances of the *U-19*'s valves giving away long before this point—I didn't know, and certainly I no longer cared, nor did any of us. *We brought it off!* I thought, grinning up at the others. Then I turned to stare out over the darkened water at the dim, almost invisible silhouette of the *U-19*'s tower. *And now we've got our submarine,* I thought; then I heard the chatter of Frank Lauffnauer's teeth, and when I turned to look back at him and at the others, there along the rail, I was no longer smiling.

Someone had to ride the sub, and I'd volunteered. There was nothing I or anyone could do if she started to founder, except to sing out; but if the towline broke, Moreno's boat would shoot ahead for no telling how many dozens of yards before she could reverse, and the sub might be lost in the dark. In that case, we needed someone aboard with a flashlight, to locate the sub again. I'd volunteered, I didn't quite know why; her deck awash, there was no place to ride except the little conning tower, and it would be slimed and wet and scaly with rust. But that's where I wanted to be, and Moreno was in the cabin getting me a set of boots and oilskins to protect my clothes and keep me dry. Forward in the boat, I saw Vic and Linc sprawled on the deck; they were wearing heavy jackets of some sort now; I couldn't see them too clearly. Just above me, Frank Lauffnauer stood, quickly dressing, staring back at the ancient German sub he'd served in more than half a lifetime before, and I wondered what he was thinking. Rosa stood on deck leaning against a wall of the little cabin, and I saw Moreno come out and say something to her. I couldn't hear what it was, and in the faint reflected gleam of the running lights I saw her shrug. He murmured something again, and she replied—in Italian, I realized now—then she stood up, walked to the door of the cabin, and ducking her head, stepped down inside. Moreno followed, said something else in Italian, and I heard Rosa reply angrily; a moment later she stepped out, her arms draped with a bulk I couldn't make out, and walked toward me. She stopped at the rail, and I saw she was carrying oilskins, boots, and a blanket. "I'm going with you," she said quietly, "if you don't mind."

"Sure," I said after a moment, surprised. "Glad to have you." Then Moreno stepped to the rail and dropped my gear, almost flinging it, into the bottom of the boat, and walked away. Rosa laughed aloud at him, handed her gear down to me, then swung a leg over the rail, and I reached up to help her into the boat.

I rowed back to the sub, then, and sitting in the boat, we struggled awkwardly into our boots and oilskins. Holding to the conning tower, I helped Rosa up, then passed her the blankets. I tied the boat to the conning-tower rail with a dozen feet of line, then climbed in beside Rosa, and hailed Moreno.

The diesel rumbling at low speed then, Moreno very carefully maneuvered his boat, keeping the towline slack—he handled her beautifully, I had to admit—till he lay directly ahead of the drifting sub. Then he moved forward, very cautiously and very slowly, and the arc of the heavy towline slowly lifted from the water, and we heard it dripping. Slowly the arc flattened, we heard the creak of the gradually tightening line, then it was taut, angling up from the sub's bow to the boat in the darkness ahead. Carefully and evenly, Moreno opened the throttle, and almost imperceptibly we were moving. Steadily the speed built up, and standing there in the dank little tower, we could feel the beginning breeze of our movement on our cheeks, and now I could hear the ripple of water at the base of the tower. We moved ahead then, curving gradually onto a southeast course, at a steady eight or nine knots, I judged.

There was no moon yet, and it would be less than a quarter-moon when finally it appeared. This night had been chosen for that reason among others; from any more than thirty or forty feet, only the boat's running light would be visible. The danger of our sub being seen by anyone was almost nonexistent.

Rosa's oilskins rustled, and I glanced down to see her tugging something from her pocket; then she brought out a thermos full of coffee, and I grinned. "You're a bright girl," I said, and she unscrewed the plastic top, then poured it half full.

"There is no cream, and no sugar," she said, offering me the cup. "Do you mind?"

"No, I like it that way. Go ahead, have yours, then I'll have mine."

"We will have it together," she said, shrugging a shoulder. "Unless you wish not to; you Americans worry so about germs."

"Suits me," I said, and she took a sip or two, then offered me the cup, and I had some; it was good coffee, nice and hot. Then I passed the cup back to her.

We had two cups of coffee that way, and there was something pleasant and companionable about sharing a cup as we did, and I was very aware of this handsome young woman beside me. There was something exhilarating, too, about this strange journey through the dark, across the smooth water, our feet actually lower than the ocean level, standing in a space no larger than a small closet. "It's not too comfortable here," I said, "and it won't get any better. Why'd you come out, Rosa? Okay if I call you Rosa?"

She smiled, shifting her position a little. "This would be a strange place to be formal; yes, call me Rosa. I will say Hugh. I came out here because I did not wish to be there." She nodded at the vague shape of the boat ahead.

"Was Moreno annoying you?"

She laughed contemptuously. "Not as you mean. He is careful, he wants to marry me, so he speaks and looks carefully; I made him understand that he must. But he hungers after me; all the time; he cannot hide it. And I am sick of it. This Vic of yours understands better; he knows how I am feeling, and he is pleasant and polite, nothing more.

But he also is just waiting his time, and I do not like even this just now."

"And Linc and Frank?"

She shrugged. "They live in dreams; I am nothing to them."

"That leaves only me."

She smiled. "We will see about you; this is a good place to find out, is it not?" Then she stopped smiling, and said, "I am a widow, Hugh; of four months; I do not want men just now. In time I will again, and when I do I will welcome attention. I do not understand these women; they dress so beautifully, they spend so much money and time on their hair and faces, they make their figures beautiful. Then a man looks at them, enjoying what he sees and showing it, and they are insulted, their faces grow cold. What is the reason for that? I do not understand it. Now, my husband just dead, I am not ready for men looking and staring at me, so I do not dress for it."

"You must have been in love with him."

"Love, love." She shrugged a shoulder, her oilskins crackling. "He was my husband, and I was his wife. Whether I loved him or not, that is less important than you think."

"Okay, okay," I said. "You're twenty-two or three, no older, and I'm twenty-six. But you talk as though you were fifty, and I were fifteen."

She just smiled—laughing at me again—and didn't say anything, and I felt my face flush angrily, then I laughed, too.

It was a long night, a very strange one, and it was oddly enjoyable. The stars came out in full force presently, looking a lot closer, as always, on the water than they ever do on land. And after a while a curved sliver of moon came out, making a faint glittering path on the water. We slept a little, from time to time, taking turns sitting down in the confined damp little space and using the blanket as padding over the outer hatch cover. We'd tried sitting down at the same time, but we were jammed tight against each other in our slickers, and while Rosa might have been the girl you'd most want to be confined with in a conning tower, it was just plain uncomfortable, and we gave it up. At times, leaning on the rail, or lounging back in the little tower, we talked a little. Rosa learned something of my previous history, and when I asked her, she told me something about Italy, and her life over here. Her marriage to Moreno's cousin, I learned, had been arranged by an uncle, in a correspondence from Italy; she'd never seen him, only photographs, before she came over to marry him. I thought that was strange, but apparently she didn't think so.

Once, without any preliminaries—we'd been silent for some minutes—Rosa said, "My father, a brother, a cousin, my sister, and my mother were shot by the Germans in Naples. They were partisans, we all were; and they were betrayed, arrested at home, and shot within half an hour. I was not home, and I never returned; I stayed with an aunt and uncle in a suburb across the bay. And I acted as a courier for eight more months, until the Americans drove the Germans from Italy. Once I carried through Naples in a basket the grenades that destroyed a German staff car, killing four officers."

"When was that?"

"In 1944."

"You were—how old?"

"Nine, nearly ten." She glanced up at my face for a moment—we were leaning on the conning-tower rail facing forward—then burst into laughter. "Look at you!" she said. "You are picturing a little girl in pigtails; wearing an Alice in Wonderland dress, perhaps. Isn't it so?"

"Well . . . I don't know; something like that, maybe. I was thinking of—well, you *were* scared, weren't you?" I said irritably.

"Yes. Of course," she said quietly. "But if you are picturing a terrified, frightened, innocent little nine-year-old, it was not like that." She smiled a little, staring ahead over the water. "I was frightened, but I was excited, too, and I liked it. I carried messages, sometimes written, sometimes remembered. And I carried weapons, clothes, food, forged military passes. I loved it, Hugh, and I knew what would happen to me if I were caught; I was no ordinary child. And I am no ordinary woman. I look forward to what we are going to do; for the money, and what I will be able to do with it; and for the danger and excitement of it, too. You could not keep me from it."

"You're right," I said, nodding. "You're not exactly a typical Brownie or Camp Fire Girl."

"What is that?"

"Never mind," I said. "You wouldn't be interested."

All night we moved through the water at a steady eight or nine knots, and not once did we see a boat or even a set of running lights. Twice we saw planes, far overhead, the sounds of their motors fading slowly, their lights blinking regularly. Every once in a while someone from the boat would hail, and I'd answer.

A half hour before daylight we curved in toward the shore. I couldn't see anything different about this stretch of coastline. It was as dark, formless, and as lightless as it had been for some miles now, but obviously it was different to Moreno. Several hundred yards out, he reduced speed so slowly and expertly that while the towline went slack, it never touched the water until we were nearly dead stopped. He shut down the diesel then, the two boats drifting with hardly any way, and it was the sub, all her bulk under the water, that stopped first, of course, the towline tightening till it creaked, then slacking off again.

We waited, then, for dawn. Once Moreno had to start up his engine, and tow us in a wide sweeping circle back to our starting point; the two boats had drifted too close. At the very first hint of whitening sky to the east, I hauled the small boat up to the conning tower, then Rosa and I rowed back to the big boat, and she got out. Vic climbed down into my boat, a thick coil of half-inch line looped around his forearm, and we rowed—fast, now—to the sub. We hailed the boat, and they pulled in the towline, then Vic knotted an end of his line to the towing eye, and I rowed for shore, Vic paying out the line as we moved.

On shore, in the first faint light, I could see the vague bulk of the dock I was heading for. We reached it, and I saw that it was typical of its kind. It looked like a house, or perhaps a small-sized barn, set on piles in the water at the very edge of the shore. It had a steep gabled roof, shingled with wood, old, weathered, and a little green with mold. There were several large, dusty windows under each of its eaves, and the entire end of the structure facing the water was a big double wood door, its bottom a foot or so under water just now. Standing in the boat, Vic unlocked the padlock, and with me backstroking the boat, he pulled the doors open. Inside, two feet above the water—the tide was high now—two platforms, each about four feet wide, extended the length of the building, one on each side and about a dozen feet apart. Between them was water, and at the far end of the building, the two platforms were connected by a third which extended across the back of the building.

We rowed inside, climbed out, and tied up the boat just outside the door. Then, the line over our shoulders, we began to pull; and we didn't move. With the sub a dead weight in the water, we could not overcome her inertia. Our upper bodies almost parallel with the dock planking, the rope biting into our shoulders, we heaved and strained till the sweat poured into our eyes, and we didn't gain a single inch.

The sky was lightening fast, there was a hint of orange sun just under the horizon, and now I saw a chain hoist hanging from the center beam, about where you'd need it to work on the boat's engine. We found a fourteen-foot plank lying against a side wall, shoved an end of it over to the opposite side, and using it as a bridge I got under the hoist, caught the chain, and lowered it enough to tie on our line. And now, the chain rattling through the pulleys, we started the little sub moving easily. Once it started, we pulled it by hand, the little conning tower moving steadily through the white dawn toward us. It had dried during the night, and now I saw for the first time that under the slime that coated it, it was red with rust.

There were a couple of fending poles lying on nails in the wall, and while Vic stood on the platform at the far end of the building, hauling in the line, I shoved on the sub's side with the pole and guided her into the slip. She was shorter than Rosa's boat, narrower in the beam, and she came in easily; and now there she lay, deck submerged, gently nudging the buffing of old tires nailed to the sides of the slip.

In two trips with the small boat, Vic ferried in the others, and then —Rosa's boat anchored two hundred yards beyond low-tide line—we all stood lined up on the dock in the first full bright daylight, staring in silence at the ancient little submarine. "Well, here she is," Linc murmured then. "Next question; will she ever operate again?"

I said, "How we going to raise her? After forty years, the valves'll probably stick, if we try to blow her."

Lauffnauer nodded at the water. "We piled concrete blocks in the slip at low tide. Three layers of them on the bottom, more on the sides. There are only a few inches of water between her and the blocks now. When the tide goes out, she will rest on the blocks; a crude drydock. You have props ready, Ed?" He turned to Moreno.

"Right there." Moreno nodded at the end wall—his face sullen, I thought; he hadn't once looked at Rosa or me—and now I saw a couple of dozen newly cut two-by-fours piled neatly against the wall.

We propped the conning tower right away: a couple of long two-by-fours on each side, one end of each resting against the tower, the other ends lying on the platforms about an inch from the walls, the two-by-fours angling upward slightly toward the tower. As the tide ran out and the sub lowered, the two-by-fours would move down toward the parallel, wedging themselves tight against the walls. They'd been cut carefully to size for this; Moreno had measured the conning tower under water, and the distance between the dock walls.

About a hundred and fifty yards behind the dock was a two-room shack, with a small septic-tank bathroom. A plank walkway led from a rear door at the side of the enclosed dock, across the swampy shore-land and up a gradual incline for fifty yards or so to solid dry ground. Then a path continued across the rocky weed-clustered earth to the door of the shack. Rosa's husband had kept a few cots in here, a secondhand electric refrigerator—there was a power line into the place, which continued on to the dock—a two-burner hot plate, and a few cooking utensils. He and his one- or two-man crew had slept here occasionally, when they were going out to fish before dawn, or when they'd come in very late. Now Rosa went on up to the shack to fix us some breakfast. They'd laid supplies in for that, and—I learned later—extra cots for us all.

The rest of us stayed, watching the sub inch downward in the slip, as the tide lowered. The conning-tower props moved slowly to the parallel, as we guided and kept them in position. Presently their ends touched the walls; then they began to squeak and groan against the wall studs as the pressure tightened. The slimed deck planking began to break the surface of the water, and we knew the sub's bottom had touched the concrete block floor underneath her.

There were two handsaws, newly sharpened, hanging from nails in the wall, and now Moreno took a small cardboard box lying on a wall studding. There were five brand-new metal tape measures in it; we each took one, and Vic and Linc each took a saw. Saw in hand, Vic knelt at the edge of the platform on one side of the sub, Linc on the other, each with several lengths of two-by-fours beside them. Then, as the waterline sank, exposing the sub's sides, the rest of us measured distances between the platform pilings and the sub's sides, calling them off to Vic or Linc. They sawed off the short lengths required, and we wedged them into place, stomping them down with the heels of our shoes, pounding them tight. Finally, a short prop between every piling and the sides of the sub, we were finished, and again we sat on the dock staring and silent, watching in fascination as more and more of the ancient little sub came into view.

Rosa walked in with a big battered metal tray loaded with fried-egg and scrambled-egg sandwiches on paper napkins, an assortment of old jelly glasses filled with canned orange or grapefruit juice, a big gray enamel coffeepot, and a stack of chipped cups, mostly handleless. We ate then, sitting in a row, legs dangling over the sides of the platform, and again—it was curious—we said hardly a word. We simply sat, chewing and sipping in silence, staring in wonder at the old sub, watching the waterline slowly sink. The water was well down now, the ballast tanks half exposed. The upper portions of the sub's sides were drying, and as they dried the red rust revealed itself under the slime. Drying, it changed from black to dull orange to a bright vivid orange finally, and it was thick and scaly, the sides deeply pitted. I wondered how much of the thickness of the pressure hull was gone, where it was most thin, and what pressures it would and would not withstand now.

The same thoughts were in everyone's mind, I'm sure, for in just that moment Vic murmured—absently, speaking to no one in particular, "She doesn't leak too much, we know that, but . . ." He stopped, slowly shaking his head, and Frank Lauffnauer spoke. His thin face was grave, and the lines down his cheeks seemed deeper.

"Now it is time to look inside," he said. "And I will go first. I saw almost nothing last night; there was no time, and it was hard to see with the mask on."

We scrambled to our feet then, suddenly excited—Linc tossed the last of his sandwich into the water, not bothering to finish it, and Moreno was grinning, his sullenness forgotten. Vic's black eyes were flashing; he was wild to get into the sub, and Moreno snatched a long coil of heavy black extension cord from the wall, a caged hundred-watt bulb at one end, and plugged it into a wall outlet. Then he handed it to Lauffnauer, who took it, and jumped across the few feet of water right over the cable railing onto the deck. And now, with the sub out of the water, and the full unsupported weight of his body dropping onto the rotted and pulpy wooden deck gratings, his feet went through them as though they'd been soft cheese. He fell to his knees, and his knees too plunged through the sodden wood. It must have hurt, but he didn't show it. He got right to his feet, stumbling a little, his feet going through again, then got to the conning tower, and climbed into it.

We waited—this was his right—and I saw him stoop, his head and shoulders disappearing, then I heard him grunt, and knew he was tugging at the hatch cover. It creaked, then snapped open, striking the conning-tower wall with a dull clang, and I waited for the sound of Frank's steps down the inner ladder.

Instead he stood suddenly upright, hurling himself away from the newly opened hatch, his face contorting, and we stood staring, astounded. Then he thrust his upper body over the edge of the conning tower as far as he could get, and began coughing deep in his chest, inhaling harshly in great retching gasps.

[74]

The odor reached us then, and we ran, ducking low, stumbling, bumping into one another, to the open doors of the dock, where we stood leaning out over the water, breathing in the fresh morning air. Behind us, I heard Frank stumbling across the sub deck, feet breaking through the sodden planking; then he was running, his shoes pounding the dock planking to join the rest of us, and gulp in new air. It wasn't strong, the queer odor that drove us from the sub; but it was unbearable. As it permeated the whole dock, it drove us out; holding our breaths, hands clapped over our mouths, we ran the length of the dock one at a time, and out the back door, stumbling up the plank walkway, gasping. It was like nothing else I've ever encountered—made up of a kind of awful sweetness, a dryness, a harsh acrid quality, and—there simply is no describing it. Rosa looked stricken, standing on the path, bent at the waist, her eyes closed, her palms on the knees of her black slacks, and breathing deeply. We were all shaken, glancing at each other and shaking our heads; even Linc's dark skin had a sickly grayish color, and Lauffnauer stood muttering in German, his eyes haunted.

We knew what it was, but no one talked about it. "You got a pump?" I said presently to Moreno. "Any kind." He nodded, grimacing, went up to the shack, then came back down dragging a long length of discarded gasoline hosing, and a hand bilge pump.

We worked half an hour then, up on a bare patch of ground back of the marshy tideland, all of us but Rosa, who went into the shack. We took the pump apart, oiled the leather valve, then put it together again, and connected it to an end of the hose with friction tape. Then I held the end of the hose out to Vic. "You like adventure?" I said sourly, and he smiled a little, took the hose, and went into the dock, a hand tight over his face. He shoved the hose-end as deep into the open hatch as he could get it, then we all pumped, outside the dock in the sunlight, for a full hour and a half, spelling each other at ten-minute intervals. The pump wasn't very effective; it was made to pump water, not air; and our joint wasn't airtight. But nevertheless, each stroke of the pump forced a column of air from the mouth of the hose, and by ten o'clock the air in the dock was fresh again.

Once more Frank Lauffnauer climbed into the conning tower, leaned over the open hatch, and very cautiously inhaled; the rest of us watching. He paused as though listening, took a deeper sniff, then got down on his knees, and we could hear him inhale deeply. A moment later we heard the small clatter of his feet on the inside rungs and the drag of the extension cord he took with him. Then, faint and muffled, we heard his voice inside the sub. *"Gott,"* we heard him mutter, his voice awed, *"Mein Gott, mein Gott."*

"What is it?" Moreno called, and I knew from the quality of his voice that he was superstitiously frightened. Frank didn't answer, and for a moment it didn't seem to occur to any of us, standing in the dock staring at the conning tower, that we could move and go down into the sub ourselves. Then we heard Lauffnauer's shoes on the rungs, and a moment later his face appeared over the edge of the tower, white and staring. For some reason he nodded several times, the rest of us motionless, then he beckoned. We swarmed aboard then, feet crushing the sodden deck gratings, and climbed down the ladder, following Frank.

The hundred-watt bulb glared in my eyes as we all crowded, shoulder bumping shoulder, into the little control room. Frank had strung the cord through some overhead piping, the caged bulb hanging just barely over our heads. Then my eyes, blinking, accustomed themselves to the light, and I stood, as we all did, looking around me, and now I muttered in English what Frank had said in German. "My God," I said softly, staring at the figure of a man sitting as he had forty years before when he'd taken his last dying look at the world he was leaving.

One hand still resting on the periscope housing, he sat before the housed scope on a padded leather seat, held erect by a shoulder pressed against the brass housing, head slumped on his chest, the face invisible. The hand was skeletal, an ivory-yellow claw enclosed in tight-fitting parchment, on the back of which, in dark blue and faded red, lay the tattooed and wrinkled image of the Imperial German eagle. We stood facing his back, the dark-blue cloth of his jacket looking jet-black in this light, and spotted with little islands and flecks of dry brown mold. We saw the back hair—dark, long, and untrimmed—protruding from under the soiled white cap on his head; and just below it the knitted ribs of the dirty white collar of a turtle-neck sweater above the collar of his uniform jacket. *"Kapitänleutnant* Keller," Lauffnauer said gently. "He was dying and we left him here—at his own orders. It was he who filled the ballast tanks, then sat staring through the periscope as the sub slowly sank. Then he lowered the scope and sat waiting to die. And now, for him," he said softly, "it is only one moment later; he does not even know we lost the war. While I have become twice as old as he."

We heard a sound—a catch of breath in the throat—and turned; Rosa stood staring at the figure seated at the periscope, her upper lip caught between her teeth, a tear running down her cheek. "Don't cry for him!" Lauffnauer said harshly. "He would not thank you!" Then more gently he said, "He was not really a very good commander, I know now; never sure of himself; he did not like command. But he did his best, and needs no sympathy now."

We edged forward a little then, feet shuffling on the metal deck, stepping around the periscope well. Now, stooping a little, I could see the unshaven, staring face. And the face was a skull, wrapped tightly in dry and minutely wrinkled mummified skin; the teeth, exposed by the shrunken skin, grimacing; the eyes—and I was grateful for this— closed. On the soiled white cap cover above his face, the gold strap and the cap ornament of the Imperial German Navy were an absolute and solid green, not a fleck of the long-tarnished gilt visible; and so were the brass buttons and two sleeve stripes, surmounted by a crown, of the uniform jacket.

I don't know how long we stood staring at the body of this man from the past. Then Moreno came to life. "All right," he said gruffly, "let's look through the damn boat, and see what we've got."

One at a time, then, we stepped over the hatch combings, forward into the next compartment, and for a moment I was astonished—it was the *only* forward compartment, and we were in the torpedo room. After a moment Vic said, "I feel like a jet pilot looking over a World War One biplane," and I nodded. Any submarine is complex; almost every square inch of every bulkhead crammed with valves or dials, levers, wheels, piping, cables—something. But this submarine was primitive, everything we saw crude and rudimentary by every standard we'd known. At each side of the compartment were two spare torpedoes, lashed into their racks with chains, one above the other; and they were little by comparison with those I knew—eighteen-inchers, I imagined; I'd never seen one before. Overhead, mounted on a simple trolley any blacksmith could duplicate, hung an ordinary chain hoist, the trolley leading to the two forward torpedo tubes—the *only* tubes in the ship. And this whole section, the entire forward half of the ship, was hardly larger than the messroom in a World War Two ordinary S-type sub. The inside of the sub was damp, and there was plenty of rust to be seen, but it was surface rust only, not deep at all, and I saw nothing that looked badly damaged.

"She is in good condition," Lauffnauer said. "As good as we could dare hope." Then he glanced up at a hammock strung over the spare torpedoes at about shoulder height, walked over to it, and stood looking into it.

Just behind me, I heard Rosa say, "Oh!" very softly, a sad little moan, and I turned to see her looking past Frank's shoulder into the hammock he was staring at. Then I looked, too. Dressed in blues with a wide white collar, a man lay on his back in the hammock—a boy, really; the beardless skeletal face was young, or had been. His hands lay clasped on his stomach, the eyes closed, as though he were taking a nap. Frank glanced up at us, then down at the figure in the hammock again. "Rudi Koeppler," he murmured. "Still young; still seventeen. He knew he was dying, and was angry; he cursed for hours on the day he died."

On the boy's chest lay two opened envelopes, each with a canceled red stamp on which was pictured a double-headed eagle, and three photographs face up, mounted on stiff cardboard, printed in sepia. "His girl," Frank said, "and I suppose his father and mother." Vic reached out to pick them up, and we stood staring at them. One was a head-and-shoulders profile of a bald, bearded man, looking fiercely ahead. Another was a head-and-shoulders front view of a somber middle-aged woman in a high-necked dress, a cameo brooch at her throat, her long straight hair parted severely in the middle and wound into two huge buns covering her ears. The third was of a plain-looking girl, smiling artificially, her dress and hair very similar to the older woman's. Printed in gold script at the bottom of each photograph was *Krampf, Stuttgart.* We passed them around, looking at them silently, then as Moreno started to toss them back into the hammock, Lauffnauer reached out, took them, and put them, with the letters, into his coat pocket.

A man lay in the other hammock, on his side, his back to us, his knees drawn up, a rumpled blanket over his legs; and we didn't touch him. "Donner," Lauffnauer said quietly. "I put that blanket there, just as it lies now—when I was fifteen years old. He was the comedian of the crew, for the first few days at least. Donner, his name was." Frank paused, then shook his head. "I no longer remember his first name; perhaps no one in the world does, any more." Lying beside the dead man, against the white collar of his uniform, was a blue flat-topped sailor's cap, unusually wide, and with two long notched black ribbons at the back. Frank picked it up, and glanced at it; on the cap band, in green tarnished letters, in the kind of ornate script I've always thought of as old English, were the words, *Kriegsmarine-Unterseeboot.* Then Frank tossed it back into the hammock.

This was also the forward battery compartment, and now Linc walked ahead, then stooped to lift the hatch cover. Squatting on the deck, he stared down at the batteries, and Vic and Moreno edged past to join him. Moreno said, "Damn, damn!—if they'll only take a charge," but I wasn't interested just then.

I touched Lauffnauer's shoulder, and when he turned, I said quietly, "Tell me about this, Frank," gesturing around me at the boat. "Or maybe you don't remember too well."

"No," he said, "I remember very well." Glancing at the figure in the hammock beside us, he cried suddenly, *"Nicht wahr, Rudi!"*—not sentimentally, but jokingly, almost gaily. Turning back to me, he said, "But there is much also, that I myself do not know." Walking forward, he beckoned, and I followed, Rosa just behind me. Edging past the others at the open battery hatch, Frank stepped up to a small steel locker and opened it. On a shelf lay three large books, bound in lead covers, and Frank glanced at the words on their spines. "The signal, code, and log books," he said, and smiled. "We should have jettisoned them, but forgot." Then he pulled out one of the books, opened it, and glanced up at me. "You wish to know all that happened here on this ship? Forty years ago? Well—" he glanced down at the open book again—"let the ship's log tell you."

And now the others turned away from the battery hatch, Linc dropping the hatch cover, and we all gathered silently around Frank Lauffnauer, and stood like children waiting to hear a story. Then, a forefinger on the stiff, angular, Germanic script—written, I could see, in lusterless but unfaded jet-black ink—Frank began speaking slowly, his eyes rapidly scanning the loose-leaf page, his forefinger following the words. "'June third, nineteen eighteen,'" he said, and raised his eyes momentarily to add, "I remember." His eyes dropped to the page again. "'We sailed from Bremerhaven at 6:04 A.M. on an ebb tide, leaving shorthanded.'" Again he glanced up at us. "Manpower was scarce in Germany by then." He smiled. "That is why they accepted me at fifteen." Scanning the text again, he continued, "There are only nine men on the roster, a *Leutnant*—Lieutenant—who was Executive Officer, and the *Kapitänleutnant,* which is lieutenant-commander." For several moments he was silent, then he turned a page. "The log is well kept," he said presently, glancing up at us again, and turning back to the first page. "Very complete, and containing what you would expect.

He lists changes of course, headings, speeds. He lists weather; wind forces, on the Beaufort scale; condition of the sea, noon positions on Greenwich time—sometimes these are DR positions—and sightings—everything you would expect. I understood none of this then; now I do. I will omit such things, however, and translate from the rest.

" 'At 11:09 A.M. a destroyer is sighted in the North Sea, off the English coast; presumably it is English or American.' Poor judgment," Lauffnauer murmured. " 'We are heading for the English Channel. We submerged to periscope depth, surfacing one hour later. Change of course. Sighted horizon smoke at 4:00, and again at 4:30 P.M., submerging for twenty minutes each time. Recharged batteries at 9:00 P.M., lying on surface for two hours; crew allowed on deck three men at a time.' I remember that. 'Karl Hauptmann, seaman, relieved of first watch, and confined to hammock with slight fever and headache.' " Frank looked up. "I trained with Hauptmann; a big stupid farm boy. Already we'd begun calling him *Kerl,* which means lout; he did not like it. 'Distance at noon, Greenwich time, seventy-one miles.' "

Frank glanced around at us. "We did not know or even suspect this, of course, but now the ship is doomed. 'June fourth,' " he read then, " 'nineteen eighteen. We enter the Channel, approaching Orkney Island, traveling surfaced but—in the American phrase—riding the vents, ready to dive. Course remains steady all day; no sightings.' " Frank glanced up, first at us, then aft toward the silent figure of his long-dead commander. "I wonder if he suspected how very lucky we were in that. 'Recharged at midnight,' " he continued from the log. " 'Karl Hauptmann, seaman, delirious with fever, and I believe that he has *la grippe,* and have ordered him sponged hourly until fever reduces. And now at 4:00 P.M., Willi Strang, seaman, reports sick with headache, chills, and fever. I expect this to spread through the crew,' writes the captain, 'and trust the first to take sick will recover before the last of them catch it. Distance at noon, one hundred and ninety-four miles.' " Frank turned a page.

We stood around him, silently listening; Moreno and Linc leaning against the bulkhead, Vic squatting on the deck looking up at Frank, and I was aware, once again, of the old familiar submarine odor of oil and sea water. " 'June sixth,' " Frank's voice continued, " 'Karl Hauptmann, seaman, very seriously ill; high fever persists, and we cannot reduce it. The captain now believes he has pneumonia. Willi Strang, seaman, still sick, but fever lessening. Rest of crew well, *Gott sei dank.* We sighted a small freighter at daybreak'—I remember the excitement

—'estimated at six thousand tons. Followed, surfaced, but could not close. Freighter altered course at noon to west southwest, and we closed to a thousand yards. The freighter draws away on new course at forced draft, estimated three knots greater speed. Fired one torpedo, but could not follow track. Believe it hit, but suspect defective torpedo.'"

"Bull." Moreno grinned. "He missed; a stern shot with the freighter drawing away."

Lauffnauer nodded, smiling a little. "I think so too, now, though I did not then. 'Recharged at midnight,'" he continued from the log. "'Last fresh beef tonight. Distance at noon, two hundred and one miles.'"

Again he turned a page, then another. "Well, we kept on," he said. "Kept a rendezvous with a *Deutsches* sub-tender off Iceland, finally, and refueled and reprovisioned at night. The food was very poor," he said, glancing up at us. "Worse, even, than the provisions we took on in Germany. And now—" he returned to the log—"the seaman died, Hauptmann, *unser kerl,* and was buried at sea. I remember how lonely I felt out there on deck at the ceremony; a boy again for a few minutes, wishing I were home. Strang recovered. Very weak, *aber . . .* able to perform some duties. And—here it comes, now. The *Unteroffizier,* the Chief, is sick. Has fever, but . . . continues his duties. 'Inspiration to men,' writes the captain. Two others are sick; one delirious, one not so bad. We are shorthanded at the refueling, and the captain of the sub-tender—I did not know this—urges our captain to return to Germany. But Keller says no; brave and foolish. Hauptmann, he says in the log, reassuring himself, was big but soft; actually frail. He is sure the others will recover quickly, and . . . since the rest are not sick yet, that they will not be. It was not true, however; I felt weak and sick at the refueling, but said nothing; brave, perhaps, and foolish, also." Lauffnauer turned a page, read silently for some seconds, then glanced up at the rest of us again, and we looked at him, eyes wide, waiting.

"Here it is," Frank said quietly. "And this is new to me, for I was by now delirious with fever. For the first time the captain refers to the sickness in his ship as influenza; we are caught, he understands now, in the influenza epidemic of 1918 which is killing millions of others throughout the world. The Chief has collapsed. He is carried to his hammock unconscious. We are off Newfoundland now, some distance yet from the beginning of our operation. Seaman Strang is fully recovered. The captain himself, he says, is well, but . . . very tired." Lauffnauer looked up. "It is showing in his handwriting now; he is

[81]

sick, too, but does not know it or will not admit it. Seamen Koeppler, Donner, and Wurtz are still well. The other five are sick, including the *Leutnant;* the Chief is dying."

He flipped a page. "Off Halifax, now. Four men are dead, and buried at sea. All but Strang and Donner are sick now. The others, including the captain, get up from our hammocks when we can, to go on as long as we are able, then collapsing into hammocks again." He shook his head. "This was terrible; even yet I remember like a very bad dream, stumbling about in this ship—" he glanced around him—"feverish, and wondering if I, too, were to die, and hardly caring." Again he looked down at the log. "We are running the submarine as best we can, upon instructions from the captain between bouts of delirium. I remember he raved about his wife and about money, cautioning her against extravagance. And once he argued with his father. I was better soon, but very weak. We ran only on the surface, helpless against any sighting; diving was too much for us. I could not even twist a wheel, but I tended the sick." Frank pointed to the black script in the book he held. "The handwriting has changed, it is Strang's; the captain is dictating the log."

He scanned two pages, turning them, then glanced up at the rest of us again. "Donner is now sick, but two others—I am one of them—are obviously recovering. The captain is mostly unconscious, and when he is not, is usually delirious. He is still occasionally lucid, though; briefly able to give orders. Two more have died." He looked up. "Those we simply dumped overboard without ceremony. There was no time for anything else; we were desperate. We were somewhere off the coast of America, but we did not know where; none of us could navigate. We were finally able to submerge to periscope depth." He nodded down at the book. "It is Strang writing the log now, the captain can no longer dictate. There are no headings, no courses, weather, or anything else of the sort. The log is only a brief scribbled account of what is happening, undated. At dusk, Strang writes—we had held a council; Strang, Biehler and I—we plan to move in toward shore, anchor, then row to shore in a life raft, surrender, and get help for the captain.

"But we did not." Frank closed the book. "The coast seemed inhabited, but when we paddled ashore we found the houses unoccupied or unlighted; perhaps there was a blackout. But we found no one to surrender to, returned to the submarine, and found the captain lucid. He was dying, but clear-headed again, and he gave us our orders. We must escape somehow to Germany, impossible as that seemed, so that our submarine might be recovered to fight again. We must leave immediately; he would stay aboard and submerge. We protested, but he shook his head. He was dying, we could not help him, and those were his orders. We were not to bury the others at sea, or the bodies might be found. Then the Americans would hunt for the submarine, and perhaps find her from the air. They had zeppelins, I remember him saying, the poor, dying, foolish man. He ordered us to dress him then, and dictated his orders into the log and signed them. Then he stood up, we saluted, he returned it, and there we left him, watching us climb out, forty years ago. We left also Koeppler and Donner who were already dead. From our life raft we watched the *U-19* submerge, its periscope turning." For a few moments Lauffnauer was silent, his eyes moving slowly over the old sub. Then he smiled suddenly, engagingly. "And so America was saved some shipping, perhaps; and today we have a submarine. It is an ill wind, you say, which blows no one good; and the tragedy of my youth is our good fortune now." Again his eyes roamed the sub, and he shook his head. "Incredible," he murmured, "that I should stand here again."

I said, "How'd you get off the island, Frank?"

"We entered one of the unoccupied houses, and lived three days on canned food we found there, reconnoitering at night. We discovered that it was an island, and that there was a public ferry leaving at night, though few people lived here. We entered a number of houses, searching for money and clothes, and found it; a little money in each of several houses, and civilian clothes in abundance. One at a time, then, each on a different day, we took the ferry to Long Island. I took a train to New York and went to the home of an uncle, whose name and address I found in the phone book. I stayed hidden in his home till the war ended, and on Armistice Day I cheered on the streets of New York with the Americans. It took me nearly four years to save passage for home; I had no passport, and I had to bribe the mate of a freighter to take me." He stood waiting then, but no one said anything, and after a moment Frank opened the log book again, and turned through several pages.

"There is only one last entry," he said, "and it is in the captain's handwriting again, but very shaky, scrawled like a blind old man's." He pointed, and we crowded around to look over his shoulders. "Strang wrote out the plan, then the captain added this." There were two scribbled words I could not read, and Lauffnauer said, "They read, 'Keller, *Kapitän*.'" We stared at them for a few moments—the ink still jet-black—then Frank slowly closed the book, letting the pages fall together, and turned to look aft toward the control room, and the figure slumped there at the periscope. "Not the worst way to die," he said softly. "At his post. In uniform. Listed as lost in action. His ship taken care of to the best of his ability, such as it was. It is better than dying in a rented room," he murmured, "a waiter, like me, with flat feet and broken veins. But perhaps, *Herr Kapitän,*" he said, raising his voice a little, and smiling, "you have helped me avoid that, too." Then he swung to Moreno. "You had a large flat crate in back of the house," he said crisply, and I suddenly knew how he'd sounded commanding his own ship. "It was about six feet by five, and a foot deep."

"I still got it," Moreno said, nodding. "I made it to store nets in."

"Make another; I want this one. We will bury these men at sea."

"Sure." Moreno nodded. "Best thing we can do with them."

We looked through the whole boat then, moving through the control room into the aft battery compartment, which contained provision lockers, a switchboard, and mess gear. Stacked on a folding shelf were two unwashed plates and forks, the food which had once stained them now dry crusts of mold.

In the rapidly-narrowing aft compartment were the main engines, two small primitive diesels, labeled *Krupp,* their shafts connected in a straight line to the propellers; behind them were the main motor, generator, the air compressor, propeller clutch, and so on. The ship was drying rapidly, and while there was rust, it wasn't serious anywhere; there hadn't been oxygen enough for any extensive corrosion. Throughout the ship everything seemed in reasonable order, as far as we could tell, though we knew there was bound to be a good deal of work to be done. The depth gauge showed zero as it should; but we didn't know whether it was actually working or not. I looked at the adjusting pump motor—this pumps water into or out of the trim tanks, to level the ship at the start of a voyage, and to adjust the trim as fuel, supplies, and torpedoes are expended—and it looked new and undamaged.

The fuel tanks were pretty full; we rapped their sides. But whether they were filled with fuel or sea water, Frank didn't know. Sea water is sometimes pumped into the fuel tanks of a submarine as the fuel is used, to compensate for the lost weight; it doesn't mix with the fuel. The fresh-water tank was empty, and I was glad to see that; it might have rusted inside, otherwise. The valves on this ship were old Kingstons; hand-operated by a row of levers set into the deck, and looking like old-style automobile emergency brakes, only much larger. Lauffnauer and Vic tried a few tentatively, and they seemed to work, though stiffly. They were labeled in German, but of course Frank knew how to operate them.

The big hand wheels for operating the diving planes, and the hand steering gear, were absolutely immovable, and we knew all planes and the rudder were rusted tight. We inspected everything visible throughout the ship: switchboard, bilge pumps, engine clutch, electric range, torpedoes—the tubes each contained a torpedo—the vent valves, Kingstons, oil and fuel pumps, torpedo spare parts, water and air manifolds, hand pumps, the periscope dry-air system, steering engine, the waste locker, which was empty, periscope telescoping gear and motor, and everything else. There was a compass reflector, and none of us knew what it was, except Lauffnauer and Linc; Linc had once seen one on an old British sub. There was a watertight compass on the bridge, he explained, Frank nodding, as far from the magnetic influence of the ship as possible, and a system of mirrors reflected its readings to the control room; there was no gyrocompass in the sub. There was a stack of German magazines and newspapers in a locker, and Frank poked through them, a little smile on his lips; one had a photograph of a fierce-looking officer, von Moltke, the caption said, and another had a photograph of Hindenburg and Graf Spee. Another had a caricature of Woodrow Wilson, pictured as a vulture wearing a silk top hat.

It was noon when we finally left the little sub. Then all of us stood in the dock staring at her, and Lauffnauer said, "Well, what do you think? I think she looks good; as good as we could reasonably expect."

Moreno said, "Yeah; on the inside," then he nodded down at the sub. The tide was very low, and two-thirds of the ship was out of water; we could see the concrete blocks on which she rested, just under the surface. And now all the dry surfaces of the ship were a dull orange with rust. "But look at the rust," Moreno continued. "Can we chip loose all movable parts? And if we do, how far can we trust them, everything half eaten away?"

Lauffnauer shrugged, and said, "We'll find out; that's all we can do. It's the batteries I worry about. Hugh, what about them?"

After a moment I said, "Well, I'm doubtful; in fact, I don't have much hope at all. I'm damn sure you couldn't have washed the elements free of electrolyte, did you, Frank?"

"It would never have entered our heads," he said.

"You couldn't have done it, anyway; not three men. It's an enormous job, and I don't actually think it could be done aboard a sub at all. The batteries would have had to be hoisted out."

Vic said, "What if they'd been able to wash them?"

I shook my head. "Even then I don't think the batteries would be any good after forty years, or anything like it. I don't know—" I shrugged. "There's been no experience on it. Batteries are funny; you can't always predict them. Occasionally some will hold a charge or take a charge long after you'd think it was impossible. Particularly if they're kept cold, and these were never warm, down where they were. But I wouldn't have hoped for that after forty years. Even under expert care in a laboratory, I don't think they could be made to last that long, or even come close."

"So as it is, we're finished, then," Linc said. "Before we start. We've got to have batteries."

"We're not finished," Vic said shortly. "Hugh, you'll think of something. I didn't bring you into this for nothing." He smiled. "You'll figure this out one way or another."

I smiled, shrugging. "Thanks, pal," I said, and though I didn't know what I could do about it if those batteries were hopelessly dead, as I felt certain they were, Vic's words gave me a little surge of hope that somehow I'd be able to do something.

After lunch, which Rosa prepared up in the shack from supplies she'd laid in, Frank Lauffnauer and I ferried the three bodies—strangely light in weight—out to Rosa's boat, in the rowboat. On the way Frank said suddenly, "I owe him ten marks; I have just remembered." He'd changed to a gray sweater and blue denims in the shack.

"Which one?" I was rowing and Frank sat in the bow.

"Koeppler." He nodded over his shoulder at the three figures lying under a tarpaulin. "He bet me the war would be over by Christmas."

"He doesn't know he won."

Frank nodded, and I rowed on then, in silence.

In two more trips we carried out perhaps a hundred and fifty pounds of small smooth boulders, towing the big crate behind us on the last trip. We ferried the others aboard then, and as Moreno headed the boat out to sea and deep water, Frank Lauffnauer, with Rosa helping him, laid the three bodies—they were small men, all of them—in the crate in a row, their hands lying crossed at the wrists. Then we all, except Moreno at the wheel, fitted the little boulders into the crate, filling every empty space. Linc had found a few wild flowers around the shack, and he laid them in. From his coat pocket, Frank brought out the photographs and letters he'd taken from the submarine, and tucked them into the crate, and I caught a glimpse, again, of the old—

fashioned face of the girl in the photograph. I wondered if she were still alive somewhere now, as we were burying her young fiancé; she'd be a woman in her sixties, if she were.

We were a good mile or so out, now, and Moreno shut down the engine, and we lay drifting on the swell. From under his gray sweater, where he'd tucked it into his belt, Frank pulled a thick folded cloth, and stood holding it for a moment, glancing around at the rest of us. "This I found in a locker aboard the submarine," he said. "It is the old German ensign." Then he shook it out, spreading it completely over the three long-dead men, and we saw the flag in the afternoon sun, still bright in the creases it had lain in for forty years: a white flag divided into quarters by two broad red stripes, one vertical, one horizontal. The black maltese cross stood in the upper left quadrant on a background of horizontal red, white and black stripes, the Imperial eagle superimposed on the center. Quickly, then, Frank nailed on the lid of the crate, the hammer blows sounding flatly over the water, the rest of us standing watching him more or less awkwardly. We were none of us sure what Frank was going to do, and kept stealing glances at each other. I thought possibly he might be going to pray, and I wished that he wouldn't. I had nothing against these long-dead Germans; in a way, possibly, I could feel a little sorry for them, though not very strongly. What had happened to them was long ago and remote from this world, and beyond a dignified burial for them, I hoped Frank wouldn't make a ceremony of it.

He didn't. He stood up quickly, then stooped and lifted an edge of the crate. *"Auf wiedersehen,"* he said in an almost normally pleasant and cheerful tone, then tilted the crate, splashing, into the water. For a moment we could still see it—the orange-white pine under the green water, sinking fast. Then it was gone, and Frank turned to smile at us. "Now!" he said. "Let us get the *U-19* to sailing again."

Six

THERE IS an enormous loss we all of us suffer, growing up—we stop playing. The things adults call play very seldom are. With hardly an exception they're competitions, even hunting or fishing, even golf, all alone. Rarely ever again do we experience pure play, doing something for its own sake completely, utterly absorbed and lost in it, nothing else mattering.

But we had it now, or very nearly—Frank Lauffnauer, Linc Langley, Vic DeRossier, Ed Moreno and I. We were about to start work on our submarine, and while it had a purpose we weren't thinking of that at all. Back in the dock, staring down at our rusting little sub, we no more wanted to leave it now than a kid wants to leave his new train Christmas morning. Looking at it, maybe reaching out to scrape the side of a shoe sole along a reddened ballast tank, all any of us really wanted to do was climb down into it and begin work, not stopping for anything. It was the most exciting toy any of us had ever had, and until now, just past one o'clock, I'd even forgotten I had a job, and had been due at it since eight-thirty this morning.

Now I had to leave our toy; most of us did. Most of us had jobs; no one had quit his till we knew for sure that the old sub could be raised and transported. And now all of us but Moreno and Rosa had to go back to New York: to break leases, check out of hotels, or leave rooming houses; to quit jobs or resign positions; to sell securities, close out bank accounts, withdraw postal savings, or raise cash at a pawnshop. Moreno had an old jeep in a little shed back of the shack, and after a last look at the sub—the tide was rising again, slowly blackening her sides—we all walked up the path, climbed into the jeep, and he drove us to the railroad station, some miles away.

Back in New York, I took a cab to my bank, where I withdrew all the money I had in both my savings and checking accounts. Then I made it over to my hotel, where I showered and changed, packed my sea bag, and checked out. By four I was at my office, stepping out of the elevator, grinning at the receptionist. I walked right through, past the stenographers' desks, to my new boss's office. I had no trouble resigning; summer was coming, slack season for our department and the whole broadcasting industry. And when I suggested giving up the two-week vacation I had coming in exchange for not giving notice, it was okay with him. He was sorry to lose me, he said, wanted to know what I was going to do, and when I told him I was going to drive out West somewhere, just for the hell of it, he nodded and said that if he weren't married with kids to support, he'd come along. He phoned the accountant then, who came in in a little while with a check for my last nine days. After a round of handshaking and goodbyes outside, I was out of the office, a free man.

In the record department, Herb, the big kid in charge of putting records back on the shelves more or less in their proper places, was sitting at his little desk. He had his feet up on an open drawer, and was drinking a Coke from a paper cup, a little radio in the drawer broadcasting a spring-training ball game. "That's a rival network," I said, nodding down at the radio. "You're fired."

"I tune out the commercials," he answered, then leaned back in his chair, looking into the stacks, and whistled shrilly between his teeth. A moment or so later, dusting her hands, Alice Muir walked out, then stopped and stood looking at me. She wore a white linen sleeveless dress, a green jade brooch at the square neckline, and she looked wonderful.

"Hello," she said, frowning a little.

"I just quit," I said. "Got time for a coffee?"

She looked at Herb, who said, "I'll add your duties to my other responsibilities; go ahead," and Alice walked around the little counter —she was wearing brown-and-white high-heeled shoes, her legs bare and very smooth and shapely—and we walked out to the elevators.

We didn't speak till we were down at the little lunch counter just off the main lobby, seated around at the far side of the horseshoe-shaped counter that filled the little room. There was only one other customer, a salesman, briefcase at his feet, hat shoved back; it was well past coffee time.

My coffee came, and Alice's Coke. The clerk went over to the salesman, and Alice—unwrapping her straw, not looking at me—said, "So you quit. You didn't need to for my sake, Hugh; I was going to ask tomorrow for an early vacation."

I wondered why she hadn't asked today, but I said, "Well, you can take your time now; I won't be back."

She nodded, taking a sip of her Coke. Then, still without looking at me, she said, "All right; I meant what I said Friday—" she looked up at me now—"but I was hoping you didn't. That's why I didn't ask about my vacation this morning."

She turned back to her Coke, and I sat looking down at the top of her head, at her straw-yellow hair and the clean white scalp at the part. "Maybe I'm crazy," I said quietly. "I have the feeling now that if I'd just let go a little, just relaxed a bit, I'd have fallen crazy in l—"

"Don't," she said. "I don't want to hear it; you don't know how sad I feel right now. I'd have married you in a minute; I still would, and I wonder if I'll ever get over you. But you're not sad; you're excited. I don't know about what, but you are." She shrugged a shoulder. "Right now, sitting beside me looking at me, you're wondering for a moment whether you made a mistake. And maybe you have. But you're going to do what you want to do, anyway." She drew herself up, spine erect, shoulders back, and turned to me, her chin lifting, her eyes sad but proud too. "Look at me, Hugh," she said softly, and I did, my eyes meeting hers then. "This is what you could have had: me. For the asking. You can't do much better, and you may do far worse." My face must have shown something, because she suddenly relaxed her posture, reaching out to touch my hand on the counter, and said, "But I haven't any right to put you through this; I haven't any claim on you. You simply came to say goodbye. And I'm glad you did."

All I could say was, "So am I, Alice. We had a lot of fun."

"Yes." She was nodding rapidly, looking straight ahead. "Maybe you'd better go now, Hugh; I'll stay and finish my Coke. Please do; please go now, Hugh."

"All right." I knew she'd be crying if I didn't, and there was nothing else to do or say, anyway. I stood up from the stool, put money on the counter to pay for the coffee and Coke, then I reached out for her hand and squeezed it. She squeezed back, hard, then dropped my hand abruptly, turning away; and I walked on out, through the lobby to the street, knowing I'd lost something, but not tempted for a moment to turn back.

Book Two

Book Two

Seven

Lincoln Langley sat smoking a cigar in the jeep, parked in the shadows beside the little country station, when Vic and I got off the train that night. Lugging our sea bags, we walked toward him along the narrow wood platform; it was dark out, the station closed, a single bulb lighted inside it. We were the only passengers to get off, the nearly empty little three-car train already pulling away, the lights from its windows sliding across us. It was funny, really—I thought about this later and was amused—we wasted no time in greeting each other. I liked Linc, and felt cordial to him, but reaching the jeep a step or two ahead of Vic, heaving my sea bag into the end, the first thing I said was, "How is she?"

And Linc had no trouble understanding me. "Good," he said eagerly, yanking the cigar from his mouth. "Moreno's got cotton waste wrapped around every movable part on the outside. Tied on with wire, and soaked with penetrating oil. He's already chipping rust."

I nodded, climbing in beside him. Vic got in back as Linc started the motor, swinging around to look to the rear, then backing out into the empty little main street of the village. "Lauffnauer back?" Vic said, and Linc nodded, shifting gears.

"Came back with me; we've been here an hour," he said, driving slowly down the street. It was a block long with a dozen wood-front stores, all closed now expect for the bar. "We've started work on the Kingstons." We passed under the single street light, a naked bulb mounted high on a wood pole, and now I saw that Linc's blue denims and work shirt were already streaked with grease. We hit the end of the speed-limit zone, and Linc jammed his cigar in his mouth, clenching it in his teeth, and shoved down the accelerator, barreling the old jeep down the asphalt county highway, and I grinned.

"In a hurry, Linc?" I said, and he flashed a smile at me.

"You're lucky you didn't have to walk," he said. "I'm going to hate having to waste time in sleep tonight; I begrudge every moment away from her."

From the back seat Vic said quietly, "What do you think, Hugh?" and I saw Linc turn to me, his mouth opening a little, waiting intently for my answer.

But all I could do was shrug, and say, "We'll know in a few minutes now." Vic was asking about the batteries; they were the all-important question. For without electrical power the sub couldn't run underwater, or run at all, for that matter; the diesels couldn't be started at sea without current from the batteries.

We reached the shack, bumping down the quarter-mile rut road that led to it from the highway, then parking at the back. Linc yanked up the hand brake, snapped off the lights and ignition, and as the motor died we heard, ringing dully through the night air, the steady clink of hammer on chisel, chipping rust down at the dock.

The shack was lighted, illuminating the path beside it, and down the hill at the shore every crack of the dock building was brightly defined, two rectangles of yellow light from the dusty windows high under the eaves lying on the black water beside the building. "See you," Linc said, and, actually trotting down the path, he hurried back to the submarine.

Rosa, in her black slacks and sweater, was making up the last of five metal cots lined up along one wall of the shack. As we walked in with our sea bags, she was pulling an olive-drab blanket taut. Deftly tucking it in, she glanced up to smile at us. "They are waiting for you," she said to me, nodding in the direction of the dock, "like children. Can you make their toy run for them, Papa?"

I nodded, lifting my sack onto the cot she'd just finished with. "Sure," I said, "I'll make it run, one way or another."

Vic put his sack on the end cot, and Rosa said, "I have found even night tables for you, in the village today," and now I noticed five empty orange crates, one beside each cot, their tops neatly covered with paper napkins. Three of them, to the left of mine, were stacked with the toilet articles and small personal possessions of the others. Propped on the top of the crate beside the cot next to mine was a rectangular sepia photograph showing a much younger Frank

Lauffnauer with a four- or five-year-old boy on his lap; beside him sat a smiling round-faced woman holding a year-old baby. "I do not think they are alive," Rosa murmured. "He has never mentioned them." Several envelopes and a postcard, all with canceled British stamps—Linc's undoubtedly—lay on the crate beyond Lauffnauer's cot. On the last in line, Moreno's, stood a calendar mounted on a cardboard easel with a date ringed in pencil; I couldn't make out the date but from its position on the page I knew it was May 17.

"Where you sleeping, Rosa?" Vic said. He was sitting on the edge of his cot, pulling blue denims and a work shirt from his sea bag.

"In my own house," she said shortly, "alone." Then she walked ahead into the little area that served as a kitchen, and sat down at an enamel-topped table there, her back to us. On a wall shelf beside the table was a small radio, and she snapped it on. Without turning around she said, "Go ahead, get dressed; they are waiting for you."

I glanced at Vic, shrugging, then sat down, untied my bag, and began tugging out a pair of denim pants and a sun-tan shirt. They came out suddenly, yanking my old Navy cap out with them, and it fell, bouncing on the floor. I picked it up, and straightened the grommet—it had been crushed in the sack—and sat looking at it for a moment. The white cover was a little soiled on one edge, and I tried to brush it off, but only made it worse. Then on a sudden impulse, I put the cap on. Once again I was about to board a sub I expected to sail on, and my old cap felt good on my head once more, it felt right, and I stood up, tilting the cap to the angle at which I'd always worn it.

There was a mirror fastened to the wall above the little sink, and I walked over to it to look at myself, Rosa at the table glancing up to grin at me. "Very handsome, Lieutenant," she said, but I didn't answer or look at her. As I stood at the mirror staring at my face and the black-visored cap just above it, the cap no longer felt right on my head, and it took me several moments to understand why.

I'd never been conscious of feeling anything more about my hitch in the Navy than that it was a fairly interesting chore. Nevertheless, now, staring at the cap I'd just put on my head in preparation for what I was about to begin, I suddenly reached up and yanked the cap off. Then I unscrewed the cap device—the shield, eagle, and anchor that made this a Navy cap—walked back to my cot, and shoved the emblem deep out of sight into my bag. And now my cap was just a cap, and I was able to wear it.

We changed clothes quickly, then, and walked down the path to the dock. Inside it, Moreno, wearing dirty tan coveralls and an old felt hat, was standing down in the water in hip boots beside the orange-red sub, chipping rust from the aft dive-plane mountings. He glanced up as we walked in, nodding shortly, and began climbing out of the water as Vic and I walked across the plank to the conning tower, then climbed down the ladder through the open hatch. Lauffnauer and Linc, working in the control room with socket wrenches, were twisting bolts from the stuffing box of one of the big Kingstons, and then I saw that of course I hadn't been the only one to remember his old Navy cap.

Shoved back on Linc's head was the small-crowned white cap of a British Chief; and he, too, had removed the cap ornament. So had Lauffnauer. On his knees on the steel deck in white coveralls, glancing up to smile at us, Lauffnauer was wearing the flaring, peculiarly high-crowned white cap of an officer in the German Navy, the black visor edged with gold. The white cover was very soiled, except at the front just above the visor. There very plainly, in white silhouette, was the shape of the straight-winged eagle that had been removed from the cap; and I knew that in a circle just under that missing eagle there lay the Nazi swastika.

For as long as four or five seconds we stared at each other, and—Lauffnauer was no fool—he read something in my face and eyes. Then he smiled. "We are not children," he said gently, glancing from me to Linc, "playing with a toy and dressing up for our parts. Though perhaps we have been acting like it. But let us put away childish things now, and go to work." Reaching up he took off his cap, then got to his feet, and stepped into the galley just aft of the control room. There he opened a small shelved locker, tossed his cap onto one of the shelves, and stood smiling, holding the door open. After a moment I followed him, took off my cap, and set it on a shelf. Linc did the same with his cap then, grinning, and Lauffnauer closed the door. "So!" he said. "The past is past, and now we are all of the same navy; our own." He grinned, reached up to clap a hand on my shoulder, and I smiled back. He was a likable man, and I felt a kind of unwilling respect for him.

Moreno's feet were sounding on the iron rungs of the ladder just behind us, and he came climbing down, and I squatted on the deck. Under the hatch cover set into the deck beside me were batteries, others in the forward compartment. Grouping themselves beside and just behind me, the others stood silent and watching, waiting for what I'd have to say. Now Rosa began climbing down into the sub, and I lifted the hatch cover.

A submarine's batteries are huge, as tall as a man, in a modern sub, and even these ancient batteries were four feet tall. And they weigh tons; they're actually an important part of a submarine's ballast. Sitting down on the deck now, my feet in the open hatch on top of the big batteries, I began the routine of inspecting, then testing them, without any real hope. Again as before I was wishing that somehow the sub's crew, or what had been left of it, had been able to wash the elements free of electrolyte, and dry them, but of course they couldn't have. There was acid in the batteries, I found, as I'd expected; it doesn't evaporate to amount to anything. Now all I could do was to see if, miraculously, the batteries had somehow held a charge for forty years. I didn't bother taking a hydrometer reading, but simply tested each cell at the volt-meter panel of the switchboard here in the aft compartment. There was no reason I could think of why there'd be anything wrong with it, or any of the electrical lines and circuits in the sub, for that matter; the sub had been fairly dry and dust free. And now I threw the old knife-blade switch, and tested the first cell.

The needle barely flickered, indicating just a trivial difference in potential. I tried each of the other cells then, everyone watching my face. But I avoided their eyes, walked back to the open hatch, and inspected the battery plates and separators—all of them I could reach. They weren't in bad condition, and the separators hadn't deteriorated to amount to anything; these had been good batteries. Then, squatting there, staring at the feet of the others in a half circle around me, I thought about trying to charge these old batteries. We could run power in to the diesels, rig them to run, and try a charge. But I knew in my bones that it would be so much waste motion, and after a few moments I glanced up at the others, and slowly shook my head.

Moreno began to curse, quietly and viciously, then Rosa gave him a little push, and he shut up. The others swung away from the hatch, Lauffnauer jamming his hands into his white coverall pockets, slowly shaking his head; Vic muttered something angrily, and the life seemed to have gone out of Linc's face. For a moment Rosa stood watching me, then she said, "All right, Papa; how are you going to fix it for us?" and the others turned back to stare down at me again.

I shrugged, looking up at them. "There's only one thing I know of to try," I said, "and I don't like it. But there's not another single thing we can do."

"All right, all right," Moreno said irritably, "let's have it; what can we do?" He was staring down at me, his eyes sharp with a hope he didn't really have.

"Use automobile batteries."

It was actually a little comical; they were frowning, their mouths opening in astonishment. Vic said, "*Car* batteries? Ordinary car batteries?"

"Sure." I had to smile, looking at their faces. "The sub doesn't care where the power comes from. A few big batteries, or a lot of little ones, the sub doesn't care; get the juice to the motor, and it'll turn."

"Hugh, are you *sure*?" Lauffnauer said, both doubtful and eager, wanting to believe me but on guard against a second disappointment. Then he laughed, the beginning of relief in his voice. "It just does not seem possible, that's all."

I shrugged, sitting there on the deck by the open hatch, and tapped the big sub battery with my foot. "This is only a 240-cell battery," I said. "That's nothing nowadays, but it's what this boat had. Well, a hundred and sixty ordinary six-volt automobile batteries will give us a 480-cell bank of batteries. And I can hook them up so that we'll have, in effect, two batteries of 240 cells paralleled for operation."

"And it'll be the equivalent of the sub's batteries?" Linc said eagerly.

"No; lord, no." I shook my head. "It'll give us maybe ten to fifteen per cent of the normal operating potential of the big one, at best."

"And what the hell does all that mean?" Moreno said angrily.

I grinned at him. "It means that if you need power you can get it from any battery, regardless of its nature. Including car batteries. But not for long. We'll get all the power of the big batteries from the hundred and sixty little ones, but not for anywhere near the same length of time. They won't begin to store the power of the big ones; it's like a bucket compared to a great big tank. We can go under for—" I hesitated, then shrugged—"twenty minutes, say. Maybe a little longer, though I'd hate having to try getting more than a half hour out of them. And get this straight—" I glanced around at all of them—"we can go under *one time only*. Then our batteries will be as dead as this—" I patted one of the big cells beside me—"and there'll be no recharging them; not at sea, anyway."

"Why not?" Vic said.

I stood up, stepping up onto the deck. "With what?" I said. "The ship's generator would pour in more juice than any little car battery could take; it'd be like trying to fill a washbasin with a high-pressure fire hose. They're still little six-volt batteries no matter how we hook them up, and you use anything much more than an ordinary car-battery charger, you could burn them out. We put a full charge in them here, then we go out; and we can dive once. And for about twenty minutes, and fifteen would be safer. And that, my little ones—" I grinned at Rosa—"is the very best that Papa can do."

After a moment or so, Lauffnauer said softly, "And those batteries will cost what?"

"We need good ones, Frank. Just about the biggest storage capacity we can get. And we'll need chargers; fast chargers and overnight chargers with a capacity of several batteries at a time. Plus connectors, and so on. No way in the world to do it, short of stealing the batteries, for any less than three thousand dollars."

Linc whistled slowly, then we all looked at Moreno. "Well," he said, shrugging, "everyone who can is to turn in a thousand bucks, as you all know. I can, just barely. And Rosa can; you got insurance money left, haven't you?" He looked at her and she nodded shortly. "Vic?" he said then.

"Yeah." He nodded. "I've got it with me."

"So have I," I said, "in my sea bag."

"And I can't," said Linc.

Moreno nodded. "And Linc can't. He told us that from the beginning; he just hasn't got it, not a dime, and that's that. Frank turned over eight hundred dollars to me an hour ago. It's every cent he's got, and after all—" Moreno smiled—"he's contributing the sub. So we have forty-eight hundred dollars to get this boat operating, and to live on. I could scrape up a little more, maybe. And maybe Rosa could, too. How about you, Vic?"

"Yeah; maybe another five hundred. But that'd be the end of the line."

"Hugh?"

"About the same; maybe a little less."

"Okay." Moreno shoved his hat back off his forehead. "We got forty-eight hundred bucks now. And say sixty-five hundred tops if we need it. So we'll spend three thousand dollars for power because we've got to have it and there's not another damn thing we can do about it. We'll get by on what's left if we have to quit eating." He grinned tightly and momentarily. "Linc, what about the radio?"

"All it needs, I feel sure, is new tubes, but I doubt if there's a tube to fit this wireless in the entire world any longer. I could make it work, however, with certain new parts, and modern tubes; even improve it,

I daresay." He shrugged. "But we don't need this type of wireless. We need only a small portable outfit of very limited range; nothing fancy or expensive. Our best bet is to buy it, and forget this one. I'd say perhaps a hundred pounds; three hundred dollars. Maybe less; I haven't priced them in America lately." He smiled.

"All right." Moreno nodded. "We've got plenty of fuel; I checked it today. So now we start buying batteries at every gas station, garage, and auto-supply place for fifteen miles around. And in New York, every time someone has to go in. And from the mail-order houses. We'll buy no more than two at a time at any one purchase; and we'll take turns buying." He glanced up at me. "You'll take care of the chargers?"

"Yeah; I'll run into New York with the jeep for them."

"Okay. Bring back as many batteries as you have room for, too; maybe Linc can run in with you, and bring back his radio and a couple of rafts. Now, let's get organized." He held up one hand and began ticking off on his fingers the next things to be done. "We'll start work on the diesels right away. Soon as we get enough batteries, we can test-run and adjust them. Then overhaul the Kingstons, the air compressor, and all vents. Get the engines and air compressor working, refill the air flasks, and we can test the tanks a few dozen times."

"What about the rudder and dive planes?" I said.

"I'm freeing them now. We'll have to use a blowtorch some places, but they'll work. Oh, what the hell—" he shrugged, grinning up at me —"they're half rusted away; all mountings, fittings, and surfaces corroded, pitted, and flaking to beat hell. The sub commander of the most fifth-rate navy in the world would drop dead after one close look at the outside of this sub. And we're going out in her, and dive her with car batteries." He laughed, just a short bark of sound, and we all grinned a little with one side of our mouths. "No use kidding ourselves," Moreno said then. "We're going to be repairing, improvising, patching up, making do, doing without, and maybe even reinventing. It'll be makeshift all down the line; the damnedest excuse for a submarine anyone ever sailed in. But so what?" He moved one of his heavy shoulders under the rust-streaked coveralls. "We're not going on a world cruise in her, either. Or standing inspection. This tub's like an old jalopy; if it gets us there and back, that's all we need."

"If," Linc murmured, and I saw Rosa's lips move, and she very quickly, surreptitiously, made the sign of the cross on her forehead with a thumbnail.

But Lauffnauer was smiling faintly, his eyes absent and reminiscent. "She is a good ship," he murmured, glancing slowly around the ancient little sub. "I trusted her once, and I will trust her again." He said it with such simple, absolute faith that sudden conviction surged through us all. We were nodding then—looking at each other, grinning, and nodding our heads in sudden happy certainty that we could not fail. And when Moreno, smiling too, now said, "Okay, gang, let's get to work," I actually tossed him a mock salute, delighted to obey.

He and I and Vic climbed out then, and Moreno got down in the water beside the sub to resume chipping rust from the aft hydroplanes, his hat shoved back on his head, and whistling softly. Vic and I each picked out an open-ended wrench from the tools, such as he had, which Moreno had laid out on the dock. And when we climbed back to start work on the diesels in the engine room, Lauffnauer and Linc were hard at work on the Kingstons again, discussing the difference between these and those Linc had seen on a British sub. At this moment, I loved these people—all of them. And I began then, unscrewing a bolt from a diesel water jacket, the best moments and days of my entire life, the happiest I will ever have, in many ways, I'm certain; and I think the others felt the same way.

I don't suppose I can really explain why. But I wonder if the happiest men who live through a life in this world aren't those completely absorbed in hard challenging work they enjoy. I suspect that it's man's natural state; that it's the reason we're here, if there's any purpose to life at all. We began work before eight-thirty that night, and only minutes later, so it seemed, heard Rosa call out from the path just outside the dock. It was twelve-thirty, she said, and she was taking the jeep to go home—and Vic and I looked up from the engine we were kneeling beside to stare at each other in simple astonishment. Then he shook his head slowly, and smiled. "I'm dead," he said, "exhausted. But I didn't know it till now."

"Yeah." I nodded. "Me, too." I was bone-tired; I hadn't really slept for over thirty-six hours, and I suddenly knew I could have lain down on that steel deck and dropped instantly to sleep. Yet I hated to put down my wrench.

Walking up the path with the others then, toward the shack and our cots, the lights out in the dock behind us, the quarter-moon high and pale in the sky, I was stumbling with weariness but I begrudged every hour of sleep ahead of me. Not since I was a kid had I had the feeling that I did now, that I couldn't wait for the next day. And when

Moreno, sitting on the edge of his cot under the single overhead bulb, winding an alarm clock, said, "What time do you want to start?" I looked up to answer immediately.

"Dawn; first light," I said, and the others—unbuttoning shirts, wearily pulling off shoes—all nodded or murmured in agreement.

For ten days, then, the pattern hardly varied. Frank, for some reason of his own, had resumed the old log of the *U-19,* briefly recording in it each night what had happened that day; and his records varied only in details. We'd awaken in darkness, dragged out of sleep by the ruthless insistent rattle of that alarm; I can hear it yet. There'd be a moment of drugged confusion; my muscles, for the first few days at least, stiffened and begging for more rest. Then the same single thought would flare up in my mind again—"The boat!"—and my eyes would pop open, a surge of deep pleasure bringing me wide awake. Rosa would arrive within minutes then, quickly prepare our breakfasts, then it was down to the sub again, and work, work, work, till eleven at night, till twelve, till after one o'clock sometimes. Meals were only an irritating interruption, the working time between them always too short, and we ate them bolting our food, discussing only the sub; and often as not we ate on the job—sandwiches and coffee—not stopping for a moment all day and half the night till we fell into bed again.

We none of us shaved, and we almost quit bathing until Rosa, one morning, arrived, opened the door, stood staring at us for a moment, then stamped her foot on the floor in sudden fury. We were dressed, sitting on our cots or wandering about the room, waiting our turns to get into the bathroom, and we all swung to stare at her. She was wearing a tweed skirt, low-heeled shoes, and a short, bright red coat with wood peg buttons. Her hair was in a pigtail down her back, tied with a red ribbon, and she looked like an angry schoolgirl. "You are pigs!" she said as she stamped her foot. "And I will not fix another meal, I will not come here again, until you all bathe!" She glared at us for a moment, and Vic came out of the bathroom, toothbrush in hand, to see what the trouble was. "I will fix breakfast," she said, her eyes black and flashing, "then each of you will take a bath; I will heat water. You will put on clean clothes, and I will wash the old ones today, and your blankets." Then she took off her coat, tossed it angrily to a chair, and turned to the refrigerator. We all grinned, and shrugged at each other, and Rosa heaved up the two kitchen windows, opening them as wide as possible.

That morning we worked in the sub until Rosa called us, each of us in turn. Then we'd go, one at a time, up to the shack, and bathe outdoors in a laundry tub in back of the shack, which Rosa had filled with warm water. After lunch she took home a mass of dirty clothes and blankets, and all afternoon washed and dried them in her electric machine and clothes-dryer.

But otherwise the days and the nights were the same, and I think we forgot, in the absolute absorption of restoring that submarine to life, why we were doing it. The world contracted to the acre or so we lived and worked on, and I've never been happier.

We had to interrupt work occasionally, one or the other of us taking the jeep to a nearby village or town for groceries, a tool, a piece of equipment. And once Moreno and Rosa made the trip to Fire Island and our rented cottage again, taking over several suitcases full of city clothes for each of us, food, razors, toothbrushes, and other supplies. Each time any of us went out, we bought batteries, at a dozen or more garages, filling stations, and stores for ten or fifteen miles around, and in New York. And we ordered batteries by mail, Rosa filling out and mailing the orders. They were shipped in by express to various nearby towns to invented names, and during the afternoons Rosa drove around picking them up, paying for them with cash; we aimed at acquiring a dozen or so a day.

Most of the time, for some reason, we stayed paired up as we'd started out; Vic and I usually working together, and Lauffnauer and Linc. And Moreno generally worked alone, Rosa sometimes chattering with him in Italian, though she used to laugh at him because his Italian, she said, wasn't really very good.

One afternoon Vic and I were testing the diving-plane wheels in the control room; we got along well, though I didn't have any feeling that I knew him much better than I ever had. Lauffnauer and Linc were old friends by now, though, and we could hear them in the forward compartment working on the trim-tank pump. We were all feeling pretty happy these days, and Lauffnauer suddenly burst into a song, in German, his voice exuberant. I'd never heard the tune before, but after a moment I realized that I'd heard the words or read them somewhere. "*Wir fahren gegen England!*" Frank sang happily, if I have the words right, and I remembered that these were the words of an old German war song, and that they meant, *We sail against England!* He sang away happily for some several seconds, then, very softly, Linc began to whistle; just a quiet soft little whistle through his front teeth. I think Lauffnauer and I recognized what he was whistling in the same instant; for Frank abruptly stopped singing just as I realized that Lincoln Langley, almost in counterpoint, was whistling "Rule, Britannia." Then Lauffnauer burst into laughter, howling with delight, and we could hear Linc's soft chuckle underneath it, and Vic and I grinned at each other.

We got an incredible amount of work done. Lauffnauer and Linc pulled the provision and china lockers out of the compartment aft of the control room, then built a rough frame of pine two-by-fours big enough to hold a hundred and sixty batteries stacked four layers deep, leaving just enough room to sidle past them. As we acquired batteries, we began stacking them there, in what had been the galley. The galley, incidentally, surprised me. It was equipped with electric plug-in cooking appliances; sauce pans, kettles, frying pans, each fitted with a plug to heat electrically. They might have been the remote ancestors of what we think of as among the most modern kitchen appliances of today, though you wouldn't have thought it from their appearance. They were of black cast iron, very crudely and roughly formed, and though Frank said they'd worked fine, I took them right out of the sub; I wasn't risking anyone even trying to use them, and burning out a line for all I knew.

With the first of the batteries Vic and I started, tested, and then adjusted the diesels. We'd found nothing really wrong with them; they'd been in good condition forty years ago, and nothing had happened to them since. But the gaskets for the water jackets enclosing the cylinders were copper and asbestos; they were squeezed flat by forty years of constant pressure, all elasticity gone, and we had no way of replacing them. All Vic and I could do was tighten the bolts to the last fraction of possible turn, but they leaked still, and we knew our engines might run hot.

A lot of what we did, in fact, was makeshift, improvised, utterly unacceptable by the standards of any navy in the world. The valves of the air compressor, for example—Moreno worked on that—should have been replaced, but that wasn't possible either. And when Vic and I had the diesels running, and we tested the compressor, it wouldn't deliver full pressure, so we couldn't fill our air flasks completely. Several of the air-flask valves leaked, too, and no crew would have sailed, let alone dive, in a submarine with valves in the condition ours were.

These were big hand-lever-operated Kingstons. There were four of them in the ship, and when they were opened, together with the air vents on top of the tanks, sea water would flood into the ballast tanks; when closed, the big valves kept the water out. So they had to be tightly seated, like the valves of an automobile engine, and while these were made of bronze, forty years of sea water had nevertheless corroded them. They had to be reground, using valve-grinding compound, and we all worked at that, taking turns, because part of the job had to be done underneath the submarine. On this tiny grandfather of today's complex subs, the valves came right through the hull, and we had to pull out some of the concrete blocks under the ship, and lie on planks in the ooze under the sub at low tide, regrinding the valves and valve seats. We had to repack the valve stems, too; the big rods rose through a stuffing box which had to be watertight. That was easy enough, but we were simply not able, under the conditions we had to work in, to regrind the valves to anything near the perfection they should have had. They leaked, and the only reason the tanks hadn't filled with water long since, sinking the sub to the bottom off Fire Island years before, was that the air vents on the topside of the ballast tanks had held tight, holding the trapped air inside which kept the water out. But once we began using those air vents, opening and closing them again and again, we knew they'd probably start leaking, too, no matter what we did to them. Then water would constantly leak into our ballast tanks, and we'd have to blow them regularly from our partially filled air flasks; and maintaining a depth while submerged might be difficult.

As Linc said one night, lying on his cot in the darkness just after Frank turned off the light, the sub should have been in drydock, if there'd been a navy in the world that would want to refit it. Then a score or more of skilled men with all the tools, skills, and equipment they needed, could have worked for weeks—spending thousands of man-hours and dollars—stripping that sub down, and completely refitting it; practically rebuilding it from bow to stern. Even then, I don't know what they could have done about the hull. It probably hadn't been built, in 1918, for much more than two hundred feet of pressure; Lauffnauer said they'd never dived more than a hundred and fifty feet. Now we simply didn't know how thin it might have rusted in places; what pressures it could still take, or for how long. If it had lain where we found it for one month longer perhaps, then for all we knew, that corroded, pitted hull might finally have yielded at its thinnest point, a needle-thin jet of black water suddenly shooting inside, growing quickly to pencil thickness, and then, the hull crumbling, a gout of black water flooding the ship.

Weeks of work, tons of equipment, and a not-so-small fortune could have been spent restoring that sub to complete fitness. Yet in ten days of hard work we finished most of all that we were able to do, and if any really major repair job had been vital, it would have been beyond us. We fixed the sub up—patched it up—as well as we could, and that's all we could do. One afternoon, all of us lying under the sub grinding valves, we started talking about the countless things that were wrong or half wrong with the ship. Linc started to laugh quietly, then we all burst into sudden laughter; there was nothing else to do. Rosa was there at the time, lying on the dock near the doorway in the sun, reading, and she looked down at us, shaking her head and smiling sardonically, almost fondly, as though we were a bunch of kids.

Rosa spent most of her spare time, which wasn't much—besides cooking, laundering, and housekeeping for us, she did most of the errands in the jeep—down in the dock, or inside the sub. She'd watch one or another of us at whatever he was doing, asking an occasional question, passing a tool over, even helping when she could, not afraid to get dirty at it. We were busy, working hard and concentratedly, and without much conversation. But still—I've never liked the unrelieved company of nothing but men for too long a time—it was nice having Rosa around.

Eight

ALL OF A SUDDEN one day, I was sick of nothing but work. Late in an afternoon, climbing up out of the sub for the hundredth time, to get a tool from the dock, I turned at the top of the ladder, and stood staring out at the ocean instead. Below me I could hear the delicate steady tap of a screwdriver blade on metal—Lauffnauer adjusting a piston on a trim-tank pump, then the sudden clatter of a tool dropped on the metal deck, and Moreno cursing deep inside the sub somewhere. But now, suddenly—the ocean before me a brilliant green, flashing in the sun—I was no longer interested in the sub. It was as though I'd come climbing up out of her after ten days, and taken a look at the rest of the world. I stood staring out at the water, fingering my new beard—I couldn't get used to the feel of it—and saw Rosa, sitting on the dock in her black slacks and sweater, hands clasped around her knees, looking up at me.

I acted on impulse. Beckoning to her with my chin, I climbed down, jumped over to the dock, and walked out, up the path toward the shack and the jeep parked in back of it, Rosa following. I climbed in under the wheel, Rosa watching me questioningly. "Got the keys?" I said. She nodded, and I said, "Get in, then," and held out my hand for the keys.

Driving fast over the two-lane country road, I went into the village, parking on the main street just out of the business district; we always tried to draw no more attention to ourselves than possible, but Rosa lived in the area, and they knew her long since. I had a little over forty dollars in the wallet in my denims, and I took it out and handed it to her. "Get some liquor," I said. "Whisky, gin, highball mixes, potato chips, olives, cold cuts, and all the rest of it. Get plenty, and get a big sack of ice cubes; I'll pick you up outside the liquor store." I grinned at her. "Tonight we're having a party."

Her eyes lit up, and she climbed out, nodding eagerly; then standing beside the jeep, she frowned. "Do you think we should?"

"Hell, yes. We're on schedule; ahead of it, in fact. We'll make May 17 with a couple days to spare. Go ahead, get the stuff; we're having a party."

We didn't even eat supper that night. Back at the shack while Rosa was setting out our supplies on the kitchen table, I went out and down to the dock, picked up a wrench, and banged on the hull. "Come on out," I yelled, "up to the shack! Everybody out!"

Someone yelled, "What?" but I simply repeated it, and when Vic's black-bearded face—he no longer looked unshaven; it was beginning to be a beard—rose up out of the tower, I just beckoned and walked on out, up toward the shack, and I heard Vic calling the others.

Moreno didn't like it. He stood in the kitchen in his dirty tan coveralls, looking down at the table covered with food, liquor, glasses, ice in a big crockery bowl; then he swung to me. "What's the matter?" he said. "Ten days work more'n you can take? You tired, or something?" Suddenly his face flushed, the cords in his neck standing out as he yelled, "We haven't got time!"

Lauffnauer touched his arm, and when Moreno's head swung around, Frank nodded three or four times before speaking, the point of his spiky little beard touching his blue work shirt each time. "Yes, we have," he said softly. "And we will work better for this; it is a good idea, Ed."

Moreno yanked his arm away, his mouth opening to answer, then Linc reached past him, picked up a glass, dropped an ice cube into it, and called over to Rosa who stood leaning against a wall, arms folded on her chest, glaring at Moreno. "What'll you have, Rosa?" Linc said quietly.

She smiled, pushing herself from the wall to step over to the table. "Whisky," she said, "with ginger ale," and stood waiting while Linc began mixing her drink, and Moreno swung around and walked out the door.

I went after him. I caught up with him on the path, and said, "Wait a second, Ed." He turned swiftly, jaw muscles working, eyes narrowed, and I said, "You're wrong. You're a good commander; you've bulled this through in ten days, and we're nearly done. You've organized the work, done a beautiful job, forgot nothing. A good commander, but still a mustang. Put stripes on your sleeve, and you're tougher than any officer ever was before you; drive, drive, drive, to prove you can command." I grinned at him. "But leave's important, too, and that's what this is; leave in port just before the fight. And tonight that's as important as the work; you'll have a better crew for it. That's something a commander ought to know, too. Now, come on back, and have a drink."

He stood looking at me, jaw muscles still working, eyes narrowed, but he made himself weigh what I'd said. It must have been hard for a man like him; all his life, I suppose, he'd simply lashed out when opposed. But he was commanding now, and not his own emotions but the good of the cause was what had to count, and he made himself think about that. Then he said it—sullenly, reluctantly—but saying it. "All right; I made a mistake. It's time to knock off for a night." He was thinking aloud. "It's true; we got to be a good crew; damn good. And this'll help." He nodded shortly, not wanting to but doing it. "Okay, Lieutenant, let's go back."

We had a good time. We drank a toast first, standing around the kitchen table holding our first drinks. "To the *U-19*," Vic said, standing there black-bearded and grinning in his grease-streaked blue denims, one sleeve of his work shirt ripped from shoulder to elbow, but somehow seeming dapper and jaunty as ever. "May she have a lot better hunting her second trip out."

We drank then, and it tasted good; I felt two weeks' tension begin to drain out of my nerves, and I lifted my glass again. "To the captain," I said. "He's an uncouth bastard, but he may do all right just the same."

"What's this 'uncouth' business?" Moreno growled, but he grinned a little.

"It means you need a shave," I said, then I reached for a potato chip, and the party was started. Like a bunch of office workers at a party, we talked at first only about the work we did together; lounging on the cots, wandering back to the table for food or drinks. Presently Vic said something about a jammed induction valve he'd been working on, and it reminded Frank Lauffnauer of a story. On the brief training cruise he'd had in World War One, he'd reported a tank empty. The only gauge it had was an old-style water gauge; just a glass tube outside the tank, the water level in it matching the level in the tank. Actually the tank was full, but the water in the tube being clear and filling it completely, Frank thought it was empty. When they dived—

in harbor—they went down like a rock, striking bottom, and Frank lost a leave, and the Chief was broken. It was a typical submarine story, and it reminded Linc of another. He'd accidentally dropped an anchor in harbor, fouling it and swinging the sub broadside to another one following, and they'd nearly been struck. Then all of us had sub stories to tell, and we might have spent the evening that way, just talking and relaxing with our drinks.

But Rosa got bored after a while, and she walked over to the radio, turned it on, and found some dance music. Then she stood swaying beside the radio, softly snapping her fingers in time to the music, looking very graceful in her black slacks and sweater. Lounging on a cot, Vic watched her for a few moments, then asked her to dance, and they did; down along the line of cots.

We all danced with her then, except Moreno. He didn't know how to dance, he muttered, and when Rosa offered to teach him, he just shook his head and got up to mix another drink, his face tight and sullen. He couldn't hide his jealousy of Rosa, couldn't control the way he felt, seeing her in another man's arms, even just to dance. The rest of us continued to dance with her though, and time, the way it does at a party, passed very fast. Lauffnauer finished dancing with Rosa—he was very graceful; he and Vic the best dancers among us—and he bowed from the waist as they stopped, European style, and Rosa smiled, her black eyes sparkling, pleased at the gesture. "It's eleven-thirty," Moreno said then, "let's knock it off now; we got work to do in the morning," and the rest of us looked up, surprised; no one else had been watching the time.

I don't blame myself for what happened then. Our little party was over, and Rosa, smiling at something Linc was saying, stood shrugging into her red jacket with the peg buttons. Then she pulled the jeep keys from her pocket, and stood with them dangling from her fingers, as Linc finished. Rosa had gone home every night by herself, in the jeep. It wasn't practical for anyone to see her home; she usually left well before we'd finished work, and we all knew she didn't think it was necessary anyway. But standing at the table, taking a last potato chip from the bowl, watching Rosa get ready to leave, it seemed to me someone should see her home tonight. We'd had a party, she was a girl going home, and tonight it seemed inappropriate, almost boorish, to let her just walk out the door by herself, while we went to bed. I looked over at Moreno who was walking toward his cot, trying to catch his eye and suggest with a nod that he ought to drive Rosa home. But he sat down, lifted a foot to the edge of his cot, and began untying his shoelace, and I got mad. It would never enter his thick peasant head, I thought, to make any sort of gracious gesture to anyone, not even the girl he was hoping to marry. He hadn't even the elementary courtesy to wait till she'd left before starting to get ready for bed, and I walked around the table, and touched Rosa's arm. "I'll see you home," I said. "You were the belle of the ball, and deserve an escort."

She smiled, bowing her head in acknowledgment, but I saw her glance at Moreno from the corner of her eye before replying. He wouldn't look at her; still unknotting his shoelace, he wouldn't glance up or acknowledge that he'd heard, but I saw the muscles bunch at the corners of his mouth. "Thank you," Rosa said to me then, handing me the keys. She turned to call a general good night to the others, they answered, and we walked out.

In the jeep we crawled along our own rut road for a quarter mile. Then turning onto the asphalt county highway, I shoved down the accelerator till we touched sixty-five, and held it there. The top was down, so was the windshield, and the cool night air flowed over our faces, wonderfully exhilarating after the heat of the little cabin, and I felt alive and excited, back in the world again after ten days in the submarine. But only a minute or so later we were slowing, pulling into the dirt driveway beside Rosa's house, and I hated to stop, unwilling to end the evening, go home and to bed, and back to the submarine in the morning. And when Rosa turned to me, eyes still sparkling from the drive, to ask if I'd like coffee, I was glad to accept. She lived in a small frame bungalow set fifty yards back from the road, and I looked at it curiously as we walked toward it from the driveway. Her husband had built it himself, I'd heard her tell Vic and Frank Lauffnauer one day at the sub; a plain, solid, little white-painted building without any charm or grace. Rosa unlocked the back door, and we went directly into the kitchen; a big one with a huge, round wooden table at its center. This room had been the center of the life of the household, I imagined.

Rosa put coffee on to boil immediately, then took off her coat, and hung it on a nail on the back of the door. I sat down at the table, and she got out cream, sugar, cups and spoons, then sat down across from me, and I took out cigarettes, gave her one, and lighted them. Then, exhaling a jet of smoke, she set an elbow on the table, her chin cupped in her palm, cigarette in her hand, the smoke rising past her hair, and smiled happily. "I had a wonderful time dancing," she said. "I was almost forgetting I was a woman till tonight."

"Well, you are that," I said, and grinned at her.

"Yes—" She nodded slowly. "And being escorted home; that completes it. You make me feel very good tonight, Hugh."

I just nodded, smiling pleasantly; I wasn't trying to start anything. But Rosa sat staring at me. She hadn't had a lot to drink tonight, but she'd had some; and it was also the first really good time, I think, that she'd had in months. Now her eyes were happy, exuberant, and she smiled at me mischievously. "Would you like to kiss me?" she said. Her eyes laughing at me, she added, "You made me feel like a woman again, with your party tonight; it is your fault."

I looked at her, sitting there across from me in that high-necked black sweater, ripe and desirable, her olive-skinned face still flushed at the cheekbones from the wind. "Sure," I said carefully, "any man would."

"Oh?" Her brows rose and she nodded. "I see." She was still laughing at me, teasing me. "So it is any man, and you are simply no different from any other; you do not commit yourself personally. Well, then—" she leaned toward me suddenly, across the table top—"go ahead, Mr. Anyman; kiss me."

I leaned forward till our lips met, our hands on the table top supporting us as we leaned far over it, not touching in any other way. Then I kissed her, feeling the soft fullness of her lips, our mouths pressing hard together, our heads moving. Then I yanked my face away, knowing I had to if I were ever going to stop, and as I sat back again slowly I could feel my face flushing, and was glad a beard covered part of it.

Rosa—a magnificently handsome, full-figured woman sitting across from me—folded her arms on the table top, and smiled. "So," she said. "That is better. I did not wish to be taken home by Mr. Anyman just because I am any woman." She picked up her cigarette from the saucer in which she'd laid it, and stood up. "Now we will have our coffee."

We just sat talking then, drinking our coffee. What was New York like, Rosa wanted to know, and once again I was astonished at this girl. She spoke excellent idiomatic English with very little accent. She learned languages easily, she'd once told me when I asked about it; speaking French well, knowing some German though she refused to speak it; and within a year after reaching the States she spoke and understood English far better than her husband had. She dressed like an American girl, too, liking American styles, and wearing them with a flair. A week or so ago she'd arrived at the shack wearing a tailored gray skirt, a white blouse, and a pink cardigan sweater, looking like a college girl, and even the black sweater and slacks she wore now were smart-looking. She seemed very Americanized, in short; yet now she told me that most of the people she knew in this area were Italian-born, only a handful first-generation Americans. And she'd hardly been out of this area since she'd come to this country; the only times she'd been in New York even briefly were the day she arrived from Italy, and traveling to and from Fire Island twice. This, I realized, was still a girl from a little Italian fishing viliage, alone and widowed in a foreign country, courageous and self-reliant; and sitting there talking and sipping coffee, I felt very fond of her.

I finished my coffee, and stood up, thanking Rosa for it, and she walked to the door with me. At the door she thanked me again for taking her home; it meant more to her than I'd realized, I understood now, and I wondered what her husband could have been like. Standing in the doorway, I put an arm around her waist, drew her to me, and kissed her again. But she responded only slightly, fondly but almost absently, her mind somewhere else, and I let her go; the party was over, and I set out to walk home.

I'd been there twenty minutes, I suppose; it took me another twenty to walk home, along the county road which more or less paralleled the coast; and the drive to Rosa's house couldn't have taken more than four or five minutes. So when I turned off the road to walk the quarter-mile or less down to the shack, I'd been gone about forty-five minutes. The shack was dark, I saw, walking toward it, then I saw a cigarette glow on the little stoop that led into the big room that was our dormitory, and I knew Moreno was waiting for me.

He stood up when I was a hundred yards or so from the shack, and walked toward me, and when we met on the path, we stopped, facing each other. "Well?" I said.

"Where you been?" he said quietly, bringing his cigarette up to his mouth; then it glowed, and I saw his bristle-bearded face for a moment, slit-eyed and hostile.

"You know where I've been; taking Rosa home."

"Take you this long to walk back?"

I was about to explain that we'd had coffee, but I stopped myself; I owed Moreno no explanations. "What's it to you," I said, "how long I take?"

He was silent for a moment or two, and I knew he was keeping a grip on himself, forcing himself to reply quietly. "You know damn well what it is to me," he said then. "I'm going to marry Rosa, and you or nobody else is going to start hanging around her."

"Why, sure," I said pleasantly. "Of course. I won't spend another second alone with Rosa. Or say any more than hello, goodbye, and how are you—"

"See that you don't."

"—from the moment she tells me what you've said. Just have your fiancée tell me, Moreno, that she's going to marry you. And from then on I won't even look sideways at her."

"She doesn't have to tell you; *I'm* telling—"

"Oh, yes, she does." I leaned down a little to stare into his eyes. *"She* has to tell me. You been talking about marrying Rosa for a long time now, but I haven't heard her say a word about it. You just have your fiancée say so, Moreno, next time I ask to take her home. Because there's sure as hell going to be a next time now." I stood staring at him, waiting for whatever he wanted to say or do.

He grinned a little in the faint starlight; mean and nasty. "You want trouble, pretty boy?" he said softly. "You'll get it; a lot more than you want." Then he turned and walked back to the shack. I followed, and inside the shack we got undressed in the darkness without another word, and went to bed.

First thing in the morning we hoisted the torpedoes out of the ship through the torpedo hatch, using the chain hoist in the dock; an awkward, but not very hard job. There were four spares plus two in the tubes, and we hauled all six of them out, and lowered them to the dock along one side of the sub, and Moreno began working on one of them.

This was his field, his specialty, and though I watched him from time to time, as we all did, I didn't even try to understand what he was doing. But his job was to convert at least one torpedo to a dummy; to take off the warhead, remove the TNT, and replace it with a small flash charge. We'd often used dummies in the Navy for practice firings; they go off with a flash and a lot of smoke, for easy sighting, but with no force to speak of. They don't even wreck the torpedoes, and you recover them afterward.

Actually, a practice-head is different from a warhead, but Moreno said he could make these do, and I knew he could. Just the same, I'll admit it made me a little nervous, standing on the dock with Vic, Lauffnauer, and Linc, watching him get ready to remove that blunt and deadly red-painted warhead from the first of the torpedoes. He grinned up at me nastily, so I made a point of standing there watching, even after the others left. I stood watching him remove the detonator in the war nose first, then unscrew the warhead, and—working with wrenches and several screwdrivers—open up the compartment which held the TNT. It's strange-looking stuff, like big perforated sticks of horehound candy, and there was a lot of it. These were small short-range torpedoes, only a thousand yards, but each of them held over four hundred pounds of TNT, a terrible and devastating force when exploded. Presently Linc rowed the small boat into the dock alongside the sub, and Moreno laid the big candylike sticks in the bottom; then Linc rowed far out to sea to dump them overboard.

Moreno had bought whatever he needed for the harmless flash charge; the difference in weight between it and the big charge he'd removed would be made up, he'd said, with ordinary sea water. Once the TNT was out of the warhead, I didn't hang around; Moreno and I weren't speaking any more than necessary, and today the rest of us were to begin testing the sub.

We weren't finished working on her; not quite. There were still odds and ends to finish up yet. But the engines and motor were working—beautifully, and in perfect adjustment. The compressor worked as well as it ever would, and the tanks held air. All valves and vents were in reasonably good working order; and all fuel, air, water, and electrical lines were in excellent condition. The periscope worked smoothly; all we'd had to do was clean and oil it. And my switchboard worked perfectly the first time I tried it. All outside parts were free and moving again, though they were terribly eroded, pitted, and worked loosely.

But though it wasn't a lot, we'd done just about all we could. Lauffnauer had stripped off the sodden deck gratings, and was going to knock together a new set made of two-by-fours. We had two inflatable rafts to buy, Linc had a radio to buy, and I had to get chargers. But essentially we were finished; now we had to test what we'd done.

Inside the submarine, we blew the tanks, and the sub rose to float high in the dock, gently nudging the old tires nailed to the sides. This much we'd known would happen; we knew we could blow the tanks. Then we opened the dock doors, and Lauffnauer, in the tower, searched the water with a pair of Navy binoculars that belonged to Moreno; stolen, I imagined. There was nothing in sight, and the rest of us shoved the sub out with poles; there was a fresh breeze and the water was choppy today, but we didn't want to test her only under ideal conditions anyway. I climbed down inside to the engines, Linc coming along to take the rudder wheel; Vic stayed on deck with his poles to fend her off if necessary. Lauffnauer hadn't replaced the old deck gratings yet, and Vic had a job staying on deck. Then I started the diesels, Linc swung the rudder wheel, and we curved out to sea. Vic came down then, Lauffnauer still in the tower. We went a mile out, cruising back and forth along the coast for half a mile in either direction, testing the engines at various speeds, Linc and Vic getting used to the way the rudder responded. We had all our batteries, and we'd bought them charged, and after a time I tested the motor. We'd used up some of the battery charge, and not all of them had been charged to capacity in the first place. So I ran the motors for only a minute; they worked fine.

From time to time we flooded to just above negative buoyancy, then blew the tanks, testing them over and over. Then, finally, we made our first dive test, in twenty-five feet of water. Moreno had told us where to find clean bottom at that depth, and we sounded with a line and found it right away. We expected no trouble; the tanks had blown when we raised the sub; and in any case we could flood and escape at this depth without even using aqua-lungs. I threw out the engine clutch, Frank came down, closing the hatches behind him, and we flooded the tanks, very slowly. We sank then, the tanks not completely filled, at just below positive buoyancy, and the depth gauge worked. The needle moved to five, then ten, then fifteen feet; and a moment or so after we felt the sub's keel nudge the bottom, the needle stopped at twenty-six feet. We didn't move; we held our breaths, listening. But there was no sound of water, either inside the hull, or from the ballast tanks. Then we moved through the sub inspecting for leaks, and found none. We hadn't expected to; the sub, after all, had withstood the pressure of a hundred-foot depth for forty years. It was our work on the ballast-tank valves we'd come down to test; if they failed to work now, if the tanks wouldn't blow, we'd have to flood, and escape, leaving the sunken submarine forever.

Finally Lauffnauer gave the word, Vic yanked the air-flask levers, and we heard the gush of sound—always wonderful to hear, always a relief—of sea water forced out by the rush of air into the tanks, and we felt the sub stir, and saw the depth-gauge needle quiver and begin to move back, and knew we were rising. Vic shut off the air then, closed the valves, and I started the motors, as Lauffnauer and Vic took the fore and aft dive-plane wheels. Then, at just above negative buoyancy, we maneuvered the little submarine at about fifteen feet depth, Lauffnauer commanding. We rose toward the surface, then nosed down toward the bottom, the sub responding well, as Frank and Vic heaved at their wheels, Linc steering. We kept it up for only two minutes, then I shut down my motors; I wasn't risking running out of juice for the trip back. The sub rose of its own buoyancy then, we surfaced, and as Lauffnauer broke open the hatches we were grinning at each other. We still had other, and far more severe and dangerous, tests to make, but our submarine was operating so far, and we felt certain in that moment that it would continue to do so. Then I connected the diesels, started them, and we headed for home. I wanted the batteries fully charged for the rest of our tests, and I hadn't yet had a chance to get chargers, so we were through for the day.

Moreno had two torpedoes ready when we got back, and was working on a third; he'd already paddled out and dumped the TNT, he said, grinning up at me, as though I were the one who needed reassuring about that. He'd decided to convert all six, he said then; we were standing in the dock watching him. Without facilities we didn't have, we couldn't really test these torpedoes, and while we needed only one dummy, there was no point in depending on only one of them, when we had five spares on hand. He'd convert them all, he said, and the rest of us nodded and agreed.

For a few minutes then, we stood watching Moreno carefully reassembling this third torpedo. These were early old-style torpedoes, and they used grain alcohol and distilled water for power. The alcohol burned in a steady, intensely hot little flame under a flash pan. The big air flask which formed the main bulk of the torpedo sprayed a mist of distilled water onto the flash pan, where it was instantaneously converted into live steam. The steam drove the turbine which turned the twin screws; actually a torpedo is a tiny submarine, a marvel of ingenious compression. There was nothing wrong with the torpedoes that he could detect, Moreno said; there was actually water and alcohol still in those he'd opened, they were so tightly built and sealed, though he'd added more to each of the two he'd finished, as he would to this. The turbines seemed all right, but just as important as the turbine, in a torpedo, are the automatic devices which keep it on course, and at whatever depth it's been set for. A gyroscope holds it on course, automatically moving the rudders to keep it moving in a straight line. And a hydrostatic piston, instantly responding to any changes in depth pressures, regulates the little fins beside the rudders, moving them up or down as necessary to keep the torpedo at its pre-set depth. These Moreno couldn't test. They looked all right, he said; they seemed to be in good working order, and he was certain they were. Just the same, he told us, we couldn't rely on any one torpedo to work when the time came, so he was going to continue work on the others.

"Hugh," he said then, glancing up at me, and I was surprised; his voice was pleasant and he even smiled agreeably. "This might be the best time to pick up your chargers and the rafts. Linc can go along to pick up his radio. What's on your schedule, Frank?"

"I will make the new gratings. I can ride along to the village, order the two-by-fours, and ride back with the lumber truck. I will buy paint, too, and bring it back."

"Okay." Sitting on the dock beside his partly assembled torpedo, Moreno nodded. "Hugh? Linc? That okay with you?" he said, and we nodded; I didn't quite trust this new friendliness, though I couldn't imagine what he was up to. "Vic," he went on, "maybe you could give Frank a hand on the deck gratings."

"Sure," Vic said, and Moreno yanked open the first couple of snap fasteners at the neck of his tan coveralls, then pulled out a little leather sack hanging from a chain around his neck. He took a thick roll of bills from the sack, carefully counted out seven hundred and fifty dollars, mostly in twenties, then handed it up to me.

"Bring back the change," he said, grinning, and I took it, not answering. Then Linc and I left, to go up to the shack and get dressed for the city.

In the little bathroom, washing, I decided not to shave. It would have been hard—I'd have had to use scissors first—and a beard, I discovered, staring into the mirror, turning my head to look at it, is a hard thing to part with. It suited my face, I thought; it was thick and stubby, slightly curly, and yellow-brown like my hair. It made me look older, harder, and I was pleased with it. I dressed in clean denims and work shirt; Rosa had washed and ironed them. Then I went out to wait, while Linc washed and dressed.

Rosa had a cheese sandwich and a glass of milk ready for me, and I sat at the kitchen table eating, watching her prepare a sandwich for Linc. It was the first moment I'd been alone with her since I'd been at her house, and now I thought about last night; and about my encounter with Moreno on my way home. In a way I didn't want to do this; a quarrel among any of us was a dangerous thing now. And while I liked Rosa—she was a nice girl—that was all I felt. But Moreno had forced this issue; he'd warned me off with no right to do so. He had no right either, I thought, to limit Rosa's company or pleasure; why the hell hadn't he taken this girl to visit New York long since? Since he hadn't, I was going to. I didn't want to, not really; but I wanted even less to feel the way I knew I would if I let Moreno's warning keep me from doing it. Rosa was slicing Linc's sandwich in half, standing at the drainboard of the sink, wearing a high-necked yellow sweater, the sleeves pushed up over her elbows, a dark-green skirt, and low-heeled shoes. Her hair coiled in braids on top of her head, she looked very, very pretty. "Want to ride along, Rosa?" I said casually. "Spend a couple hours in New York?"

She swung around, her eyes lighting up; then her lower lip crept in between her teeth, and she frowned and glanced out the window toward the dock.

"Listen," I said angrily, "are you marrying that guy? If you are, I wish you'd say so."

"He says I am." A slow mischievous smile crept over her face. "He asked me again this morning; even before breakfast, as soon as I arrived. He told me, that is; this time he didn't ask."

"And what did you tell him?" If she were going to marry Moreno I wanted to know. I'd let her strictly alone then, and—I had to admit to myself—I'd be almost relieved to be able to.

"Nothing." She shrugged. "I'm not ready to be married again; my husband is dead only four months. But in time I will marry again."

"Moreno?" I persisted.

"Maybe."

"Don't marry Moreno," I heard myself saying, and Rosa smiled, her brows rising.

"Oh?" she said. "Are *you* proposing to me, then?"

"No, I'm not. But you can do a hell of a lot better than Moreno."

"And a lot worse!" she said suddenly, angrily, leaning toward me, her hands on her hips, her black eyes glittering. "You don't like him, but I could do much worse; a very great deal!"

I shrugged, and stood up. "Suit yourself," I said, and just to irritate her, because I felt angry myself, I added, "You'll have plenty of money to console you, anyway."

She just laughed at me; a single contemptuous snort of laughter, her head tossing. "Money," she said. "You are like children, all of you; Moreno, too. You think money changes things. What would it do for me? If my husband has money, will he lie around the house and not work? And what should I do? Money or no money, I will do the same thing—make a home for my husband, and raise his children. There is nothing else for a woman; it is what she is for. And the women who think not pay for it with their lives. Useless wasted women. For myself, that is all I want, and I think I will not marry any of you; you are stupid, all of you. Yes, I will go to New York with you!"

I had to laugh at her, at this fiery girl standing with her hands on her hips glaring up at me; I never knew what she was going to do or say. "Fine," I said, laughing. "Come on along." And she glared for a moment longer, then threw her head back, hands still on her hips, and burst into laughter, too.

Linc came out a moment later, wearing clean wash clothes, but unshaven, too. He didn't know what we were laughing at, of course, but he grinned at us amiably, and his smile, together with his beginning beard—tightly curled and close-fitting like his hair—made him look like a chocolate-colored saint. I yelled for Lauffnauer then, and a moment or so later when he came plodding up the path, we all walked out, turning toward the back of the shack and the jeep. We climbed in, and as Lauffnauer approached the jeep, he glanced at Rosa beside me, then at me—warningly, his eyes narrowed—but he said nothing, and got into the back with Linc.

We didn't do anything special in New York. At the first gas station outside the tunnel, I stopped, and Linc and I copied half a dozen addresses each, from the classified section of the phone book; radio- and auto-supply houses, and a couple of surplus stores. I put Rosa in a cab then; she was going to Fifth Avenue, at Linc's suggestion, walk up it, and we'd pick her up in Central Park, across the street from the Plaza Hotel.

It took Linc and me a little over two hours to buy what we needed. I got my chargers right away, and then two small inflatable Air Force life rafts at a surplus store in the same block. But Linc and I visited half a dozen radio-supply places before Linc—looking over radios, asking questions, and pricing them—found what he wanted. I waited, in the stores at first, then later just sitting outside in the jeep.

We picked up Rosa then—it was a little past five—and started back for the tunnel. She'd had a good time, she said, and I suggested stopping for a drink somewhere, but perfunctorily, not really meaning it. We weren't dressed for it, and Linc said no, he didn't care for one, but he offered to wait in the jeep. Rosa shook her head though, and I nodded; we weren't in the city for anything but business, and it was time to go back.

But I felt dissatisfied, somehow, all the way home, and wished I had thought to plan this trip differently. If I were going to ask Rosa to come with me to New York, risking trouble with Moreno, as I'd felt obliged to do, then somehow the trip should have been less routine. We could have gone dancing, maybe, if I'd planned this differently, or at least had lunch. As it was I'd started trouble to no point at all, and felt cheated. It was dusk, almost dark, when we reached the shack, finally, and Linc hopped right out of the jeep, picked up the carton containing his radio, surprisingly small and compact, and carried it around the corner of the shack toward the dock. Then—I was startled, and had just time to wonder if she'd been thinking as I had—Rosa turned to me, lifting her arms easily and naturally, as though there were nothing else that could occur, and my arms slid around her, and I was kissing her. I held her tight to me, and kissed her long and hard, and when we stopped, it was only for an instant. Then I was straining her to me, kissing her again, and it was wildly exciting—this trip was worth while!—and I never wanted to stop.

But as suddenly as she'd begun, Rosa was pulling loose, and she leaned back against the door away from me, a hand rising to her hair, the other hand holding me off, and I got mad. "What the hell was that for?" I said.

"I don't know." She shrugged. "No reason. I just felt like it; is everything you do for a reason? Perhaps I was just trying to find out how I feel; you cannot remain a widow forever, and I will remain one only as long as I feel like one." She frowned angrily. "Anyway, Ed Moreno doesn't own me. Not yet."

I grinned at her. "I guess that answers my question; you weren't kissing me, you were just defying Moreno."

"You think too much."

"Maybe; so let's quit thinking." I leaned toward her, putting an arm around her waist, drawing her toward me, and said, "No thinking now; this time it's just for the fun of it." She hesitated, frowning a little, then raised her arms, and I grabbed her to me, and kissed her once more; this time long and lingeringly, enjoying it, the blood pounding in my temples.

Then she broke loose, twisting suddenly and angrily from my arms. "This is stupid!" she said, glaring at me. "Like children! You don't love me! And I don't love you! You are nothing but a big good-looking man, and I am ashamed of myself!"

I reached forward and put a hand on her arm. "Now who's thinking too much?" I said gently, smiling at her, and after a moment she smiled back, but grudgingly.

"There is lipstick on your face," she said shortly. "Wipe it off." Then she sat waiting, a hand on the door handle.

I reached for the handkerchief in my back pocket, then stopped. I don't know how I suddenly knew that Moreno was waiting somewhere in the almost complete darkness around us; I don't think there'd been a sound of any sort, though maybe there was. But I knew, and I said, "You go on ahead; I've got to haul the rafts and chargers down to the dock."

Rosa nodded, and got out, and before she reached the door of the shack, I opened my door, and moved quickly out away from the jeep, onto the rut road and in the clear—crouched, turning, watching every direction. But Moreno didn't rush me. There were no stars, no moon, but there was still light, the very last of the day, high in the sky. And now the indistinct silhouette of Moreno's squat powerful figure walked out from behind the shack; how long he'd been there watching and listening I didn't know. Then, in the faint diffused light, I saw the dull shine of the knife in his hand.

I don't know anything about knife fighting beyond the little I've read here and there; which is that it can be highly skilled, a whole system of offensive and defensive lunges and parries. In any case, I didn't have a knife of my own. But I was certain Moreno was skilled with a knife; the very way he held it, walking slowly toward me, seemed professional and deadly. Standing half crouched, my hands out and open, watching him move closer, I knew that this time there'd be no talking; that he was going to use that knife to kill me if he could.

I was—quietly and with utter calm—very frightened. I don't think my pulse beat even increased; I couldn't let my fear affect me. If I was going to survive the next minute, I had to be as deadly and purposely thoughtful as the man with the knife—not four yards away now—walking toward me, the haft in his fist held at stomach level, the blade pointing at me. Now, silently, not saying a word, he was ten feet away, and I whirled and ran; purposely awkward and stumbling, simulating blind panic. I ran three or four steps, up the road away from the shack, then darted a look over my shoulder. Moreno was running hard after me, but not gaining, and I stumbled again, my outthrust hand brushing the tall grass beside the rut as though I were about to fall, letting him come closer. Then, my feet pounding in the dry powdery dust of the deep rut, I stooped, still running, grabbed up a thick handful of dust, and whirled to face Moreno. Very fast but with absolutely careful aim, I shot my arm out, opening my fist, and flung the handful of dust squarely into Moreno's face. He came after me still, but stumbling, blinded, his free hand swiping across his eyes, and as I backed carefully away, maintaining a yard's distance between us, he began to curse, not loudly. He was shaking his head violently, eyes blinking rapidly, the knife still outthrust, and now I kicked. With all my strength, aiming with the very point of my toe, my foot flashed upward and the blunt tip of my workshoe caught his hand squarely. The force of it flung his arm straight overhead, the knife flashing up out of his hand. Then I hit him, with every ounce of force I had, aiming for the belly but missing and catching him squarely in the chest, knocking him over and rolling in the road.

He continued to roll, very quickly, out of my way, and onto his knees and feet, arms and fists out, low and in front of his belly as he crouched. He was blinking still—I could see the whites of his eyes—but I knew from the way he moved that he could see, and I stood waiting for him.

We fought, then, for a long time, through many minutes, though I don't know how many. I've laughed and will again at fights I've seen on television and in movies—blow after tremendous blow landing squarely on the jaw or deep into the belly, any one of which would finish most men. But still the fight goes on, furniture crashing. We weren't that good; few men, if any, are. We swung at each other's jaws, and struck a shoulder bone instead, or grazed a head, or missed completely, stumbling against each other and struggling frantically for balance, feet sliding. We clinched awkwardly, holding each other up. We grunted with effort, heaving for breath, and we both went down again and again, half knocked down by a blow, half stumbling and falling. We grazed chins and cheekbones, necks, shoulders, and arms, and once, somehow, Moreno hit me squarely on top of the head, and I actually punched him hard on the knee.

Nothing I know of exhausts a man more quickly—in real life, anyway—than a fight. A skilled professional fighter at the peak of his youth fights only three-minute rounds. In between, attended by half a dozen experts, he rests completely for a full minute. And even when fighting, long seconds often pass with no blow struck or received, the fighters slowly and warily shuffling, arms nearly motionless. Yet even after a fight like that, a fight for which they have trained and rested and brought their legs and bodies to the peak of endurance, the men are worn out. They lie outstretched then, back in their dressing rooms, rib cages heaving for oxygen, eyes closed, and deadly tired.

We weren't trained, we weren't professionals, and we burned up energy—grappling, heaving at each other, swinging blows at full strength, slipping on the trampled weeds, tripping in the ruts of the road—at a rate no professional could possibly permit himself. And the fight didn't end at all; it just dwindled to a stop. We were standing in the darkness pressed against each other, arms hanging onto each other, and I think that if either of us had been able to step aside, the other would have fallen on his face in the road. I couldn't lift my arms; there is no better way to describe it than to say they were like lead. They hung from my shoulders, clutching Moreno, and their weight was palpable as though they weren't a part of me, my muscles utterly without strength to lift them. My legs were exhausted stumps, my knee muscles fluttering, and if I had once let my knees bend, I could never have straightened them and would have sagged to the ground.

We couldn't talk; we stood slumped together, holding each other erect, the breath actually whistling in our throats, chests swelling and collapsing in struggle for air. Our shirts were soaked with sweat. Moments passed, then we staggered apart, and stood swaying, staring at each other. Then—not a word had been spoken—we stumbled down the road toward the shack, arms actually around each other's waist holding ourselves up.

Rosa was alone in the cabin, standing at the sink rinsing dishes. As we stumbled in through the door, she turned to look at us, and her eyes widened, but she didn't ask needless questions. She swung around, yanked two chairs out from the kitchen table, and pulled them to the sink, gesturing at them with her head. We sat down, fell into them actually, and Rosa took two clean dishtowels from the little shelf over the sink made of an old crate nailed to the wall. Soaking them under the tap, she said, "Take off your shirts," and we each began fumbling at them. The tails were out long since, the shirts ripped and grass-stained, most of the buttons missing. But they were wet and clinging with sweat, neither of us could get them off, and Rosa helped us, peeling them down our backs, then lifting our arms by the wrists to tug the sleeves off. Then Moreno and I slumped in our chairs, heads resting on the backs, our faces upturned, still gasping. Rosa stood before us, a wrung-out towel in each hand, and washed our faces—roughly and mercilessly, not sparing the bruises. She flung the towels in our laps then, telling us to sponge ourselves off, and stood, her weight on one hip, arms folded on her chest, grinning down at us. "Idiots," she said. "*Stupidi!* Look at you; like pigs in the mud. I wouldn't touch either of you with gloves. Clean yourselves up!" Then she walked out, and we could hear her steps crunch on the path leading down to the dock.

We mopped away at our chests and arms for a little time, our breathing quieting down. Then Moreno said, "You're out of condition, Lieutenant; if you could of gone one more round you could of killed me."

"One more round would have killed me," I muttered, glancing up at him; then our eyes met, and Moreno grinned.

"I was mad," he said. "Really mad. I'd of killed you." He smiled and shook his head. "But the fight must of drained it out of me; I got nothin' left now. Maybe it's Rosa who needs a boot in the tail."

I nodded. "I wouldn't be surprised."

We were silent for a moment; I wanted a cigarette, but didn't feel like moving. Then Moreno said quietly, "Let's cut it out now; that all right with you? There's too damn much at stake to fool around."

"Suits me." I nodded.

Nine

WE WORKED THAT NIGHT, but only till about ten. Frank had knocked together a set of deck gratings during the afternoon, and now, propping them up against the end of the dock, he and Vic began to paint them, black. And I rigged my chargers down in the sub—beginning to ache and stiffen from the fight—and got them started. But mostly we just wandered through the sub, all of us, looking her over, fooling with this or that, not doing much of anything really. There wasn't much left to do any more, and we had two more days and nights left; this was May 14, and we were to sail on the morning of the seventeenth.

Around noon the next day, we tested the sub. We moved out as before, this time towing the rowboat, and found a hundred feet, sounding with the boat's anchor line. Then Vic and I climbed into the boat, untied her, and paddled clear. Moreno was back at the dock finishing up his torpedoes; Lauffnauer and Linc were going to make a stationary test dive alone.

They went under—Linc climbed down, and we heard the hatch slam after him. Then, waiting a hundred and fifty yards away, we saw the deck lower, disappear, then the water creep up the rusting side of the tower and close over it. We waited; five minutes, then six, then seven. Suddenly the water boiled, continued to boil, and the conning tower broke surface, then the decks, the water gurgling from the sub's drainholes. Linc broke open the hatch then and waved his arms, hands clasped together, and we rowed over to her.

She'd tested out as we expected, yet just the same, the sub back in the dock, drying from black to dull orange again. I stood staring down at her with the others, wondering what was going to happen out in the ocean in this little boat, far beyond any help. She was so little! Standing on the dock beside her, I knew I could jump over onto her bow, and actually make her bob in the water from my weight. And she was old, incredibly antiquated, dangerous to sail in the day she was launched, and far more so now. I thought of all that was wrong and half-wrong with this ancient, obsolete little submarine. Then, my eyes roving back and forth along the length of her, I looked at the rust, already orange again on the conning tower, at the fragmentary remains of black paint in patchy streaks and scaling blotches here and there, and at the faded-out rust-speckled white paint on the side of the tiny tower that spelled *U-19*. There wasn't much paint left, white or black; mostly she was vivid with rust, thick and scaling. Scrape your fingers along a side as all of us often had, and your nails were bright orange. No one had ever gone to sea in a submarine like this, and it seemed suddenly unbelievable to me that we were going to try, and for a moment there, I hoped that something, anything, would keep us from ever trying. "Damn it to hell!" I said, swinging angrily to the others. "Let's get this thing painted so it at least looks like a sub!"

Moreno nodded, standing beside me, arms folded on his chest, face bruised black, blue, and orange from the fight. "Yeah," he said, and grinned. "I'll feel better, too. You get the paint, Frank?" Frank nodded, and Moreno said, "We'll paint her today, soon as she's dry, right after lunch." He grinned again. "Maybe the paint'll help hold her together."

The next day, the sixteenth, there was almost nothing to do. We'd painted her the day before, right down to the waterline at low tide, using ordinary gray house paint, and just slapping it on; we didn't care how long it lasted. After lunch we laid on the new deck gratings, fastening them down; then we lashed our two deflated rubber rafts to the gratings just forward of the tower. I had batteries recharging, and from time to time I uncoupled fully charged batteries and hooked up others. Moreno stowed our chart, sextant, chronometer, and instruments in a locker, and Frank and Vic carried half a dozen stubby canoe paddles down into the forward compartment. Linc brought down our two underwater flashlights, and hung them by their thongs in the control room.

After lunch we loaded the torpedoes in, lowering them down into the sub one at a time with the chain hoist in the dock, then man-handling them forward until we could lift them with the sub's hoist in the forward compartment. We loaded the first two right into the firing tubes, and Moreno scratched an X into the paint just above one of the tubes. "This is the one we'll try first," he said, "just for luck. I think it's in the best condition."

Then, suddenly, in the late afternoon, there was nothing more to do. Rosa brought down a plastic hamper full of sandwiches, fruit and cookies. And she had three thermos bottles washed and drying on the drainboard of the sink, ready to fill with hot coffee in the morning. At supper, we ate in almost a complete silence, staring off at nothing, each busy with his own thoughts. Then Rosa and Moreno set up an extra cot, in the kitchen; Rosa was staying here tonight. Moreno, Linc, and Rosa began a rummy game then, sitting on a cot, dealing the cards out on a blanket; while Vic, Frank, and I lay on our cots, or wandered around the room.

The rummy game died around nine o'clock, and we gave up trying to do anything but wait out the time; talking a little, smoking a lot, drinking coffee. Around ten Moreno said, "Let's have a drink," and Rosa got out our half-filled whisky bottle from a cupboard, and we all had a drink, straight, without ice or water. "Here's luck," Moreno said quietly. "We'll sure as hell need it," and we all managed to grin, a little wryly, and tossed the drinks down. Then Moreno set his glass on the wooden drainboard of the sink. "To bed, now; everybody," he said. From his pocket he brought out a little brown-tinted bottle, unscrewed the white plastic top, and began shaking the little capsules it contained toward the bottle mouth. "Here," he said then, offering them around, "these are seconal tablets; I want a full night's sleep for everyone," and we all held out our palms. I was glad to have one; I was wide-eyed and tense—rigid—with excitement, and sleep would have been impossible without it. We went to bed then, still half dressed; Rosa in her black slacks and sweater fully dressed; and well before ten-thirty the little shack was silent. Then I was asleep.

Ten

WE SAILED in the dark, just past high water on an ebb tide. Our one alarm clock had rung thirty minutes before, in the dead of night, and I turned my face into my pillow, shaking my head; suddenly I didn't want to wake up to this day. Almost immediately Moreno shut off the alarm; it was beside his bed, and he must have been lying awake waiting for it. Someone moaned, coming out of sleep —Linc, probably; he'd done it before—then I heard the slap of bare feet, Frank Lauffnauer, and the overhead light snapped on, a single naked glaring bulb, and I wanted to shout at him to turn it off. Vic said, "Well, this is it!" parodying the worn-out phrase, and I knew he was alive with excitement, actually happy, and I could have killed him. Moreno growled, "Yeah," and I heard Rosa sigh and mutter something.

I'm never at my best in the morning; I'm awake but not functioning well, ready to be irritable if I don't watch myself, and getting up before daybreak is even worse. Now, sitting on the edge of my cot, buttoning my shirt, my fingers still clumsy—Lauffnauer coughing steadily and irritatingly—I wanted nothing but to crawl back into bed, and I knew with a positive, angry certainty that we were about to sail out into disaster.

We took turns washing, quickly; Rosa first so that she could prepare toast and coffee. Then we ate quickly, too; standing up in the little kitchen area, forcing the food down, swallowing the hot coffee, not bothering to talk beyond a few muttered good mornings. We looked like a submarine crew all right, I thought morosely, standing there drugged with sleep and the after-effects of seconal, chewing toast without wanting it—a crew a good ten days out at that.

Rosa said irritably, "Someone should wear a black eye patch; you look like pirates." It was true; bearded, we looked tough and hard and disreputable. Lauffnauer, standing beside me sipping coffee, eyes absent and staring, had a close-fitting brown beard that slimmed down to a point, making his hawklike face even longer, thinner, and more saturnine. Moreno's was black, wiry, and bristling; staring out into the night toward the dock, chewing toast, he looked like a murderer. Linc's beard was short and curly, close to his face, and Vic's was jet-black, already quite long and very silky, making him more darkly handsome than ever. Mine was stubby and bluntly pointed, thick and blondish, close to my skin and a little wavy; and it made me look older. We looked like pirates, and we seemed bigger today, too, I thought, because of the way we were dressed, I supposed. We all wore heavy-knit pull-over sweaters, mine and Linc's gray, the others' navy blue. Vic, Lauffnauer, and I wore navy-blue pants, and Linc and Moreno blue denims, and we all had heavy high-topped workshoes of unfinished leather, our pants stuffed into them, and bloused over their tops. In appearance, anyway, we were a submarine crew—hard, dangerous, and competent—and that's what we were in fact, too, I thought, feeling a little better now, the coffee inside me.

"All right, let's move," Moreno growled, setting his empty cup on the drainboard of the little sink. I had a little left, and just stood there, holding my cup. But when the others straggled through the doorway, I set my cup down, turned out the light, and moved with them, pulling the shack door closed behind me. If we were ever to reach the end of this day, I knew we had to behave like a crew, the best crew we knew how to be. Rosa was carrying three thermos bottles of coffee, and I caught up with her, took a couple of them and we straggled along the path in the darkness, showing no light, six figures under the stars feeling their way down the path toward the *U-19*, waiting at the edge of the sea.

The sub was ready. There was nothing to do but start. Even the rudders were already in position, and we all, except Moreno, who stayed in the tower, climbed down into her, and I went directly back to the engines. They were cold, of course, and it took me several minutes to start them, and I cursed and muttered at them, but all the time, in the back of my mind, lay the hope that somehow they wouldn't start at all. Then presently they stuttered into life, I nursed them along, warming them, then shouted up to Moreno. "Engines ready!"

"All right," he called down, "let's go," and, the old diesels growling rhythmically, we moved out of the dock to sea. A thousand yards out, curving onto a northeast course, Moreno ordered, "Blow main ballasts," and the air surged into the tanks, the deck pushing against my feet, and we rode high in the water, as we would till first dawn.

There wasn't much to do now. I had my engines to watch, making sure they didn't run too hot, but they seemed all right, and I walked forward to the switchboard just aft of the control room, and checked my batteries; they showed a good full charge. Lauffnauer had the trim tanks to handle, adjusting them as needed to compensate for fuel loss. Linc sat at his radio in the control room, his headset covering one ear only, slowly twisting a dial, monitoring whatever transmissions he could hear, which weren't many, he said. Vic sat at the rudder wheel, and Rosa stood by. We wouldn't need Rosa at all unless we had to crash dive; she'd heave the levers then—Moreno had drilled her—which would flood the main ballast tanks.

Frank and Vic started a game of rummy, Frank sitting on the deck in the control room beside Vic at the wheel. Rosa, standing at the little sink in what had been the galley, just aft of the control room, was pouring coffee into paper cups from a thermos. I had nothing to do then—I'd just checked the batteries at the switchboard directly behind her—and I stepped over beside her to take a cup. "Hello, sucker," I said, and she turned to glance up at me, grinning.

"I think you are right," she said, nodding. "We are crazy. Are you frightened?"

"Sure," I said, but it wasn't true. I was awake now, feeling fine, the coffee I'd just tasted very good, and I wasn't scared. "Are you?"

She thought about it for a moment, then shrugged, turning to resume pouring coffee, and I knew she wasn't frightened either. I suppose none of us was just then. Nothing was threatening us, and we weren't taking action, or at least it didn't seem like it; we were simply moving along through the water and the last of the night, the diesels behind us rumbling hypnotically. It wasn't possible for me to really believe yet that we were actually going to attempt what I knew we were.

Moreno called down occasionally, whenever he saw running lights. But he saw very few, and never very close; we were well out to sea now. I checked my engines every ten minutes or so, but they were running nicely, and not too hot, though I thought they might if we had to run at full speed.

About an hour out, I climbed up for a look around, crowding into the little tower beside Moreno. The starlight was good, and I could see the sea around us; a little choppy, but not rough, the waves foot-high at most, and running southeasterly. To the east, off the port side, I saw the very first hint of white; false dawn, I knew, the real dawn soon to come. "Nice, isn't it?" Moreno murmured beside me, and I nodded. "I could have stayed in the Navy, and liked it okay," he said, "if there'd been any kind of career in it for me."

"Maybe there would have been."

"Nah." He shook his head, smiling. "I was too much of a damn fool, a wild young kid, when I was young enough to try for an Annapolis appointment. And too old by the time I got sense. I like it at sea, though—" He looked around him. "The Navy, fishing, or something else; it's the only place for me."

"Be tough on you if we all end up in a prison somewhere."

"I'll kill myself then," he said quietly, "first chance I get," and I knew he meant it. Lauffnauer's head poked up then, through the open hatch at our feet, and I stepped down onto the ladder, sidling past him as he swung out on the ladder to make room for me.

"How do you feel, Hugh?" he said softly, and without waiting for an answer, he went on, "I feel lucky; it's a good day." Then, surprisingly, he added—and I realized he was charged with contained excitement—"Just before the surrender my family was killed in the bombing of Hamburg. For the first time since then, I feel alive again." He wasn't really talking to me, I realized, but to himself, and would hardly have heard an answer. I smiled at him, climbing down past him, then turned away from the ladder to check my engines again.

We moved on, then, a black speck crawling steadily across the vast face of the ocean in the beginning dawn; and for hour after hour through the morning we continued, at a steady eight-and-a-half to nine knots, the coast just visible far to port. Twelve times we sighted ships: freighters, an ocean-going tug, a Navy transport, two destroyers, several Coast Guard cutters. But they were far off, and we knew our little tower, half submerged now, was invisible to them.

Somewhere around noon, Rosa began laying out sandwiches from the hamper she'd brought, and opening warm Cokes on the drainboard of the little galley sink. I was sitting on the control-room deck, hands loosely clasped around my knees, staring absently at Vic, who was sitting on the periscope seat idly rubbing at the brass housing with a thumb. Lauffnauer was forward, adjusting his trim tanks, and Linc sat, one side of his headset to an ear, reading a paperback book; I'd glanced at the title—it was *Heidi*—and been amused. Now I got to my feet and stepped over the control-room combing into the aft compartment, to check my batteries.

At least I told myself that's what I was doing, and I did; they were okay. I turned and looked at Rosa, her back to me, for a moment; then I stepped over beside her, and she looked up at me questioningly. I put my hands on her waist, just over the swell of her hips, and turned her toward me. Then my arms moved around her, and I drew her to me. She neither resisted nor helped; her hips close to mine, she hung back from the waist, almost limply, looking up at me expressionlessly, arms hanging at her sides; in one hand, I noticed, she still held a bottle opener. "We are coming closer now," she murmured very quietly. "Soon it will begin, and you are frightened." After a moment I nodded. I was frightened—not panicked, but with a perfectly healthy fear, a realistic awareness of what was coming—and now Rosa nodded, too. "And I may be the last woman you'll have a chance to touch," she said then. "All right; I am frightened, too, now. Go ahead, Hugh," she whispered, "hold me, kiss me," and she lifted her arms to my neck, and drew herself tight to me. I kissed her, then, and she kissed me, hard, and we had a long, long moment in which everything else was blotted out and disappeared. I wondered if I were in love with her.

Then our arms relaxed, she drew back again, and we stood, eyes searching each other's face. I began to draw her toward me again, my breathing shallow and rapid, but Rosa stepped back, twisting out of my hands. "There must be no more trouble," she said, "not today. Go back to your engines, and wipe your face." Then she turned to the little sink, uncapped a bottle, and I walked back toward my engines, pulling a handkerchief from my hip pocket, and smiling; I felt fine, ready for whatever was going to happen.

It was much later, well after three o'clock, when Lauffnauer in the control tower with a sextant—he'd relieved Moreno for the past forty minutes—called down a sighting. Vic sat waiting at the little chart table in the forward compartment just beyond the control room, his instruments ready on the chart before him. Now he worked out our position, then called through the ship what we knew he would say. "We're there," he said, "or close enough, anyway." Moreno had the rudder wheel now, and called for quarter speed, and as I walked back toward the engines, he began heaving on the wheel, turning the sub's bow into the swell. Then we lay floating, maintaining our position on the vast gray-green surface of the Atlantic, and began to wait.

[133]

No one pretended now that he wasn't nervous. Moreno, in the tower again, checked our drift regularly, occasionally calling for a change in position, singing out the commands; then we'd maneuver the sub, getting her back into position. Over and again I inspected the batteries, checking the connections, checking the voltmeter; and twice Moreno turned over the bridge to Lauffnauer, and came below deck to fuss with his torpedoes. And all of us prowled the sub, below deck and on it, someone climbing up or down the ladder all the time. Now Linc came down from the deck; Vic was spelling him at the radio. As he stepped off the ladder I stood waiting to climb up; he winked at me as though we shared some very funny secret. We'd all of us been making frequent nervous little jokes, and as I climbed the ladder, and stepped out into the little tower beside Lauffnauer, I heard a burst of laughter from below.

We were riding high now, the decks above water. The sky, I saw, was clear, and the sun was warm on my face; except for a little easterly breeze it would have been hot. We lay riding the gentle swell, the choppiness and spray gone, the deck gratings drying, and I climbed out onto the deck. Smiling, Lauffnauer said, "Let us just stay here, Hugh, all of us, out at sea forever; there is nothing on the land for any sensible man."

"Suits me," I said, nodding; I knew what he meant. It was wonderful out here, level with the sea, almost a part of it—except for what we knew was coming.

Vic appeared now, relieved at the radio by Linc, Moreno at the rudder wheel below, and he climbed out onto the deck, and stood looking around the horizon, a real bearded submariner all in navy-blue. We had no formal lookout, beside the man in the tower. There was always someone up here now, and none of us spent more than a minute on deck without turning to study the southwest horizon. I wandered to the stern, and stood leaning on the cable railing looking off toward the almost invisible shore, and after a moment Vic joined me. I glanced up at him, and his eyes were happy. Quietly, he said, "I promised you adventure, Hugh, and now we're going to have it; no one in the world has ever done what we're going to. And whatever happens, even if I'm dead thirty minutes from now, it's worth it."

I nodded, and said, "Yeah." I wasn't really agreeing; it wasn't worth it to me if I died or went to prison for what we were about to do, but I didn't argue it.

Maybe five minutes later, Moreno relieved Lauffnauer in the tower, then called to me, and I turned. He was holding Linc's white British Chief's cap in his hands, fastening on the ornate gold-embroidered cap ornament. I came over, and he held it out to me. "Linc sent this up," he said. "Better start wearing it now," and I took it, and put it on; I was to wear it because it wouldn't fit Vic or Frank. It was the only scrap of actual uniform we had, but in our sweaters and navy-blue pants, Vic, Lauffnauer, and I looked like submarine personnel at sea anywhere.

Some twenty minutes later I was back at the engines, Vic was at the rudder wheel in the control room, Linc at his radio. Moreno was in the conning tower, Lauffnauer and Rosa on deck. Suddenly Linc's voice—raw with excitement—called through the ship. "I'm getting her!" he yelled. "Straight voice transmissions, loud and clear!"

Vic yelled—a wild and triumphant "Yahoo!" Then he shouted to Moreno. "Permission to leave the wheel, Ed! We can drift now!"

"Yeah, come on up!" Moreno shouted back, and I shut down the engines, then ran through the ship and clambered up the ladder.

They were clustered around the conning tower staring to the southwest. Then Moreno, binoculars raised, shouted loud enough for Linc to hear below, "Smoke on the starboard bow!" We stood motionless, staring, for a minute or more; I actually forgot to breathe, and had to inhale suddenly, a deep sighing breath. And then, there it was—just the tiniest unevenness, a faint alteration in the ruler-straight line of the southwest horizon, and I became aware of the steady pound of my heart in my chest. Through several long seconds we stood staring, and once again Linc called up excitedly; my eyes were narrowed, straining to see, then I blinked, and as my eyes opened again, the speck was perceptibly larger, and Moreno lowered his glasses. "That's it," he said quietly, and now we all moved, our heads turning to search one another's faces, and I don't think there was one of us who didn't wish that somehow we were anywhere but here.

"Transmitting steadily," Linc called up again, his voice quiet now. "Routine stuff only," he continued. "No code, and no scrambling." A moment later he said, "Receiving, too," also straight voice. "I'm preparing to send, Ed," he called, then repeated it, "Preparing to send." Standing staring at that tiny far-off ship, I knew Linc was twisting his dials slowly and carefully; he'd installed his radio so that it could transmit a weak signal only, detectable at no more than horizon distance. Now the distant smudge was the size of a thumbnail, and as we stood watching, it suddenly turned into a tiny ship, hull well up and moving fast; and I could feel that my face was flushed, and my neck swelling, as though it were gorged with blood that couldn't move through my veins fast enough.

As we watched, within minutes, no more than three or four, the tiny ship had swelled in size; and then suddenly it was no longer tiny, no longer distant, and I stood watching it acquire definition and color. We were in good position, I could see now; the ship, steady on her course, moving toward us at an angle that would bring her within perhaps six hundred yards of us in passing. The distance between us was steadily shrinking; clear and focused, she came ploughing through the sea, angling toward us. The incredibly long, tall black hull, the white superstructure, yellow cargo booms, and three enormous red stacks were vivid against the blue sky, and as I stood staring, the sun winked for an instant on the blur of gold at her prow that was, I knew, the string of great gilded letters which spelled *Queen Mary*. We were almost in sighting distance for her, I knew now, and I glanced up at Moreno. His binoculars raised again, he stood motionless, staring at her; then he dropped them, and yelled, "Send!" his voice exultant. "Okay, Linc; *send!*" he yelled again, and his face was dark and flushed, his eyes glittering. And now we stood, the rest of us, our eyes still on that huge ship growing and swelling through each passing second; but our heads were tilted, ears over the open hatch at Moreno's feet, listening for Linc's voice.

Eleven

H.M.S. SUBMARINE TRIDENT," he began in the quiet monotone radio operators always seem to use, "calling *Queen
Mary*. H.M.S. Submarine *Trident,* calling *Queen Mary.*" Speaking
slowly and with careful clarity, Linc's English accent was now very
pronounced. "Please reply with an extremely low-strength signal," he
continued. "We are on a secret mission in these waters. Repeat: please
reply with extremely low-strength signal. We are a British submarine on
secret mission here." He pronounced the last word *he-ah*. "We do not
wish our presence revealed; this is important. We urge that you call
your Captain before replying. Repeat: urge calling your Captain before
replying. H.M.S. Submarine *Trident* calling *Queen Mary*," he droned
on, never pausing, never giving them a chance to reply until the entire
contents and meaning of our message had been drilled into the mind of
the operator receiving it. For if he were to casually flash a reply using
the full strength of the liner's powerful transmitters, capable of being
received for many miles around us, there'd be nothing we could do
but dive immediately. Then we'd get out of sight if we could, and try
to sneak home, the whole scheme abandoned forever.

The enormous ship came steadily on, and now it dominated the
ocean, incredibly big. We could see its hundreds of portholes flashing in
the sun, and make out the long line of lifeboats in their davits, and
the great white bow wave at her towering prow, and I stood thinking
of the day I'd been aboard her. ". . . British submarine on secret
mission in these waters," Linc's voice droned on. "Do not reveal our
presence, please; reply with weakest possible signal. Request to speak
to Captain, please. Request Captain reply personally. This is H.M.S.

Trident, British submarine calling *Queen Mary.* We are a British submarine on—"

Suddenly another voice, metallically reproduced by the loud-speaker just below, interrupted Linc's monotone, and the fear flashed through me. Deep and level, every syllable hard and awesome with authority, the voice echoed loud and strange in our submarine. "This is the Captain of the *Mary.* This is the Captain of the *Queen Mary.* Who are you? What is your name and rank, please?"

"This is Commander Everett O. Cunningham, sir, R.N.," Linc replied immediately and very courteously, "commanding British submarine *Trident.*" Then Linc yelled up to us, and we knew he was either covering his microphone or had momentarily flicked it off. "Low-strength signal!" he shouted triumphantly. His voice instantly reverting to its former brisk and respectful formality, he continued. "We request help, sir. We are an experimental submarine, a new small type and newly commissioned, on a test run in these waters under Admiralty orders. Our main engine is broken down, sir. We need a part which we believe your engineers can supply. I urgently request permission to board, sir."

"Board!" The metallic static-laced voice was astounded. "You're asking me to *stop my ship,* Commander?" Pushing through the water toward us, growing ever more enormously long and tall, the great liner looked as though it could never stop growing in size.

"Yes, sir; I must, sir. I cannot overemphasize the importance of my mission, Captain—" and now Linc's voice had a note of irascible Royal Navy command and authority. "We *must* have help, and we must have it secretly from a British ship; we have been waiting on your course for three days, submerging at sight of all other ships. We are on Admiralty orders—" Linc's voice was crisp, very rapid now, and very British. "We will delay you no more than twenty minutes at most, I assure you. Request permission to board, sir! Or we will be obliged to abandon our mission, disclose our presence in American waters, and beg help from whoever will give it."

There was a long pause, the loud-speaker crackling and alive, and I stood actually holding my breath, remembering Moreno's words in the little house on Fire Island. In the face of a request like this, he had insisted quietly, the captain of absolutely any British ship in the world would be obliged to stop. *He'll have no choice,* Moreno had said, shrugging. *He'll stop; he'll damn well have to.*

And he did. There was a pause, then the Captain's voice, quiet but ominous, replied, "Very well, Commander, but you'd better know what you're doing. We will stop and render assistance if we can; but this will be reported, fully and in writing, to the Admiralty Office in Southampton as soon as we dock." Even as he spoke, I saw the great wave at the *Mary*'s bow begin to shrink, and as it slowly diminished another grew at the stern, and I knew the massive propellers—four of them, Vic had told me, each weighing tons, and three times taller than a man—were churning in reverse.

"Yes, sir," Linc was replying. "Of course, sir. And I'm very grateful. I request, if you will, sir, radio silence concerning our presence here. We do not wish to interfere with your normal transmissions, Captain. But if you will request your operators to refrain from mentioning our presence, and temporarily forbid scrambled ship-to-shore communications by passengers, who might inadvertently—"

"I have already done so, Commander," the voice in the speaker replied testily. "You've told me your mission is secret; more than once, I believe. Do you have a small boat? Can you board?"

"Yes, sir; we have a raft. Our engineering officer, his Chief, and a crewman will set out immediately."

"See that they do," said the Captain of the *Queen Mary,* having the last word, and taking no nonsense from the Royal Navy.

An instant later, and again we knew Linc had flicked off his speaker, he yelled, "Made it!" then he let out a howl of sheer animal exuberance, and we all grinned tightly; I glanced at Rosa, and her face was white, but she grinned, too, her eyes excited.

It takes time to stop a ship of nearly eighty-five thousand tons propelling itself through the water at perhaps thirty-five knots; you don't just put on the brakes as in an automobile, and for some time we could detect no least decrease in the *Mary*'s speed. Her course was angling her ever closer to us, though, and we didn't wait for her to stop. Lauffnauer was knifing through the lines that bound one of the rafts to the gratings just forward of the tower, and I turned, and clattered down the ladder for the paddles. When I came up again, the raft was inflated and floating just off the deck, Vic already in it, Lauffnauer on deck holding it. I handed them each a paddle, climbed in, then Lauffnauer jumped in, shoving us off, and we each began paddling as hard as we could, Lauffnauer steering with his paddle.

Now the *Mary* was visibly slowly losing way on a straight course, and we paddled to the northwest ahead of her, toward a point at which we judged she would stop. We were in good position; the distance between the two ships was shrinking steadily, and we had considerably less than a quarter mile to paddle. Now we could make out the black lines of her rigging against the sky ahead, and the swarming flecks of color which were thousands of passengers lining the rails to watch our approach.

There is an irresistible momentum about important human affairs; men take jobs, sign papers, commit crimes, get married, knowing sometimes that they should not, but going ahead through the foreordained actions and words as though powerless to take the simple steps that would prevent it. I could have capsized or punctured the raft, or dived overboard, but I did not and could not. It was too late, though I knew we were about to attempt the impossible. Then I stopped thinking about it, forced myself. It was too dangerous; you can paralyze yourself thinking too much about the dangers of what you know you've got to try.

We were only a hundred yards from the *Mary*'s side. Under any conditions an ocean liner is an awesome sight, but when you approach one in a small boat—a speck in the water beside her—she is enormous beyond belief. She towered over our tiny raft now, more and more with every stroke of our paddles; that black side rising up forever, the faces of the passengers a blur, they were so preposterously high above us. The length of her extended, so it seemed, from horizon to horizon, and she cut off the sky. There was nothing now but the black side of that ship before and above us; she filled the world.

She had her boarding ladder down and waiting—a flight of stairs, actually, angling up her side—and when we tied up to it, finally, we might have been standing at the base of a sheer black cliff. Vic finished tying up and I glanced at him and Lauffnauer, and knew they were afraid, as I was. Then Vic in the lead, Lauffnauer and I following, we began climbing up the side of that enormous ship.

Climb a fire escape up the face of a great apartment building, every window filled with faces staring down at you as you move, and you may understand a little of what I felt. It took several minutes—I began feeling the effort of it in my calves—to climb those hundreds of steps, and I could feel the eyes of thousands of people—the population of an entire town—on the back of my neck. Then we began angling past the rows and rows of portholes, some open and some closed, but most of them filled with silent faces staring out at us as we rose, climbing and climbing, up those stairs. I've never felt so powerless and helpless, and I made myself grin—tough and viciously, jutting my bearded chin out—and forced the feeling out of my mind. But it lay then, contracted to a knot, in the pit of my stomach. Then—I glanced at my watch—Vic stepped onto a deck, Lauffnauer and I following, and the fear was gone, left suddenly behind somewhere, and I was tautly alive, ready and alert. Vic was right—this was adventure, now it had begun, and I was ready for it.

A half dozen ship's officers, some in blues, some in whites, stood waiting, but they and the crowd of staring passengers and crew members just beyond them were only a vague background for the man, the Captain—six feet tall, wide shouldered, dressed in whites, his cap visor crusted with gold—who stood in their center. His face, lean and weathered, was grim; it would have been angry, if he had permitted it; and he glanced impatiently, inquiringly, from Vic to Lauffnauer, after only a flick of his eyes at my white British Chief's cap. "Well?" he said gruffly, then Vic—the smallest and least threatening of us, and the most ingratiating—spoke first.

He saluted, palm outward, British style, the Captain impatiently returned it, begrudging every second's delay, and Vic said briskly, "Lieutenant Follett, sir," in what seemed to me precisely the voice and intonation Linc had rehearsed him in. "And we're extremely grateful." He extended his hand, and the Captain shook it once, his mouth quirking impatiently.

"Are you an American?" he said, eyes narrowing; and my muscles tensed, ready to fight our way to the landing ladder if we had to.

But—I was astounded, and almost smiled—Vic grinned happily. "Yes, sir!" he said instantly, his voice and face apparently delighted. "I'm surprised you could still tell, sir; I've been in the Royal Navy just under four years now." I saw his eyes, and they were elated, and I knew it was no pretense; Vic was enjoying this. The Captain grunted in reply, and Vic leaned toward him. Lowering his voice, he said, "If we could speak to you privately, sir?" From the corner of his eyes, he glanced at the passengers crowding around us. "Our mission . . ." He paused, waiting respectfully, and after a moment the Captain swung to one of the officers, nodding at the ship's rail a few paces ahead.

"Clear a space for us," he said, then walked ahead to the rail. Speaking over his shoulder as we followed, he said, "Now, be quick about it, Lieutenant. I warn you; we move in twenty minutes, with you on board or off."

"Yes, sir," Vic said again, and stepped to the rail to lean on it beside the Captain. Lauffnauer stepped up to the other side of the

Captain, and I stood beside Vic. A half dozen crew members were politely urging passengers away, who obeyed quickly enough. Then, the half dozen officers standing in an irregular semicircle behind and beside us, the nearest passengers and crew members a good twenty feet away now, Vic spoke quietly. We were leaning on the rail staring at our sub, some four hundred yards out, her tiny length perpendicular to ours. "Captain, sir," Vic said, "it will save a good deal of time if we simply show you something, rather than try to explain it. But I should warn you; it will astound you, I promise; astound everyone aboard this ship. And I wish very much that you would again instruct your radio room, emphasizing that under no conditions are they to mention our presence, or what they are about to see. It is most secret."

With a quick irritated little shake of his head, the Captain swung to one of the officers just behind him. "Instruct the radio room to continue absolute silence about this submarine's presence," he said, "until ordered otherwise. Repeat that they are on secret mission, and are about to give me a demonstration of some sort. Silence about that, too. Maintain all normal transmission, however." We waited till the officer who had left returned from the radio room, then I made the irrevocable move that would turn every being aboard this ship into an enemy. Taking off my white cap, I moved it through the air several times in a slow arc, until I was certain that Moreno, watching through his glasses, must have seen me.

We were watching for it, and so we saw it first. But within seconds— I heard the gasps from the men around us—the Captain and his officers saw it, too: a sudden white line of foam flashing straight out from the nose of the sub, growing, lengthening with a terrible speed in a ruler-straight line toward the huge black side of the *Queen Mary*.

A torpedo moves astonishingly fast; far faster than most landsmen understand. And even this primitive 1918 torpedo shot through the four hundred yards of water between the sub and the side of this ship in seconds, its white wake flashing into ever greater length, like the trail of a low-flying jet. There was no time for the Captain of the *Mary* to react, beyond clutching the rail suddenly with both hands, before—his mouth open, his head moving as he helplessly followed that spurting white trail—it struck, far to the left, toward the prow, and we heard a great shuddering moan in the throats of the hundreds of people around us.

We saw the bright flash, the basketball-size puff of black smoke, and then heard the sound, no louder than and very much like the backfire of an automobile. Then I spoke, instantly, leaning across Vic to bring my lips very close to the ear of the staring man beside him. "It's a dummy, Captain," I said slowly and carefully as though speaking to a deaf man, but my voice was harsh and menacing, the politeness and pretense ended now. "It is a dummy torpedo with a small flash charge only. A dummy," I repeated once more, "and beyond a little scorched paint, no harm done to your ship at all."

His face was absolutely white with fury as he turned slowly toward me, and the men around us were crowding us, ready to grab us at a word or glance from the Captain. "I'll have you broken," he said very quietly but with utter rage, and he glanced at Vic and at Lauffnauer on his other side, to include them. "I'll have you broken and in a Naval prison from the day you land." Suddenly he shouted. "Are you *insane?*" he roared. "What in the bloody *hell* do you think you're doing!?" He swung to one of the men behind us, mouth opening to roar out an order, and now Lauffnauer reached out and grabbed his hand at the wrist.

For the first time aboard the *Mary,* then, precisely as planned, Frank Lauffnauer spoke, and it was his German accent as much as the words he spoke, that told the Captain instantly what we wanted him to know. "We are not a British submarine," he said, thrusting his face to within inches of the Captain's. "We are not English; we are in no navy at all. And that was the *only dummy torpedo we carried.*" I felt my skin chilling as the blood withdrew from it, for this was the moment, the single terrible test of everything we planned. If this tall white-uniformed man staring at Frank Lauffnauer's face rejected the lie Lauffnauer was offering him—if this enormous bluff failed—we'd be grabbed by a dozen hands within seconds, slugged to the deck, and spend years to come in an English prison, or be hanged.

"We carry twelve more torpedoes, Captain," Frank Lauffnauer was saying with a terrible intensity, "all of them live—full warheads! Four of them are in the tubes at this moment, aimed at your ship; and they cannot conceivably miss at this distance!" We had only two tubes, not four; five more torpedoes, not twelve; and every one of them, I knew, a dummy like the first; and I wasn't breathing, staring at Lauffnauer's strained face and blazing eyes. "The second and third salvos," he was saying, the words tumbling out, "can be loaded and fired before you can possibly get under way. Captain!"—the word was a cry, almost as though he were frantically begging the Captain to heed—"one dozen torpedoes fired into the side of your ship! Spaced along the entire hull!

And they are set for ten feet below your waterline!" He paused for a second, staring into the Captain's face; and I was astounded. I couldn't have done this, I knew, but Lauffnauer was acting his part with a terrible perfection. Staring at his anguished face, the muscles around his bearded mouth working, almost twitching, putting over the gigantic bluff on which everything depended, I almost believed him myself—actually felt a stab of horror in my stomach at the picture he was creating. Lowering his voice, the words husky and deep in his throat, Lauffnauer said quietly, "Will your ship sink then?" He shook his head slowly. "I do not know. Neither do you. Neither would the ship's own architects. It might. Twelve torpedoes into the side of your ship, below the waterline . . . and, Captain, the *Mary* might sink. Those torpedoes will be fired, Captain. They *will be fired*," he repeated, and if I hadn't known it was impossible, I would have believed this man, believed both his words and the agony in his face as he added, "unless you do precisely and implicitly what we tell you to do."

And now we waited, everyone on the deck beside us motionless and still, and I knew what was going through this man's mind. I knew, at least, what Lauffnauer and Moreno had insisted, and now I hungered to believe it. *There is only one possible way he can react,* Moreno had said, and Lauffnauer had nodded. *Only one action he can possibly permit himself. More important than his life, more important than any other consideration in the world—is the safety of that ship. Are you bluffing? He'll think of that; instantly. And maybe you are. Personally, he'd like to test it. Personally, he might risk his life at the snap of a finger to test it. But he simply won't dare to risk the* Queen Mary; *he can't. You might fire—you might! And to risk that just isn't a possible thing to do.*

I became aware that the Captain had spoken, and it took me an instant to get clear in my head what the words meant. "I don't believe you," he said quietly, and Frank, staring at him, did not reply. "I don't believe you," the Captain repeated sharply. "Sink this ship, you filthy bastards, and you sink with her!"

And then Frank nodded, and once more I was astounded; it was the resigned hopeless nod—to perfection!—of a condemned man. "Yes," he said quietly. "For if you refuse us, Captain, why, then as far as they are concerned—" he nodded toward the tiny sub floating on the swell a quarter mile away—"we might as well be dead. We are of no further use to them, and for them it is *better* that we die. Alive we are a menace to them, if we fail. But sunk with this ship, they can hope to escape.

We drew lots for this job, Captain." He nodded at Vic and me. "We are the three who lost."

For a moment the two men stared at each other. Then Frank, shoulders slumped, his voice dispirited and almost weary, said, "They will fire, Captain; nothing will stop them. It is part of the plan, and they will fire. *Look* at me, Captain! Look at my face and you will know that I am speaking the truth."

And in that moment—I had to keep from shaking my head in admiration of the simple perfection of Frank's performance—an enormous rush of relief welled up in me, and I knew we had succeeded. Lauffnauer and Moreno were right; to risk being mistaken, to risk this enormous ship lying helpless on the water before the torpedo tubes of the tiny submarine out there, was not a possible thing to do. This man knew that, and now so did I.

"You are a German?" he said tonelessly. It wasn't really a question, but Frank nodded.

"A former U-boat commander."

There was a moment when the Captain stood glancing around his ship almost idly: at the deck, the rails, the ship's boats in their davits —his direct responsibility, and one of the most awesome in the world. Then he looked back at Frank. "What do you want?" he said without expression, and from the men all around us I heard the sigh of held breaths gently exhaled.

Frank held up a hand, and I saw that it was trembling just a little; then it stopped. With his other hand he bent the little finger of the upheld hand down against the palm. "Radio transmission is to continue normally; you will see to that. So long as you sight no other ship, you will not say that you are stopped. If you are sighted, and any inquiry made, you will say that you are making an engine repair, and require no assistance. There will be no code messages, no scrambling. Your radio is being monitored aboard the submarine; any deviation from these instructions—" he shrugged—"and it is out of my hands, Captain; they may choose to fire."

He bent down a second finger. "The stern of your ship is under continual observation; you will not attempt to move." A third finger went down. "You will lower a motor launch and have it waiting at the side for us, its engine idling." His index finger folded against his palm. "If a ship appears, and in spite of your statement that you need no assistance, it actually changes course to approach, we are to be notified, and permitted to leave immediately. Those are the conditions,

Captain, or—and this is beyond our control—the torpedoes will begin."

"All right. And what do you propose to do?"

Lauffnauer's thumb dropped down across the folded fingers, and now the hand before the Captain's face was a fist, and he grinned. "We are going to rob the first-class passengers," he said.

I suppose a dozen things to say crowded through the Captain's mind; but his lips compressed to a thin line, and he said none of them. Now, after waiting a moment, watching the Captain's face, Vic spoke; and again, this was a part of our plan. Vic had a charm, when he chose to use it, a kind of grace, in both manner and voice, and during these moments we were smoothing the Captain's ruffled feathers; we wanted no least trouble we could avoid. Courteously, smiling pleasantly, Vic said, "Would you please have all first-class passengers requested, over your speaker system if you will, to assemble immediately in the main lounge. Have it done, please, quietly and courteously, with no least suggestion that there is any cause for alarm; simply say that the Captain has an announcement to make. And I think, sir, that the officer who leaves this group to make that announcement—" he paused momentarily, letting the pause emphasize what he went on to say—"should be a man you are quite certain will understand the pointlessness and danger of trying to warn the passengers or crew about us. Anything that risks harm to us should be avoided." Vic smiled charmingly and deprecatingly, almost in apology for having had to say anything that might possibly be thought offensive.

The officers around us, the only other men aboard the ship who understood what was happening, stood staring at us, their eyes narrowed, their lips tight. One of them in particular, a big man in blues, glanced continually from one to the other of us, his jaw muscles clenching and unclenching, his eyes like blue ice. Their bodies were tensed, ready to move at a single word or even a glance from the Captain. The Captain turned to one of them as Vic finished; he was an intelligent-faced man wearing British-type shell rim glasses, but he looked hard and very tough. The Captain looked at him for a moment, then nodded, and the man—reluctantly, his lips working; he hated to do it—turned and left, to carry out Vic's orders, and Lauffnauer went with him.

Vic murmured, as though it hardly needed to be said, "We will offer no rudeness, insult, or violence to your passengers, of course, Captain. We will be as courteous as we are allowed; we want no trouble. Now, please detail a seaman to get us five empty mail sacks, and take them to the Purser's office; just make it an order, with no explanation."

After a moment the Captain beckoned to a group of seamen who stood near the rail a dozen yards away, watching us curiously; they wore blue denims, heavy-knit sweaters, and dark-blue navy-style knit caps. The Captain pointed to one of them—a tall, blond, Scandinavian type—and the man walked over to him. "Yes, sir?" he said, and the Captain, voice gruff, told him to bring five empty mail sacks to the Purser's office, and leave them there, and the man saluted, and turned away.

Just over our heads, and at intervals all along the deck, we heard the sudden crackle of loud-speakers coming to life. There was the metallic sound, reproduced in the speakers, of a man clearing his throat. Then a voice sounded from all of the speakers simultaneously, and throughout the entire first-class section of the ship, I knew. "All first-class passengers," the voice said quietly, "are requested to assemble immediately in the main lounge; an announcement will be made there. All first-class passengers are requested to assemble—" The voice continued, but now it was almost lost in the sudden murmur, then the excited babble of the hundreds of passengers on the deck around us. They began to move then, slowly, sluggishly, through the various passageways leading into the ship; men standing politely aside to let women precede them, most of the passengers eyeing us curiously, a great many of them apprehensively. They must have been a baffled lot; these were the passengers who had seen us board, and then actually seen and heard the torpedo smash against the side of the ship. Yet it had done no harm, and we had continued to stand conversing, apparently, with the Captain himself, and a number of the ship's officers. Then, presently, they'd been quietly asked to assemble in the lounge. What they made of it, I didn't know; there were probably dozens of theories being debated. But we smiled and nodded as they looked at us, Vic even bowing a little, and I winked in as friendly and engaging a way as I could at a stout middle-aged woman who was staring at me. They didn't know what was happening; it was a sudden astonishing break in the expected routine of their voyage, and human curiosity being what it is, I knew that whatever else they felt, nothing could keep them from hurrying to the main lounge.

They flowed obediently into the ship, and a moment later Lauffnauer and the officer who had left with him came walking toward us, and silently rejoined the group. Vic said, "We'll go to the Purser's office now," and with absolute assurance that he would be followed, he stepped forward, and without glancing back said, "We will all go. No one is to leave the group, please, Captain." After a moment's hesitation, Vic already on his way, everyone followed, Frank and I bringing up the rear to make sure no one tried leaving.

Leading the way, Vic walked into the ship; he knew it, at least this portion of it, as well as the little knot of grim-faced officers trailing him. Inside, Frank left the group, and the rest of us wound our way in silence down the great main staircase. Frank was on his way to the radio room—Vic had shown him, using a printed diagram, where it was—and I knew by heart, now, what he'd say there. Over one of the ship's transmitters at low strength, he'd say, "Dog; D-o-g, Dog," which meant that everything was okay so far. He'd then say, "Bike; B-i-k-e, Bike," which meant we were about on the time schedule we'd anticipated. There were alternate words for other contingencies. We'd decided on code because it was the quickest way of conveying the information, shortening the time during which another ship might conceivably hear us; he'd be on the air no more than six or eight seconds. Even if he were overheard, it would mean nothing; and it protected us, additionally, from anyone on the ship tricking the sub by impersonating one of us. We'd picked Frank for this because his slight accent was simply one additional safeguard.

Now the rest of us were on the next lower deck, walking toward a waist-high wooden counter over which hung a sign reading PURSER. The other side of the counter was a small office space: desks, typewriters, filing cabinets, and two men and two girls working at the desks, all in blue uniform. They glanced up at us curiously, momentarily, then turned back to their work. Lying neatly folded on the counter, I saw now, lay a little stack of gray and blue sacks of heavy canvas, the top one imprinted with a blue crown, the words *Royal Mail* underneath it.

Our little group stopped a dozen yards from the counter; a few passengers were crossing the area, or coming out of the various corridors leading into it; all hurrying toward the main companionway, the enormous staircase that led up to the Promenade Deck and the main lounge, glancing at our little party as they passed. Vic turned to the Captain, and said, "When the last passengers are out of here, please have the Purser unlock all safe-deposit boxes—" He nodded toward a little steel-barred enclosure at the rear of the Purser's open office. Again the Captain looked at Vic, and his eyes were like steel; and again he said nothing. We stood there for a few moments near the center of the area, the two men and girls in the Purser's office glancing up at us from time to time, but continuing with their work. Frank came walking down the main companionway, nodding at Vic and me, then joined us. The area was empty of passengers now, but from one of the corridors we heard footsteps, moving fast, then a middle-aged man in tan slacks, a tweed coat, and a scarf at his neck, crossed the area, glancing at us to smile as he walked quickly toward the main companionway. Then he hurried up the stairs, the sound of his footsteps receding.

"All right," Vic said, "we'll go inside, please," and we all walked around to a door at the side of the Purser's office, Vic picking up the stack of empty mail sacks as we passed. Vic opened the door, and we followed him in, crowding the little office. The Purser—a man of about forty, in blues, two gold stripes on his sleeves—stood up from his desk as we walked in; the Captain told him to unlock the barred area, and then all of the safety-deposit boxes. He gave no explanation of the order, and after staring at the Captain for a moment, then glancing puzzledly around at the rest of us, the Purser took a ring of keys from his pocket and walked toward the little barred gate.

Inside it, Vic turned to one of the officers. "Take one of these mail sacks," he began, "hold it open, and stand here with—" But the Captain interrupted.

"No," he said, and he meant it. "They won't interfere; for the safety of the passengers and the ship. But they won't take part in your crime."

We could have forced the issue, and made him back down, of course; if he didn't dare risk his ship to prevent his passengers being robbed, he couldn't call our bluff over a triviality. But it was a triviality to us, too; and it gave the Captain a chance to stand up to us over a detail at least, and he deserved that much. Vic nodded instantly. "Yes, sir," he said, and opened one of the sacks, laying the others to one side on the floor.

The Purser began unlocking the boxes, one after another; they were the kind of long, slim, black-enameled boxes you see in a bank vault. Then Vic began pulling them out, handing them alternately to Lauff-nauer and me. After we'd searched the first box, Vic pushed a corner of the open mail sack into the empty space the box had occupied, then shoved the box back in, and the sack dangled there, hanging open.

A good many of the boxes were empty; the ship wasn't long out of port, and most passengers hadn't yet got around to depositing their valuables for the voyage. Other boxes, though, contained papers, documents, letters, photographs, jewelry, watches, currency, traveler's checks. One of them had a pair of baby shoes in amongst the other things; one contained an envelope stuffed with thousands of five-dollar United States postage stamps, we had no idea why; one had what looked like an ordinary handkerchief; three or four held small reels of eight- or sixteen-millimeter motion-picture film; several had bottles or boxes of pills, tablets, or colored liquids. All we did though, Frank and I, was pull out the currency, and toss it into the open sack, wasting no time on anything else, not even on the jewelry, some of which was spectacular. There was a diamond necklace which must have been worth a hundred thousand dollars; there was simply no doubt, seeing it sparkle and shimmer in Frank's hand as he tossed it back into the box, that it was real.

Over and over again—my arms actually began to feel the effort—we flipped open the black lids, pawed a hand through the contents of the box, pulled out the currency, dropped it into the sack, then flipped the lid closed, and returned the box to Vic, who'd slide it into its proper place. Most of the currency on this voyage from the United States to Europe was American; there were hardly any one-dollar bills, but there was everything else from fives, tens, and twenties to fifties, hundreds, and thousand-dollar bills. One box held a sheaf—in brand-new bills held together by a paper clip—of what must have been, though we didn't stop to count, twenty one-thousand-dollar bills.

There was Canadian currency, too, but we left that in the boxes. And there was a good deal of English money: pound notes bearing Queen Elizabeth's picture, and the big white five-pound English notes printed on one side only of sheets nearly as large as writing paper. We took all the English currency, and we took the French, which was almost entirely in long slim ten-thousand-franc notes. There was Italian currency, though not much, and a little of almost everything else—Danish, Swiss, Spanish, Dutch, German, and I don't know what all—none of which we took.

We took ten minutes, I suppose, to go through all those boxes, and the dangling mail sack was sagging when we finished, its bottom lumpy and beginning to round from the weight of what must have been ten or fifteen pounds of paper currency. I had to smile at the faces of the officers watching us; their mouths were grim, but their eyes were round with astonishment, like children's. Vic slammed the last box into place, then swung to the Purser. "All right," he said, and nodded toward a small polished-wood enclosure across the area here from the Purser's office; set into the enclosure were two barred windows, and above them a sign reading MIDLAND BANK. "Open it up," Vic said; the Purser glanced at the Captain, who nodded, and we all walked out and across to the little shipboard bank.

We spent less than two minutes inside it. The Purser unlocked the two cashier's drawers, and Frank scooped out the currency—mostly English, some American—which lay in neat wrapped bundles inside them. Then the Purser opened the small combination-lock wall safe, and as Vic held the sack open, I shoved into it from the safe what must have been a bushel-basketful of thick bundles of brand-new currency. Then, almost entirely in silence, we walked out toward the main companionway.

The little group who climbed it then, toward the Promenade Deck, was larger now; the Purser, his assistant, and the two uniformed women clerks were with us, at Vic's request to the Captain. We knew we couldn't hope to keep quiet indefinitely the knowledge of what was really happening aboard the *Queen Mary*, but it seemed only sensible to keep the secret as long as we could.

We climbed the great staircase in silence, passing a huge photograph of Queen Mary wearing a crown and ermine robe—Frank glanced up at it curiously—and walked across the cream-colored linoleum deck above. Then Vic, still in the lead, pushed open the double swinging doors that opened into the enormous lounge of the *Mary*.

Twelve

I WILL NEVER FORGET the sight of that enormous room as our group stopped just inside the doors. I'd seen this tremendous lounge, with its immense pillars and towering ceiling, its hundreds of tables and chairs and scores of settees and lounges, when it had been silent and nearly empty. Now the vast room was actually crowded. Standing, sitting, or moving slowly and with difficulty through the crowd, were hundreds of people, and the murmuring roar of their talk, the senseless hubbub of hundreds of voices—some of them rising angrily, some merely excited—was, for a moment, terrifying. The knowledge of our position—three men facing a floating, hostile city —washed over me suddenly, and I glanced at Vic, and at Frank, who had just rejoined us, to see how they were taking it.

Frank's face was wooden, staring into that crowded room; there was no telling what thoughts were moving through his mind. But Vic's eyes were darting, flashing with excitement, and his lips were actually curved in a faint smile. Staring at him momentarily, I knew he'd never been more alive; this was the biggest moment of his life.

Then I took a deep breath, and exhaled it slowly; forcing a calm on myself, closing off my thoughts and feelings to everything but what I had to do now. I was the biggest, the most impressive among us, and now it was my turn to act. I made myself step forward, and began edging past groups and clusters of people, squeezing between them, murmuring apologies. Men swung to stare at me, some wonderingly, some hostile; women stared curiously or excitedly, some of them fearfully; some smiled, and when they did I nodded in return, politely but gravely; the time for smiling was past.

I reached the center of the huge crowded room, and stopped beside a small table of polished wood, putting a hand on it, ready to climb up on it. Then a sudden intuitive idea sprang up in my mind, and I turned instead to a large davenport a step or so away. A young couple, a dark-haired man and a rather pretty woman, sat there, a newspaper lying between them. Inclining my head toward the woman in the suggestion of a polite bow, I said quietly, "Would you mind if I borrowed that newspaper, please?" Staring, she shook her head mutely, then handed me the paper, and I took it, thanking her, and turned to the little table. Taking my time, I carefully spread the paper on the polished top—covering it completely before I climbed up on it. A man who would protect the top of that table before he stepped on it, I knew, might still suggest menace, but not callousness or wanton brutality. He'd be listened to before anyone took action, and far across the room as I climbed onto the table and raised my hands, palms out and arms high, asking for silence, I saw Frank Lauffnauer grin in approval.

I don't think anyone who has never stood alone facing hundreds of people—hundreds more at his back—knowing he's got to persuade and intimidate them to his will, can understand how I felt. There was fear; this mob could drag me down and tear me apart. But overriding the fear—swelling up within me and dissolving it—was a tremendous calm exultation. My arms held high, the vast murmur of talk rapidly decreasing as people throughout the room turned and became aware of me, I was suddenly what I seemed—a big, wide-shouldered, bearded man; tough, competent, and dangerous. These people turning to stare up at me, their talk swiftly dying to a few scattered voices, were going to do what I told them to because I was going to make them.

"Ladies. Gentlemen," I said slowly, my voice deep and firm, audible, I knew, throughout the whole vast room. "A good many of you already know that I am from the submarine now lying off the starboard side of the *Queen Mary*. There is no point in trying to make you think I'm welcome here; a lot of you saw, and I'm sure all of you now know, that our submarine fired a torpedo which struck this ship. It was a dummy torpedo!" I raised my voice, overriding a beginning excited murmur. The murmur died abruptly, and I went on as before. "It carried a harmless flash charge only, and was fired as a warning. Now, let me assure everyone in this room—" again my voice rose—"every woman, every child, every elderly person, and everyone else for that matter—" once more I dropped my voice—"that no one is going to be hurt. No one is going to be harmed. No one is going to be molested, or even so much as spoken to rudely . . . *as long as you accept that warning."*

I stood silent for a moment, slowly turning on the table top, my eyes roving their silent, upturned faces, staring them down. Across the room Frank and Vic, I knew, were watching the exits, making sure no one tried to leave, though apparently no one even thought of it; they stood staring up at me. Very softly now, making them strain to hear, I resumed. "Any hotheads out there, and there are always a few; any wise guys, any heroes, any plain damn fools, listen to me now." Rapidly, matter-of-factly, I said, "The submarine beside this ship carries torpedoes, twelve of them. They are live, they carry full warheads, and there was only one dummy." Suddenly my voice rang through the room. *"Any trouble, any interference or resistance—"* I leaned toward the crowd at my feet, my voice dropping again—"and those torpedoes will be fired into the side of this ship, and they will sink it."

For a moment, bent forward at the waist, I continued to stare out at them; the room was absolutely silent. Then I stood upright to my full height, hooking my thumbs into my belt, and I smiled at them, pleasantly, cheerfully, absolutely calm and sure of myself. Again I turned slowly on the table to speak to them all. "Behave yourselves," I said conversationally, "do as you're told, and no torpedoes will be fired. We'll soon be off this ship, you'll resume your voyage, and have plenty to talk about at dinner tonight. Now, that's all for the moment, except one thing." Again I leaned forward, grinning down at them as evilly as I knew how, bearded chin outthrust. "The stupid ones among you, the little handful of damn fools who never know the truth till it kills them, might want to test me out. Wondering if the submarine out there—" I jerked my thumb over my shoulder—"really does carry torpedoes. And whether the men aboard will really fire them. To the rest of you, I say—stop any fools you may hear talking trouble from getting the rest of you killed. *You* know you're hearing the truth—" I gestured with my chin across the room to my right—"because there stands the Captain of this ship and his officers; and they are not contradicting me. They know I speak the truth; and they stand as they do to save your lives."

I gave them several long seconds—turning slowly on the table, meeting their eyes as they stared silently up at me—to take in what I'd said; to understand and accept it. Then, the moment a subdued murmur of talk began, I cut it off instantly by bringing my palms together, hard and loud, snapping them back to silent attention. "All right," I said quickly, and—I knew I could afford it now and that it was a good idea; calming the frightened, and saving face for the heroes —I spoke very courteously. "I have a request to make of you, please. It will be a great help to us if you will all occupy this side of the room." Raising my arm, I pointed to the port side of the ship. Then, continuing to hold my arm out, finger pointing commandingly, I resumed; rapidly now, getting them moving, giving them no time to do anything else. "Please hurry!" I said, raising my voice urgently. "We will appreciate it greatly! No one will be harmed or molested in any way! Hurry, please!"

They had begun to move, glancing slowly and doubtfully at each other first, then edging past or walking around furniture on the starboard side of the vast room. I saw men shrug in response to questions, and now a good many women were smiling, their faces excited. I kept talking, monotonously, hypnotically, supplying them uninterrupted leadership and command, keeping them in a pattern of compliance. "It will be a little crowded, I know, for which we are sorry. But we do need the other side of the room empty." They were flowing into the port side of the lounge now, those already there making room. "I suggest that women and elderly people be given the available seats; the younger men will stand, please." Someone tugged at my pants leg, and I glanced down. A short, stout, cheerful-looking man of middle age, wearing white slacks and a red sweater, stood looking up at me.

"What's it all about?" he said pleasantly, curiously.

"Nothing to get excited about," I answered, and gestured him on. I glanced over my shoulder; the room in back of me was nearly empty now. Before me the room was very crowded, people shifting about, finding places to sit or stand, then lifting their faces to stare up at me, waiting. Most of the women were seated, most of the men standing, very few admitting to being elderly by sitting down.

And now Frank and Vic stepped forward, walking toward me, and again I brought my hands together hard, palms cupped, the sound like a pistol shot. Instantly, before the babble had fully died, I was saying, "All right! We want your money, nothing else; the cash you have with you, and that's not worth getting killed about. You will file past this table as I motion you forward; until then, stand or sit where you are. There will be no moving about. As I signal you, you will step forward four or five at a time. We will take your money, and that will be all; no jewelry, only cash. I will be on this table watching all exits, and there are men posted outside each of them. Anyone trying to leave will be *hurt;* I guarantee that. Don't anyone try to be a hero. All right—" I gestured rapidly at a little knot of five or six people immediately before me: two men in business suits, two women and two men in casual sports clothes. "Step forward! Quickly now!"

After a moment's hesitation, glancing at each other—"Step forward, please! *Now!*" I shouted—they began walking toward me, the women worried, the men assuming forced nonchalant looks, as though to suggest they were coming forward only out of idle curiosity and of their own volition. Frank and Vic were beside my table now, facing each other about a yard apart, motioning the little group to file between them. They began to do so, the two men in business suits first. Instantly and moving very rapidly, Frank and Vic began searching them, in the procedure we'd agreed on long since. Their hands shot first into their inside coat pockets, then flashed down along their sides, feeling the outer coat pockets, then to the pants pockets, and in each case they found a wallet in the left hip pocket. If they hadn't, they'd have searched further, but these first men hadn't really had time to think of trying to hide their money. As Vic and Frank began the search, I hopped down from my table, turned to another one nearby, and picked up a heavy metal ash tray and a little stack of three or four books. With these I weighted an edge of the mail sack—the same sack, already partly filled, which we'd used in the Purser's office—to the table top, and it hung open, its bottom resting on the rug. Then I climbed back onto the table to stand facing the crowd.

Vic opened the first wallet, snatched the currency from it, dropping it into the open sack, then thrust his wallet back at the man, saying, "Walk forward, and stand clear back against the wall," already swinging to the next man. But he spoke pleasantly, smiling, and while the man frowned, he walked on between Frank and Vic, then across the empty half of the room to the opposite wall, to turn and stand, waiting. I felt a light sweat break out suddenly on my forehead, and my breath exhaled in a soundless sigh as though I'd been holding it. For this first man's action had been important; creating, we hoped, the beginning of a pattern of compliance and obedience, an atmosphere we felt these first-class passengers of the *Queen Mary* would welcome. It would become almost bad form, we hoped, to do anything but co-operate politely.

As Frank searched the second man, Vic swung to a man in sports clothes, coatless and wearing a snug-fitting sweater; and Vic went straight for his hip pocket, yanked out his wallet, and snatched out the paper money—English currency, I saw, as it dropped into the sack. Then, pleasantly, courteously, he gestured the man forward. Frank had finished with his man, and now these second two men walked on, as had the first, and a rush of enormous relief—the pattern was being established!—began to well up within me.

Then it stopped; from the corner of my eye I saw that the fourth man—Frank had just searched him—had not walked forward as instructed, and I knew that one of the two waiting women was his wife. We'd known this would happen, and as planned, they simply ignored him, allowing him to stand there making sure that no harm came to his wife. Swinging to the woman before him, Frank said, "Get out your own money, please, and avoid being searched," and the woman opened her palm to show a one-dollar bill. We had no way of knowing whether that was really all she carried or whether there was more hidden on her. But it was vital now not to interrupt for a moment the pattern of nonresistance—for the benefit of the watching hundreds still to be searched. At this point we were risking no trouble, and Frank instantly took her dollar bill, dropped it into the sack, motioning her on, and the waiting man stepped forward with her. The woman before Vic had pulled a wad of bills from the pocket of her blouse, and handed it to him; he thanked her politely, smiling charmingly. I swung to gesture the next group forward, and from then on time lost all meaning.

I consulted my watch regularly—Vic and Frank were working incredibly fast—but in between, I lost all sense of time, as they stood stripping the money from person after person after person; occasionally they'd find it concealed in money belts. There were middle-aged men, a lot of them; young men, though not so many; and a few really elderly ones. And there were women of every age. Frank or Vic simply smiled at the occasional elderly people, not searching them or even asking for money but motioning them immediately on, suggesting politely that they go sit down and not be worried or afraid. This was partly out of genuine consideration for them; I'd insisted on this, and so had Vic; but also because we didn't want to risk trouble we could avoid with any hotheaded younger men. Three or four times a couple came forward accompanied by children, and each time Vic would grin and wink at the kids, saying something like, "Now you'll have something to tell them about when you get back to school." We'd motion the mothers immediately on with the kids, not asking them for money, and in most cases the men handed their wallets over without being searched, anxious to move on with their families. They might have had most of their money hidden in a pocket, we knew; or their wives could have been carrying it, or even one of the children. But we were glad to get rid of them as quickly and quietly as possible.

The search went on. Every ten minutes I interrupted, and then, Frank and Vic alternating, one of them would hurry out to the radio room, lighting a cigarette on the way to catch a few drags. They'd contact Linc, rattle off their code words—a new set each time, which they'd memorized—then receive Linc's assurances that all was well at his end. Each time, they told me when they returned, the three or four men in the radio room tried to talk to them, but they simply shook their heads, without replying. Leaving the radio room, they'd check on the ship's boat waiting beside the *Mary,* and look around, glancing around the deck and down corridors, but the ship seemed quiet, they reported. They encountered ship's crewmen and officers, but these simply stared, not speaking.

In the lounge, the first mail sack, presently, was filled, and I jumped down, pulled the drawstrings closed, laid it on the thick rug beside the table, then hung up a second sack, and Frank and Vic began filling it. Our customers had gotten clever now, but we'd anticipated that, and after the first few dozen—those who'd stood directly under my eyes from the beginning—Frank and Vic began searching them even after they'd emptied their wallets. And they began finding money in pockets, the tops of socks, wadded into shirt fronts, pushed up into neckties, hidden under belts, in the sides of shoes, under collar bands, stuck into belt loops, jammed into shirt sleeves, held under arms, concealed in newspapers, magazines, books, cigarette packages and cases, wrapped in handkerchiefs, tucked under wrist-watch straps, and I glanced down at one man from my table—his face red and rigid, breathing hard through his nose—and told him to spit his money out into the sack, and he did so; a big wadded mouthful of green bills.

We passed up thousands of dollars in traveler's checks, a fortune in jewels, and, we felt certain, a considerable amount of perfectly good cash because we weren't able to search the women. No matter what threat we made, there'd have been trouble about that, and we knew money was walking past us stuffed into brassières, stocking tops, under girdles, and the like. Instead, we relied on guessing which women were concealing money, Frank or Vic glaring into their eyes to see if their glances wavered, or if they blushed; and a surprising number did blush guiltily as though they had no right to be hiding their own money. Looking tough and ruthless then, Frank or Vic would snarl, "All right, hand it over, or we'll search you for it right here in the middle of the room." Sometimes, then, they'd produce money from wherever they'd hidden it; but if a woman insisted she had none, there was nothing to do but motion her on, hoping not too many of the women still to be searched had seen or understood what was happening.

After a time I climbed down from my table, Vic and I trading places, to spell him for a while, and within minutes my fingers were black from handling money—American, English, and French; we took no other kind. Then we had our first trouble. A big man—about thirty years old, and well over six feet and two hundred pounds—stopped before Frank, arms hanging loose and ready. He wore a blue suit, blue button-down-collar shirt, and a dark blue tie. "Lay a finger on me," he said quietly, "and I'll break your jaw for you, torpedoes or no torpedoes." Instantly, his arm flashing, Frank had the man's shirt in his fist at the collar, fingers inside it and twisting hard so that the man's face suffused with blood, and he was choking, unable to talk. And in the same instant, his voice low and vicious, the words tumbling out, Frank was saying, "We'll knock you flat, and kick your ribs in, you son of a bitch," and the man's hands, rising to his neck, hesitated, then dropped, and Frank shoved him hard toward me as he let go. "Search the bastard," Frank growled, then turned his back to him, and began searching the next man. I searched the big man. His wallet, and it was thick with bills, was in his inside coat pocket, and as I emptied it he stood trembling with frustration and staring off past me, never meeting my eyes.

Five or six minutes later a second man, about forty years old, nodded at the woman beside him, and said quietly to me, "You touch my wife, and I'll kill you." Frank looked instantly up at the man's face, then said to me, "Let her alone." I found the man's wallet, and it had fifteen dollars in it, a ten and a five, and we both knew he'd given most of his money to his wife. But we had to let them go. The man meant what he'd said; he'd start action if we touched her, and then, threat or no threat, the room could flare into riot. He was a clever man; he saved his money; but there weren't many like him.

Once again Vic interrupted; it was time for another report to the sub. Frank walked out of the room, and I continued alone. Frank was back in five minutes; a passing freighter, Linc had told him, had just questioned the *Mary,* but the radio man replied that she was stopped for engine trouble, and required no assistance. The sub, low in the water, tower barely out, had apparently not been spotted. Then Vic climbed down to resume searching, Frank climbing to the table top to face the crowd.

We were about half finished now, both sides of the great room equally filled, a wide clear space in between the two groups, with us in the center of it. I was tired, feeling the strain. We'd been here nearly forty minutes now, and the second mail sack was nearly filled.

Monotonously the passengers filed between us, ten or twelve a minute. Nearly every one of them seemed to understand that there was nothing they could do but what they were doing. The simple presence of the ship's Captain across the room, silent and grim, arms folded across his chest, made it plain that he, the passengers, and the entire ship were helpless.

Long since, the rest of the ship had learned what was going on. We'd been aware of faces, seamen and officers, stopping outside on deck to peer through the heavy curtains into the lounge; and the first time it happened, I'd beckoned one of the ship's officers over to the table, and sent him out to explain what was happening, and tell them to keep clear. Twice passengers—and three or four times, stewards or other crew members—had come walking into the lounge to stop in their tracks and stare in astonishment. They were passengers, I supposed, who'd been asleep or in a shower or something of the sort, when the announcement to assemble in the lounge had been made; and crew members who'd been in other parts of the ship. Each time, standing on the table top, I'd smiled pleasantly, beckoning them to the table, then telling them to go over and speak to the Captain. We hadn't robbed those passengers; not knowing what was happening, they might have fought, so we let them go, knowing the Captain would explain.

The radio operators, too, knew what was going on now, Frank told us from the table top as Vic and I continued working. And by this time, we supposed, the entire ship's personnel and perhaps all other passengers knew; no one else had blundered into the lounge for the last half hour. Certainly the cabin- and tourist-class passengers must have been given some sort of explanation of why the ship was stopped.

I was sick of the sight of money, and sick of touching it, too, now. It had lost all meaning to me, and if it had been my decision, we'd have turned and left, and been satisfied; it was hard even to think any more. Twice I mechanically opened a wallet, and tossed money into the sack—once Italian, and once Spanish, I think—that we had no use for. I felt sorry for the people who had lost it; we'd simply throw it overboard eventually. But we couldn't take time to retrieve it from the sack; we'd been here a long time now and I was desperate to be finished and get off this ship; the strain was growing every minute, and it showed in Vic's face and Frank's now, and mine, too, I knew. We knew that the surprise of our assault on the *Queen Mary* was long since gone; that the Captain and his men had had plenty of time to think. We didn't know what they could possibly do; we believed there was nothing they could do; but we couldn't be certain. And standing here, mechanically stripping money from passenger after passenger, aware of the steady pound of my heart, I was afraid that at any instant the Captain would somehow understand he'd been bluffed, and that his voice would suddenly sound, ordering the men beside him to walk forward, and seize us. If he did, I wondered what I would feel; we were pirates—technically and actually. We could be hanged if caught, and probably would be, in London. Until we were back on the sub again, we were in terrible danger, and as minute after minute passed by, my fear of it grew.

We were perhaps three-quarters finished, about a hundred and fifty people between us and the moment we could turn and hurry out of this room, and now I longed for that moment as I've never longed for anything else. The very thought of it—of actually leaving this ship where we'd been forever now; and of getting out from under these hundreds of eyes—obsessed me. It was becoming unbearable, and I'd have given anything to turn and run from this room. For along with the ever-increasing fear and strain, something else had been growing. It was something I'd never before experienced in my life, and I hated it, the hatred growing each time it happened, and I simply didn't know how long I could go on taking it. It was the occasional look of pure contempt that looked out at me from the eyes of a man I was searching; and once in a while from the eyes of a woman. Each time it happened it was harder to accept.

Nearly always it came unexpectedly. From the beginning, the reactions of most of the men had followed a pattern of very little variation, and I was used to it. They'd stand before one of us, their faces set and angry, helpless and knowing it, and simply want the search over with, to be able to walk on. A few were frightened; a few curious, studying our faces; a few indignant and blustering. The women's reactions were more varied; like the men, some were wooden-faced and angry, some timid and a little frightened, some curious and staring. But in addition, a fair number of women seemed fascinated, and in various ways. Some, both young and middle-aged, were downright giggly, trying to talk to us, trying to prolong their moments of facing us, and obviously actually sorry to be obliged to walk on after only a few moments. But there was one girl—very close to being beautiful, clearly well brought up, and who may never before have felt like this in her life—who stood staring at me, and her eyes were on fire. Glancing into her eyes for a single moment, I knew I could have taken her arm and walked off to her cabin with her; that that was what she intensely wished could happen. And I knew, too, that it had nothing at all to do with me, but everything with what I was doing, and that she hated me for what she was feeling.

It happened again, a woman stood staring at me, her eyes so wide the iris was rimmed with white. She had a purse but there was no money in it, and when I handed it back to her, she whispered, "Search me; go ahead," staring at me as though she were hypnotized. I shook my head, motioning her on, and after a moment she walked slowly past me as though she were in a trance, and I hated what I was doing here, and wanted to run.

But the worst was the contempt, the occasional whiplash glances of icy scorn that humiliated me till I ground my teeth. A short, bald, haggard-faced man stood before me, motionless, his arms hanging at his sides, neither helping nor hindering me as my hands flashed over his pockets or into them. The clothes he wore had cost more than most people earn in several months' work. He wore jeweled cuff links, tie clip, and wrist watch, and the jewels were real. He had what must have been over two thousand dollars in his wallet. He was a wealthy man, and from a single glance at his face—lined, cruel, and rapacious as a vulture's—I knew with certain instinct that he had acquired his wealth ruthlessly, letting nothing stand in his way. Yanking the bills from his wallet, I was thinking, "This money doesn't really belong to him; he stole it, too." Then I handed back his wallet, my eyes met his, and I saw the look of pure contempt. He was a man who might have admired me for it, if I'd taken his money single-handedly; or if I'd cheated him out of it cleverly. Now, though, I was less than dirt to him, and it occurred to me suddenly, as though the words had been spoken and were sounding in my brain, "But it doesn't belong to me, either."

A tall, middle-aged man stopped before me, his wallet open in his hand, a sheaf of bills in the other. He tossed the currency into the open sack, then reached into his trouser pocket, brought out a small handful of change including pennies, and tossed that into the sack, too. "I haven't another cent," he said coldly, and held up his opened empty wallet. "Don't put your hands on me." For an instant we stared at each other, his eyes like blue ice; then my eyes dropped first, and I waved him on, my skin crawling under my clothes.

These people, Moreno and Lauffnauer had told me long ago sitting on the sand at Fire Island, were rich or close to it; or they had incomes twenty times bigger than the most I could ever hope to earn; otherwise they wouldn't have been here. We'd be taking only the cash they had on them, and they could all afford that, and easily, Frank and Moreno had said. No one would miss a meal or a Cadillac.

It had sounded obviously true. I'd believed it. Now I wasn't so sure. There'd been a man in a gray suit, wearing a vest with a gold watch chain stretched across it, and when I'd taken his money he'd said nothing, like most of the others, and passed on. But his eyes, as he moved past me, were sick, and for the first time it occurred to me that in robbing some of these people, I could be doing them a terrible harm.

He was the first, but there were others. There came one now, stepping up before me, a woman in her middle thirties, and unmarried, I somehow felt certain. She was frightened, she'd hung back till among the last, and she had her money in her hand, a roll of bills, and as I reached for it, her eyes went bleak. And I knew suddenly that this was a vacation trip she'd been saving years for, and that in my hand was all the money she had to spend on her trip. I glanced at Vic; he was busy, his hands running down the sides of a man's coat. Then I thrust the bills back into the woman's hands, and waved her on abruptly.

I understand very well how absurd this sounds; but nearly finished, only forty or fifty passengers still on the side of the room facing us, I suddenly understood that I was stealing. I suddenly understood that I was a thief. But of course that doesn't explain what I mean. Of course I'd known from the beginning that I was going to steal; and when you steal, you are a thief. Yet I hadn't really known that at all. Now I'd actually *done* it; was nearly finished, in fact. There on the thick rug of the *Queen Mary*'s lounge actually lay three gray-and-blue canvas sacks stuffed and lumpy with paper money. And behind me, their eyes on me, stood hundreds of living people from whom I'd helped steal it. I'd taken actual creased, soiled, and crisp new bills from leather wallets, from sweating hands, and from pockets whose cloth had brushed against my skin as my hand entered and left them; and my fingers were blackened from the dirt of those bills. There is a difference between knowing that stealing is wrong, and actually doing it; and the difference is enormous.

Let every man and women I had robbed *be* rich, I was understanding. Let every one of them be easily able to afford every cent we'd taken. And let each of them be utterly undeserving of the money we'd taken from them. It was still true—and the words spoke themselves in my brain again—the money still wasn't mine.

I wonder if most thieves, or at least far more of them than we may suspect, don't experience the emotions I felt, the first time they steal; I wonder if a considerable number of thieves don't have a moment of understanding and sorrow for what they have become?

There were no more than twenty-odd people facing us now, bunched together, most of the half of the great room in which they stood empty. And now Frank jumped down from the table, and carrying an empty mail sack, he began to search the nearly empty side of the room. Sweeping lounge and chair cushions to the floor, he'd shove his hand down back of the upholstery and move it swiftly along the back and sides. Nearly every time, the hand came out with a wad of bills, sometimes two or three. He lifted lamps to look into their bases, and pulled out money; lifted rug corners and brought out currency; looked under furniture, and took out more; shook out every book, magazine, and newspaper, and sheaves of bills dropped or fluttered from their pages. We'd expected this; it was bound to happen, and in a way it helped us. Frank moved quickly, crisscrossing the area, gathering money far faster than we'd done searching pockets for it. He found it easily; there simply weren't any very good places for hiding money, or if there were they didn't occur to us. Certainly he must have missed some, but he surely found most of it; he half filled his sack.

As Frank made his search, Vic and I continued ours. He beckoned at the little cluster of perhaps twenty-five people who were left, and half a dozen of them, men and women, walked forward as we finished with the last of the previous group. Then I turned to the new group, and once more—tiredly and automatically, estimating the time, only minutes now, until we could leave—began accepting the wallets and money that were held out to me, and searching the men. I didn't care any more whether the women were holding out money, and didn't try to find out. I didn't want to meet anyone's eyes any more, and I no longer even glanced at their faces. I looked at my watch; it was almost time once again to check the sub, and this time I wanted to go. I wanted to leave this room, I couldn't stand to be in it a moment longer, and gesturing at Vic, pointing to my watch, I turned, and actually ran from the lounge, out toward the radio room.

I reached it, burst into the room, and grabbed up the microphone, waiting for a moment while the man seated beside me, twisting a dial, lowered the signal strength. Seated behind him facing the opposite wall, and seated beside him, were two men wearing headsets and speaking quietly into microphones slung to their chests. I heard fragments of what they were saying, and as far as I could tell, this was normal ship's transmission. The walls of the room were solid radio equipment: dials, gauges, knobs, and wires which meant almost nothing to me.

The man beside me turned to nod up at me, and I said, "Deck; calling deck; please reply."

From a speaker set into the wall, Linc's voice said, "Abe; this is Abe. Go ahead."

"We're leaving," I said, "in less than ten minutes. How're things?"

"Okay, all well. Be glad to see you. How's it going?"

"Okay," I said hastily. "See you; signing off now. Deck signing off."

I ran out, toward the nearest starboard rail, and at the rail looked down. There beside our raft lay the little ship's boat tied to the foot of the ladder, its exhaust bubbling, a seaman at the foot of the ladder standing beside it, and I turned back into the ship. Inside, walking quickly back toward the lounge, I glanced around me. No one was in sight; all the corridors I could see and the big main companionway were empty and silent. There was a sound coming from the deck, apparently, on the port side of the ship. I recognized it, partially, as a sound associated in my mind with a regular, frequent, and normal shipboard activity of some sort; a steadily-sustained clacking sound a little like a Venetian blind moved by a breeze; or as though someone were dusting the blind with fairly regular rapid strokes. I knew the sound well enough, though I couldn't quite recognize at the moment what it was, and I dismissed it from my mind, and turned toward the lounge.

Thirteen

AYARD FROM THE DOOR I stopped, dead still in my tracks for an instant. Then I turned and ran, legs thrusting the deck away with all the strength of my thighs, as fast as I could possibly go, and burst out onto the portside deck so fast I had to fend myself off from the rail. The staccato clacking—I knew the sound now—was louder out here, and for an instant I couldn't locate it. The deck was nearly empty; here and there far down the immense length of the ship, a few figures, ship's crew, I supposed, lounged at the rails. Then I swung around, my back to the rail, head thrown back to stare up at the source of the sound. It was several decks above me, far beyond any hope of getting to it. Then I saw the searchlight-type lamp facing the sea, to the east, and the seaman beside it rapidly and steadily manipulating the clacking venetian-blind-like shutters which alternately covered and then revealed the face of the signal lamp. How long he'd been sending I didn't know, and it no longer mattered. I swung around, and actually leaning far over the rail, I stared out to sea, scanning the horizon; then I saw it. It was only a speck, a slight imperfection in the line dividing sea and sky. Then the speck lengthened, and narrowing my eyes I could see—either actually or in my mind—the never-to-be-mistaken sight of a destroyer, her bow wave white, heeling over in a fast racing turn. Then it shrank to a speck again, and I knew she was heading straight for us, and I pushed off from the rail, and ran into the ship.

You can think of a lot when you have to. I ran across the deck, and into the ship, and for the first half dozen strides I didn't know where I was going. I thought of getting to the radio, and warning the sub, but knew instantly that I mustn't. They'd take her under, I suddenly knew; Moreno would never wait for us; and I turned, running hard, toward the lounge. Even then, I had time to understand what had happened. The Captain had done it. Standing in the lounge with his officers, he'd instructed them all. And when I had sent one of them out to warn off others from entering the lounge, that officer had passed the word. Ever since that moment someone had manned that signal lamp, glasses on the horizon, waiting for a ship that could be signaled in the one silent way the submarine—with the whole bulk of the *Mary* between it and that ship—could not detect. I wondered if Moreno or Lauffnauer had thought of this possibility, and felt sure that they had, and were willing to risk it. Then—I thought of this, too—when I entered the lounge, I slowed to a walk.

I moved fast, but I was walking; for no one here knew yet what was happening. They might, within moments; at this instant, an officer, a seaman, or a group of them could be running through the ship, to burst into the lounge and shout out the news, and I knew there was not so much as a single second to lose. I walked in, but Vic knew from my face that something was wrong, and all I had to do was whisper, "Destroyer." He nodded, stooping instantly to the floor to snatch up two filled sacks, and thrust them into my arms. "Get into the boat, fast," he murmured. At one end of the empty side of the great room, Frank, still searching, had glanced up to watch us, and Vic stepped forward toward him as I turned toward the lounge exit—still walking, but moving fast—a money-stuffed mail sack under each arm. I didn't want this money, not any more; but I knew we had to walk out with it as planned, or the little knot of ship's officers, staring at me as I walked toward them, would sense something wrong, and surge forward to grab me.

Once out of the lounge, I ran—pounding across the inside deck, then leaping across the combing to the railed deckway outside, and swinging toward the ship's ladder that angled up, just past the railing, to the deck on which we'd boarded the ship. Tossing the sacks over the railing onto the ladder, I swarmed over the railing myself, scooping a sack up into each arm. The ladder was empty, slanting far down to the sea and the tiny launch at its foot, its exhaust muttering. Frank and Vic hadn't appeared—they might have been caught—and all I could do now was hurry down those hundreds of steps, my feet clattering. But the thick bulk of the sacks crowded me on the narrow ladder, catching and jamming against the rails beside me. I wanted to heave them over the side, and run, taking the stairs two at a time, but it would have been useless; I still had to wait for Vic and Frank. Then, perhaps two-thirds of the way down that long distance to the water, I heard the footsteps above me, clattering down after me, and Vic shouted to me to hurry. They were gaining on me, pounding down after me, then I heard voices—one or two, then suddenly scores of them shouting excitedly, and then a whole swelling babble, and I knew hundreds of passengers were pouring out onto the deck from the lounge.

The ladder was trembling now, from scores of feet pounding down it, and I knew we'd be caught, Frank and Vic bunched behind me, unless I found a way to hurry, to run as fast as the men who were after us. I heaved the two sacks around to the front of me, clasping them to my chest—packed tight with paper currency, they were bulky and very heavy—and now I couldn't see the steps before me, and I didn't dare risk a fall and a jam-up on these stairs. It simply did not occur to me that now I could heave the sacks overboard, and run, and the footsteps behind me—a lot of them now—were clattering down after us, moving very fast. Clutching my sacks to my chest and face, I ran, blindly, down the last dozen or so steps, tripped near the bottom and fell into the launch, seeing the astonished face of the seaman beside the launch staring down at me. Then, flat on my back, tangled up with the sacks, I saw Frank and Vic, each with a partially filled sack in one arm, jumping down after me, three steps at a time, a dozen ship's officers leaping down after them not twenty yards behind. Just ahead of Frank, Vic sprang into the boat, on top of me—I thought one of my ribs might have been smashed—and Frank heaved in his sack, yanked loose the line, and shoved off hard from the side, grabbing the tiller. The seaman at the foot of the ladder simply stood, open-mouthed and staring. But one of the officers actually jumped, splashing into the water, his outstretched hands grasping for our gunwales. But even as he sprang, Frank had a hand on the throttle and the motor was roaring, the stern digging deep, and the man's clawed hands scraped down the sides of the launch and then along it as we moved out from the side of the *Mary*. Struggling up from the bottom of the launch, I saw him flailing the water, shrinking in size as we shot forward; then hands were reaching, dragging him back onto the ladder, and I saw his white cap bobbing on the waves of our departure.

Vic and I untangling ourselves, Frank at the tiller, the throttle wide open, we steered straight for the sub, now three hundred yards ahead. For two or three seconds, getting up from the bottom of the launch, I tried to guess how far that destroyer had been from the *Mary* when I'd seen her; how fast she was moving; how much time had passed since then; when she would come bursting around the prow or stern of the *Mary*, and be on us; and how soon planes might arrive; but I simply didn't know. Then I tried to calculate how quickly we could be on the sub, and whether we could possibly hope to take her down before the destroyer shot past the *Mary* toward us; lobbing depth charges, maybe, if we were going under; firing with her deck guns; or even ramming us. And then I knew what we had to do.

We could not, I understood, as I sat up in the launch, lose even the half minute it would take us to unload the four sacks that lay with us in the boat, and tumble them down the sub's hatch. We simply did not have even the seconds it would take to bring this money with us. At least I told myself so; silently I insisted to myself that the money had to be abandoned to save our lives—and for no other reason. And that I couldn't say so to Vic or Frank because they wouldn't understand, as I did, the absolute necessity of saving the precious seconds that would be lost in bringing that money along. But I don't know that it was true; I wasn't sure even then, though I wouldn't say so to myself. True or not, I simply didn't want that money; not any more. The dirt of it was on my hands, my soul, and spirit, and the memory of how I'd felt in the lounge of the *Queen Mary* rose up strong. And then—I don't know how else to describe it—it burst and drained out of me, leaving me free again and almost happy for a single moment, in the knowledge that I could leave this money behind us, and that I was going to.

I glanced behind me toward the sub; we were less than a hundred yards from her, Frank already easing back the throttle, the stern lifting. Rosa and Moreno stood motionless on deck, staring at us, Linc climbing up out of the tower.

The growl of the engine was slowing then, the tiller in Frank's hand moving, and we were curving in toward the side of the submarine, Moreno leaning out from the rail to catch the prow. "Get out *fast!*" I yelled to Frank and Vic, "and I'll heave the sacks up to you!" They nodded quickly, then the launch's stern rose abruptly as the propeller reversed, Moreno's hand slapped onto the prow, and we were stopping, scraping the side of the launch, as Vic scrambled aboard the sub, Frank stumbling and lurching after him along the bottom of the launch. "Destroyer!" Vic was shouting. "After us! Get ready to dive! Dive!" Then Frank was scrabbling across the varnished hatch cover over the engine, and I moved right after him. He clambered up onto the sub's deck, and even before he could turn around I was on the deck with him, and still kneeling, I reached behind me with one foot, glancing over my shoulder, and found the launch's prow. Then I shoved—hard, with all the strength of my leg; the bow slid out from under Moreno's hand, and even as I sprang to my feet to turn and stare after it, the launch was a good two yards away, bobbing on the approaching waves of its own motion, then three yards and four, and still moving away, its propeller slowly turning, in reverse. I think Frank would have dived after it, but I grabbed him, shoving him hard into Vic and Moreno, yelling, "Get below, get below! We haven't *time,* damn you, we haven't got *time!*" The launch was a dozen yards away now, moving, stern first, in a shallow arc toward the *Mary*'s bow.

Frank shoved me away, his face absolutely white, and his eyes were wild, insane. His voice very low and quiet, he began, "*Du gottverdammt—*"

"I *saw* it!" I yelled, swinging toward the others. "I *saw* the destroyer —he didn't! And it'll *be* here—" I yelled so loud it strained my throat, and my voice broke and went husky. "Move!" I croaked. "We've got to dive, dive!" They came to life, like a stopped motion picture moving again, and we ran, even Frank—the money hopelessly gone—to the tower. I reached it first, swung a leg over into the tower, then simply dropped down the hatch, not even touching the ladder. Then I was on my feet, and as I raced through the sub back toward my engines, I heard the iron clatter of the others swarming down the ladder, then the clang of the hatch slamming shut.

It can take even a modern submarine with a trained and full crew many seconds to dive, and more long seconds to get any real depth between her and the surface; and as I ran I was picturing the destroyer, screws flashing at full speed, ripping through the surface of the water on the other side of the *Mary*. "Dive! Dive!" Moreno was shrieking, and I heard the periscope heaving up from the well. Then I was throwing the clutch, disconnecting the engines from the shaft, and connecting the motor. Running back toward my switchboard, I could hear the sub's air-intake valves clamping shut, then the heavy clatter of the hand levers opening the ballast-tank air vents.

There are two ways a submarine can dive. The ballast tanks only partly filled, the submarine still retaining a little buoyancy, it can nevertheless dive by the power of its motors. The screws revolving and the diving planes tilting, the sub forces itself under just as an airplane, tail surfaces and ailerons tilting, forces itself lower with the power of its engines. That's the slow way to dive; the submarine gliding forward as the water creeps up its tower, sinking ever lower for a considerable distance and time. But in a crash dive, the ballast tanks completely flooded as fast as the water will pour in, all buoyancy is destroyed. Even without the motors, the submarine will drop below the surface to sink to the bottom if nothing prevents it. Combine the two—use the motors and dive planes in addition—and you are crash-diving; both sinking and driving yourself under simultaneously.

Now, grabbing my switch handles, and slamming them closed, I was listening for the roar of the air vents from water gushing into the tanks through the open valves at the bottom, driving the air out through the top vents. My motor began turning, almost silently except for a steady high-pitched whine, and I felt the deck slanting under my feet, and heard the tanks filling; but not in the roaring gush I'd expected. I swung to stare into the control room just beside me. Linc was at the rudder wheel holding it steady, Vic and Frank heaving at the dive-plane wheels. Then Moreno at the periscope yelled, "Steady!" and Rosa, standing at the big Kingston levers, heaved them closed as Vic and Frank dropped their hands from the dive-rudder wheels. We weren't crash-diving at all; we were moving slowly forward at no more than three or four knots, the water level outside—I could picture it—creeping slowly up our sides. "What the hell are you doing!" I shouted at Moreno, but he didn't reply. Palms on the periscope handles, his face pressed into the eyepiece, he stood staring ahead at an angle to port, gradually lifting the periscope as the sub slowly slid under. Then he quickly walked the periscope through a hundred-and-twenty-degree arc, stared for a moment, and swung back again. He was watching the bow, then the stern of the *Mary* alternately, I understood. Now he stood upright, the periscope at full height, a good ten feet over the deck, and I knew we must be under, though how far the periscope projected above the water I couldn't tell; our depth gauge reacted slowly.

Beside him, eyes on the compass reflector, Linc sat at the big rudder wheel holding a steady course straight ahead, Vic and Lauffnauer beside him at the bow and stern rudder wheels. Rosa stood at the Kingston levers, her face pale, watching Moreno.

"There she is; at the stern!" Moreno yelled suddenly, and his periscope steadied at a port angle for a moment. Then he began walking it slowly around, turning gradually toward the stern of the sub. Following his movement I could picture the movement of the destroyer outside and above us as though I could see it, too. "U.S. destroyer," Moreno muttered, and I suddenly understood why we'd dived as we had, and I knew that we'd picked a good captain.

A destroyer can move faster and turn sharper than any other large ship, but still it can't make a right-angle turn. Moving at high speed, flashing around the *Mary*'s stern—perhaps sighting us, perhaps not—it was swinging, deck slanting, rudder hard over, heading toward where she knew we must be. But the arc of its turn was nevertheless wide, and was carrying it—as Moreno had understood it would have to—in a tight quarter-circle around toward our stern.

Abruptly he housed the periscope; we were a dozen feet under, though the depth gauge beside him was lagging behind; it showed only seven feet. How far ahead toward the *Mary* we'd moved, I could only guess. "Flood!" Moreno said. Rosa swung around to slam the big levers over, and now I heard the sea gush into the tanks and the underwater gurgle of the vents. "Bow and stern rudders, thirty degrees!" Moreno shouted; we heard the heavy clank and clatter of the diving mechanism, then the deck slanted, sharply this time, and Moreno's head swung to stare at the depth gauge. The destroyer placed now—watching her still in his mind's eye, I knew—Moreno was fighting for depth as we moved silently ahead under the ocean toward the huge sunken keel of the *Mary*, now, I was certain, no more than two hundred yards ahead.

I didn't know how deep the *Mary* lay; but I knew it could be forty feet or more. And if we didn't make that depth, if we didn't pass under her, we'd crash into her within two hundred yards, and have only a few frenzied chaotic moments left to live then. Yet I knew, standing motionless in the doorway, a hand braced on each side of it against the forward pull of the slanting sub, staring at the depth gauge, that Moreno had done the one precisely right thing to do.

He'd had to dive slowly, I understood; had had to find out where the destroyer was before we became blind. Yet he couldn't have waited on the surface; he had to begin his dive toward the *Mary;* she was our only hope of even temporary safety. If the destroyer reached us before we reached the *Mary*—and we could hear the throb of her propellers now—we'd be blasted from the water, or forever down into it; our pitted, half-destroyed hull couldn't withstand any kind of depth-charging. The depth gauge showed twenty feet now, then it crept to twenty-five. Turning to Linc, Moreno said quietly, "Rudder hard aport," and Linc began twisting the big metal wheel. Then, added to our forward slant was a sharp list to starboard, and Rosa stumbled momentarily. We were curving in toward the *Mary* as we approached her, curving toward her stern; then we heard the ping of the destroyer's asdic sounding through the sub as though it had struck the hull an actual physical blow.

Now, the ping sounding regularly, we were at thirty-five feet, the rudder still hard over, Moreno's eyes fixed unblinkingly on the compass reflector. At forty feet the ping of the asdic stopped abruptly, and I knew we were terribly close to the great sunken cliff of the *Queen Mary*'s vast hull. Our tiny submarine lost against that enormous underwater expanse of metal, the destroyer could no longer detect us, nor could she approach any closer without ramming the *Mary*. She had shut down her asdic, and now the thrash of her propellers was suddenly diminishing too, then it was gone. And I knew the destroyer—our course and position plotted—was heeling over as she turned to dash for the *Mary*'s bow or stern to intercept us on the other side.

For a moment I stood tensed and motionless, waiting for the terrible crash of our prow against the side of the *Mary*. Then I swung around and actually took a short step toward my switchboard. But I stopped, and turned slowly back to the control room instead. It was too late to stop or shut down the motors. We were about to crash or pass under; all any of us could do now was wait to see which.

"Rudder hard astarboard," Moreno said quietly—the depth gauge read forty-five feet—and again Linc heaved on the big wheel. A moment later the submarine began listing to port, and then we heard the awful sound, faint at first but swelling rapidly—the indescribable blend of humming, murmuring, growling sounds of the cityful of machinery that crowded whole sections of the *Mary*'s lower decks. We were directly beside them—feet away; their sounds, ever louder, passing through the *Mary*'s hull, through the water, and filling our little submarine. The sound grew to a chattering roar, swelled to a peak—we were about to crash if we were going to, within two, three, four seconds at most. Then, just barely perceptibly, it began to diminish, and I knew we were under—with how very few feet to spare I was glad I didn't know. For an instant Moreno's eyes flashed in triumph, and Linc swung around to grin at him, then at me, and I grinned back, but I felt the sweat on my face begin to cool.

"Level off!" Moreno said, eyes on the depth gauge which stood at fifty-five feet. Vic heaved on his wheel, and the forward end of the submarine rose, the deck coming level. "Quarter speed," Moreno said to me, and I turned to my board and reduced speed, the whine of the motor lowering in pitch. Then I leaned into the control room, glancing at Rosa who grinned at me tightly.

[173]

"Very close," she said to Moreno then. "And now what is our captain to do?" He didn't answer, and I stood motionless, listening intently. We didn't hear the destroyer's screws, and I hadn't expected we would. Moreno was maneuvering—it was a masterly performance; he could have brilliantly commanded a United States Navy submarine—in a series of S curves as tight as he could manage, to port and to starboard alternately. We were moving slowly ahead toward the *Mary*'s bow, passing under her regularly from one side to the other. Moreno listening and guiding himself, head cocked, by the alternately swelling then diminishing roar of sound from the great ship's hull, spoke his commands, and Linc heaved on the rudder wheel—starboard and port, starboard and port.

No more than any other ship can a submarine make a sharp turn, and I knew we must be passing out beyond first one side of the *Mary,* then the other. And yet not so much; the great ship just above us was immensely wide, and as Moreno stood listening to the vast chattering underwater growl of its machinery, he was calling his commands—Linc heaving instantly on the wheel in response—even before the sound swelled to a peak. So that, still in the momentum of one curve, we were heeling over for the next before the first was completed. The curves couldn't have been held tighter, and we were unapproachable, undetectable, so long as we remained where we were. The destroyer couldn't even risk a few depth charges for luck, on the off chance of damaging us; the *Mary*'s hull could be sprung, too, and we lay just underneath it.

Vic said, "What now, Ed? We'll be up to the bow pretty soon."

Absently, Moreno said, "Turn and go back the same way," then he looked at me. "How much power we got left?"

I glanced at my watch. We'd been under three minutes, and I said, "Fifteen minutes maybe; I can't really say. We'll know when the motors start slowing, and we better not be under the *Mary* when they do."

Lauffnauer said, "Ed, they will figure out what we're doing; they probably have already. Then the *Mary* will simply move off, and leave us sitting here, at just about the time we will have to surface."

Moreno nodded, slowly and thoughtfully. "That's right," he said. "You know it. And I know it." Then he jerked his thumb to point upward. "And so does the destroyer."

Then—it astonished me—Lauffnauer grinned, Vic and Linc staring at him, frowning, as I was. "Are you thinking as I am thinking?" Lauffnauer said softly.

"Hard astarboard," Moreno said to Linc, then grinned a little at Lauffnauer. "Sure," he said. "And so is the destroyer captain. If he isn't, we're finished, but I think he is. His radio's on, and he's talking to the *Mary*'s captain right now; I'll bet on it. And they're working it out. He'll get into position, lined up with the *Mary* maybe two hundred yards astern. Then, at a signal, the *Mary* moves off, as fast as she can make it, the destroyer moving ahead too, maintaining the distance, depth-charging as she goes. Lobbing them off from the sides, and rolling them off the stern, catching us for sure somewhere under the wake of the *Mary,* or forcing us out from the sides to pick us up with their asdic. Isn't that how you'd figure it?" He looked at Lauffnauer, who nodded, still smiling.

Once again the life-sound of the great ship swelled above us, then diminished, but now it was quieter and well astern, and we knew we were under the huge silent cargo holds, approaching the *Mary*'s bow. And now, Moreno calling the commands, Linc twisting the big metal wheel, we made a great figure eight under the *Queen Mary,* then began snaking along underneath her again, the underwater sound of the ship growing again as we moved slowly back toward her stern.

"Well?" I said angrily to Moreno then. "Why aren't we sailing out, then? We've got an exactly even chance that the destroyer'll be on the opposite side." I wasn't arguing exactly; I had a real respect for Moreno's captaincy, but I did want to know. "We might get pretty far out, before the destroyer—"

Moreno was shaking his head. "We could come up directly in her path, for all we know. And with the best of luck, a few hundred yards out from the side is the most we could make, and they'd pick us up with the asdic right away; we can't dive any deeper. We'd have to surface soon anyway. A hell of a fine plan that is; we'd be asking for it. Begging for it."

"All right!" I said. "But what other chance is there? Sit here, and wait to be depth-charged?"

"That's what they'll do, isn't it?" he said calmly, and I saw Lauffnauer turn to grin at me, his eyes amused. "They'll kill us, if they can, won't they?"

"Maybe." I shrugged. "I don't know. Maybe they won't depth-charge at all."

"*And maybe they will!*" Moreno shouted. "Who's commanding that destroyer! Some kid, maybe, some loot-commander; who the hell knows what he'll do? I'd depth-charge if I was him; force us up! He doesn't know what kind of death trap we're in; he thinks we're in a modern sub, a new type; that's what we told the *Mary!* Force us up, capture us; what else can he do? Sit up there, and let us sail away!"

I shrugged again. From the look on Moreno's face, he had something in mind, but I didn't know what it could be. "Still," I said, "what else can we do?"

Grinning at me, his voice almost gentle, Moreno said, "Why, we can just torpedo the bastard."

Fourteen

I STOOD STARING at him. "Torpedo him?" I said then.

"Sure," he said softly. Then deliberately misunderstanding me, as though I were merely questioning his strategy, he said, "I think I know what he's going to do. And if I do, I'll know where he is the moment I hear the *Mary*'s engines start; he'll be lined up behind her, two or three hundred yards astern. So once the *Mary* starts, out we go; off to the side, just like you said. Only then—" he grinned—"we curve back; toward the *Mary*'s stern, blowing our tanks as we go. We'll pop up heading right for the destroyer; a full broadside shot with two torpedoes ready to go. One of them will get him for sure. Right, Frank?"

"I will not miss," Lauffnauer said, nodding.

I hadn't moved; standing there looking into the control room, I was still staring at Moreno; then I looked at Vic who was watching me, and I saw the confirmation in his face. "The torpedoes are live?" I said gently to Moreno. "You didn't convert the others?"

"Starboard rudder," Moreno said, and Linc began heaving on the wheel again. Then Moreno looked at me. "Brittain," he said wearily, "you're a pretty good man in your way, but I said it from the start; you got to be ready to do anything necessary, at times; *anything*. But you're not; I know the type. There's things you'll do, and things you won't; a Boy Scout mentality! So we just didn't tell you, Lieutenant; sure the torpedoes are live! All but the first one; you saw me convert that." He grinned at me nastily. "Then I packed you off to town with Linc to get your converters—I was never too damn sure of him—while I fixed up the others live as hell! And if you hadn't asked Rosa along, I'd of sent her myself. You damn fool," he said quietly, "did you think we could bluff the *Queen Mary* with an empty gun?"

His voice soft and persuasive, Frank Lauffnauer said, "The Captain of the *Mary* fought through a war, Hugh; you can be sure of that. And when you have survived a war, you understand reality. Now he is placed in command of one of the largest ships of the world; what kind of judgment must such a man have? There is only one way to bluff such a man, Hugh, and that is not to be bluffing at all. Don't you see? We *had* to have live torpedoes! We had to mean what we said! Couldn't you tell? Couldn't you see it in my face and eyes as I spoke to him? Couldn't you hear it in my voice? The Captain of the *Mary* did! He believed me in the only way we could ever make him believe; because it was true. It *had* to be true because I had to *know* that it was true; so that listening to me, looking at me, the Captain of the *Queen Mary* would know it was true, too. There was no other way. No other way at all. Look that man in the eye and try to bluff him with dummy torpedoes, and we'd have been knocked to the deck before I was finished."

"You'd have torpedoed the *Queen Mary?*" It came out a whisper; I couldn't seem to control my voice, and I cleared my throat.

Moreno shrugged. "You're damn right," he said.

"And now you'd torpedo that destroyer?"

"I *will* torpedo it!" Fists on his hips, Moreno stood grinning at me, mocking me. Then again the tumbling roar of the *Mary*'s machinery, nearly overhead now, began to swell, and he said, "Port rudder," to Linc.

I glanced at Vic who was staring at me. "Vic," I said softly, "that's a Navy destroyer."

He bit his lip for a moment, glancing down at the deck. Then he shook his head, brows rising regretfully, and looked up at me again. "Out to get us, though, Hugh," he said, and I stared at him for a moment.

"Is this the big adventure then, Vic?" I said. "Is this what you've got boiling in your blood that makes you so much better than the poor suckers who just sit home looking for security? Why, you pitiful little bastard," I said softly. "You know what I think you've got in your blood."

I looked back at Moreno, at Lauffnauer, at the back of Linc's head, and then at Vic again, staring at the deck, and I remembered a true story I'd once heard, a joke. A man had come to work in a large prison, a new employee. On his first day he laid some cigarettes down somewhere, and they'd disappeared. Then he'd lost some money from his wallet, and finally, indignantly, he said, "Why, this place is full of thieves!" Staring at the men before me I was understanding that you don't go into a criminal venture—with anyone else but criminals. That's what these men were, no escaping it; criminals prepared to murder if they had to. It was true now, and had been from the start; and I was their partner.

"You can't," I said, staring into the control room, looking from one to another of them. "You just can't *do* it; you can't sink a Navy destroyer!" But Lauffnauer only smiled, pityingly; Linc didn't turn, and Vic didn't look up. Moreno simply turned away, contemptuously, listening as always to the once again swelling sound of the *Mary* above us.

"Hard to starboard," he said to Linc, and once more we heeled over, to continue our snakelike progress under the *Mary*'s keel.

Just beside me stood the little steel locker we'd last opened over ten days before; and now I turned, opened it, fumbled inside it, then brought out the cap I'd put there, my Navy cap with the insignia removed. "Cut out the corn," Vic said, his voice ugly, but I put the cap on, grinning at him meanly.

"Yeah," I said, "it's corn all right, that's all it is. So how come it bothers you, Vic?" Then I snarled it at them. "Call it anything you like, but I'll tell you bastards what it means; I won't let you sink that destroyer! I'll do anything I have to; *anything!* That suit you, Moreno? I'll do anything I have to now!"

We stood motionless then, muscles tensed, eyeing each other, and waiting. There were four of them, but I had this advantage; standing just outside the little control room, one hand on each side of the open doorway, they couldn't get at me except one at a time. And I knew what I was going to do while they did not; for it was something they'd never dream anyone would try.

Again the sound of the *Mary*'s machinery was swelling and growing overhead, but well behind us now; once more we were nearing the *Mary*'s bow. Moreno gave his command, and I turned my hands at the wrists, no longer leaning against the sides of the opening I stood at, but gripping the edges. Linc twisted the wheel, we heeled over once more, and I tugged with all the strength of my arms, yanking myself forward through the opening and leaping at the same time—springing into the control room, an arm reaching out for Lauffnauer. I caught him on the side of the neck with my open palm in a wide swinging motion, flinging him stumbling across the little deck into Moreno. Then I had a hand on the air valve, yanking hard, and the ballast tanks began blowing, the pressure of the air flowing into them, forcing open the Kingstons.

But of course—and I'd known this, hopelessly—there was really no chance that the tanks could even begin to empty before they were on me; except that Rosa had leaped, too. She was between me and the others, her back to me and facing them; a fighting fury in black. Kicking, gouging, her clawed hands raking at their faces in the crowded room, she fended them off, struggling and writhing to keep them from me and the air lever. Then Lauffnauer smashed her to the deck, and Moreno sprang—not swinging, but arms wide; and before I understood, he had them around me, just above the elbows, his hands gripped tight at my back, and I couldn't move my arms. I actually lifted him from his feet momentarily, swinging my body, trying to fling him off, but Lauffnauer was past us and shoving the air lever instantly, heaving open the air vents with the other hand, the water gushing into the tanks again. But nevertheless, air had replaced some of the water in the tanks and we'd begun to rise; and now as Lauffnauer reversed the process, checking our rise, we felt the jar—first the conning tower, then the sub tilting, the entire length of the submarine rising to crash against the giant hull of the *Mary,* and I heard Rosa cry out.

Then we were sprawled on the deck, all of us, tumbling and sliding helplessly across it as the sub tilted far to starboard, glass tinkling on metal, dust and cork insulation flying, the whole submarine ringing and vibrating with sound like the inside of a vast bell, and the lights went out. An instant later—I'd done my work well—the emergency lighting flashed on, and now we all of us lay where we'd sprawled, listening for our lives. For three, four, five terrible seconds the awful grinding crunching of the two metal hulls, one against the other, continued. Then it stopped as the submarine, tilting slowly to the horizontal again, began to sink.

Lauffnauer was on his knees, scrabbling across the deck, snatching up a wrench; then he was on his feet, his back to the air lever, wrench in hand ready for me if I tried again. Linc had his hands on the rudder wheel, pulling himself to the seat before it, the rest of us scrambling to our feet. They were facing me, ready now, and I grabbed Rosa by the arm, pulling her into the aft compartment, shoving her behind me, and again I stood in the doorway waiting. For a moment Moreno stood watching me, then his head swung, and he stood staring at the depth gauge. The vibrating needle, still dropping, was slowing; then it steadied and stopped at sixty feet, and Lauffnauer closed the tanks in the same moment Moreno yelled out the order. Linc working the wheel then, Moreno calling the commands, we began the figure eight that would reverse our course, and Vic turned and ran into the forward compartment.

There was nothing I could think of to do now, or even try; and I knew I had failed. We heard nothing, no sudden rush of black water; the submarine was on an even keel, and I knew we'd only nudged the *Mary,* slowly and almost gently, just as our rise had been checked, our port side against hers, scraping paint, jarring us, but with very little force. Vic stepped back into the control room, and said, "There are pressure leaks forward; several stuffing glands badly jarred, but the leaks are small. Probably the same back in his compartment—" He gestured at me.

Moreno nodded slowly, staring at me all the time. "You'd of killed us," he said to me. "Killed yourself along with us. Well—" he shook his head in a kind of scornful admiration—"I've said this before too, mister; you've got guts of a kind."

I just shook my head at him—slowly and stubbornly—and said it again. "You can't sink a Navy destroyer; you can't. Vic, damn you!" I yelled, and felt the cords of my neck spring out. "You *belonged* to the Navy that destroyer is part of! You still *do!* You're in the reserve, you're part of it yet! You probably know people on her!"

"Step in here, Hugh," Lauffnauer said softly, smiling at me—that familiar, wonderful smile; only his eyes were glittering, and they hated me now. "And I will smash in your head for you with this." He grinned again, raising the wrench in his hand, slowly beckoning with the other.

"And now you're tied up with Nazi scum," I said softly to Vic, my eyes holding his. "Working with him to sink a Navy destroyer. How low can you get; do you like your adventure now?" Then I yelled again: "How important is it to stay alive?" and Vic's teeth bared, and I knew he'd hate me forever. "Ed!" I yelled then. "Moreno! You were in the Navy, too!"

"Oh?" he said nastily. "You remembered that, did you? You finally remembered. Yeah, Lieutenant, I was in the Navy too; just as much as you were. No gold stripes, but I was in it, too." Linc glanced up at him, Moreno nodded, and once more Linc began twisting the rudder wheel. "But you're better than me just the same, aren't you, Lieutenant—" his eyes flicked past me, at Rosa standing beside and just behind me. "You always were, weren't you, from the day you were born? And in the Navy you had gold stripes to prove it. And now you've just proved it without them, haven't you?" Again his glance flicked to Rosa, then he suddenly shouted, his face flushing dark, the veins on his temples popping out. "Well, all *right,* by God! *What else can we do!* What would *you* do, you college gold-stripe son of a bitch! You tell me, brave boy! Because I've got everything you've got, and more!"

I grinned at him, narrow-eyed and mean; then I stepped over the combing into the control room, picked up my cap from the floor, and put it on again. "Do?" I said softly. "Why, I'd go out too, Moreno." Then I shouted it—"Straight out! Right through the back door the minute the *Mary* moves!" I stood staring at him for a moment, then I leaned toward him, and said softly, nastily, as infuriatingly as I knew how, "I've got the nerve to do it, and you know it. To do *anything necessary,* Moreno—to keep from murdering a Navy crew." I spit it out: "What about you, deckhand! How important is it to stay alive?"

"It's not important to me," Lincoln Langley said quietly, swinging around from his wheel. Then he gestured at Lauffnauer with his thumb, and nodded contemptuously at Vic. "Not nearly important enough to stay alive with those two by murdering better men. We took our chances getting into this, Ed," he said quietly. "I'd just as soon take them going out, too."

Moreno was staring at him, his face flushed dark, his eyes black and glittering. He glanced at me, then at Rosa, "Rudder aport," he said quietly, and Linc looked at him for a moment, then swung the wheel. Again the sub listed as it heeled, and Moreno stood, head cocked, listening intently to the growing murmur of the *Mary*'s machinery. "Starboard rudder," he said. Linc heaved on the wheel again, and the sub began righting. But before it could begin heeling again, Linc stopped the wheel in the same moment that Moreno yelled, "Dead ahead; straight rudder!" and for a moment they stared at each other, then both of them grinned.

"Yes, sir!" Linc said.

"What do you think you are doing?" Lauffnauer said quietly, but he knew the answer. The rudder straight at the moment the grumbling murmur overhead reached its peak, we were moving down the vast length of the *Queen Mary* directly under her keel, in a straight line toward her stern.

"Doing?" Moreno said. "Why, I'm getting us out of here; maybe. Just like the man said. He thinks it can be done; or he's willing to try it. And you heard what he said, Commander—" he glanced at me mockingly—"we can't sink a U.S. destroyer. It ain't cricket." Then his voice dropped. "Don't make trouble, Frank. You'll have Hugh and Rosa to take care of again; and now me and Linc, too. I think maybe even Vickie-boy will climb on the bandwagon, now."

Lauffnauer's mouth was opening to speak, then the sound overhead swelled suddenly to a giant rumbling roar, and Moreno shouted over it, "I'm in command! Stations, stations! Man the dive planes! Full motor, Hugh! Dive, dive, or we're finished!" For a single instant Vic and Lauffnauer stood staring, then Lauffnauer's wrench dropped from his hands, clattering on the deck, and they swung to their wheels as I turned to my switchboard, and brought the motors whining up to full speed.

The terrible roar of sound—the *Mary*'s giant turbines coming to sudden life, four enormous thirty-five-ton propellers ahead beginning to revolve—never stopped growing. Once at Niagara Falls I heard the flesh-shattering sound of a mighty volume of water in awful motion; now we were far closer, and now we were hearing it under the water itself. "Forty degrees! Forty degrees!" Moreno shouted; and already it was hard to hear him. The incredible roar of tons of tumbling water grew and swelled, increasing rapidly as we moved toward it and the *Mary*'s propellers chewed into it faster and faster; it was hard even to think. Slowly, slowly, the sub's bow dipped, the deck tilting under us, but a thousand rumbling express trains were moving toward us, the submarine filled with the roar, the very air we breathed writhing with sound, and I saw Moreno's lips move, his mouth open wide, but his shouted words were dissolved in the crushing roar of sound.

Standing at my board, watching my dials, I knew my motors were screaming, driving us under at the highest speed I dared feed into them, but I could detect no hint of it in that unspeakable volume of sound. The deck slanting under our feet like a roof now, I had to hang onto my board staring at my dials, and I wondered what was left in our batteries; wondered when I'd see an indicator sag down to zero, leaving us a powerless, drifting, undersea hulk.

For we were going straight through what was rushing toward us: the unimaginable turbulence created by four giant propellers pushing one of the biggest ships in the world through the water above us at a speed that was increasing to that of a cruising automobile. And now I admitted to myself that we couldn't go through it—we'd be like a needle trying to sail through the tumbling mass of water of a giant washing machine—and I turned to Rosa behind me, lurched toward her, and took her into my arms, my back braced against the control-room bulkhead. There was no need to stare at my switchboard; we either had the current we needed to drive us under, or we didn't, and I couldn't increase it, and didn't dare to decrease it. And we either had time or we did not to get below the enormous ball of writhing ocean under the *Mary*'s stern before it was upon us. If we didn't, it would toss and shake us to pieces; turn us end over end like a wisp of straw in a whirlpool, burst open and torn apart before we had time to know it was happening. And if we did get under it, our hull might still crush from the pressure.

It was approaching us now, sickeningly fast, the distorted sound of all the waterfalls of the world; there had never been such a roar. Rosa had her hands clapped to her ears, trembling and waiting; it was all any of us could do. There was no one of us who moved any longer; there was nothing more to be done. The ship was diving, as steeply as it could, as fast as possible—and moving, simultaneously, toward the undersea hurricane rushing at us.

And then we were in it. An unspeakable force shoved our stern down hard like a giant's footstep, the forward deck heaving, and we were tossed like dolls in a blanket—lifted from our feet, torn apart, flung in every direction. Instantly the lights went out, and the ship was being rolled and tossed from one side to the other like an insane pendulum, and it squealed and groaned and shuddered like an animal from prow to stern, objects flying and striking like hammer blows on the sides; and the ship clanged and vibrated, the sound of its own torture mingling with the immense astonishing roar above us, reverberating the air past endurance.

I knew we were past it, going under not through it, by the fact that we were alive; that, diving down, we must have skirted the very bottom edges of that massive ball of seething water. But whether we were sinking, the ship wounded mortally, there was no way I could tell. And the ship twisting, flinging itself about still, the tremendous roar still above us but receding, I pulled myself from where I'd been tossed, crawled across the leaping floor to my board, dragged myself upright before it, and hanging on with one hand in the darkness, I yanked at my switches, ending the terrible drain of power from our batteries.

Then Moreno had a flashlight on, shouting, "Blow all tanks, blow all tanks!" and in the sudden comparative silence I heard the liquid spurt of water under pressure jetting into the ship. Someone was heaving on the Kingston levers, and in that moment we heard the steady slow beat of the destroyer's propellers following in the wake of the turbulence above us. But—someone had the second flashlight on the dial—the depth gauge was dropping; I could see it from where I clung to my board. We were at a hundred and twenty-five, then a hundred and thirty, then a hundred and thirty-five feet deep as I watched, and we could none of us give a single thought to what was happening far overhead.

Then the air flasks were hissing, the tanks blowing; but slowly, sluggishly. And as I watched the gauge, it dropped to one-forty, then one-forty-five, and I swung to look for Rosa. In the faint gleam of the flashlights in the control room, I saw her lying flat on her back, arms outflung, eyes closed, and I could see that she was unconscious—or dead. Then I had to swing to my board, for again Moreno was shouting: "Fore and aft dive planes! Surface, surface! Forty degrees!" and I knew that in a moment he'd be calling for power. Lauffnauer shouted, then Vic, and even as Moreno swung toward me, I shoved home my switches, eyes darting over my needles, wondering if they'd flicker. The tanks had stopped blowing; they were as empty as we could get them, but we were not rising. The depth gauge again stood at a hundred and fifty-five feet, and I heard the sound of water, like a dozen pressure hoses, shooting into the sub all around me.

Then my needles were slowly and reluctantly lifting themselves, and I was twisting my dials with all of my being concentrated in my finger tips, nursing those motors to turn our screws through these last moments of waning power. They were turning—but slowly, slowly—and I swung to dart a glance at the depth gauge. It hung at a hundred and fifty-five feet still, no further lifting capacity to be had from the ballast tanks, and we didn't dare use power for the pumps.

And we weren't lifting. We hung suspended far under the ocean surface, water jetting steadily into the ship, and I knew we had to move upward—*now,* if we were ever going to—and I threw my rheostats to full power. The needles didn't move—and then they did. Very slowly, nearly imperceptibly, they lifted, the screws turned just a little faster, and then we were at a hundred and fifty, a hundred forty-five, a hundred and forty feet. As the pressure gripping the screws lessened, they turned steadily faster, and we continued to rise, rapidly now.

We broke the surface like a sodden log, and the instant we did, I cut power, and Moreno, crouched on the ladder under the hatch, broke open the conning-tower hatches, and I was running to the engine room. In the pitch darkness I threw in the clutch, engaging the engines on the shaft, Moreno shouting to me that the submarine was sinking, decks barely awash. But I had the diesels started, and as they rumbled into life we had forward motion, the diving planes lifting now, barely keeping us afloat.

We got the pumps running then, and with a portion of the hull out, ending the leaks in the upper third of the ship, we kept fairly even with the other leaks, and moved slowly ahead, toward the west and the shore eight or ten miles ahead.

No one spoke, or was capable of speaking. Suddenly there was nothing to do, and we simply stood where we happened to be—jaws hanging slack, eyes round, staring with the stupidity of animals at the circle of sky over our heads, feeling the air from the surface move down and touch our faces. All I felt was—not a wave of relief; no rush of exaltation—but an enormous apathy, a great physical weariness. One leg was throbbing, my pants were torn, and I stood, shoulders slumped, knees weak, holding to the conning-tower ladder; and I could have dropped to the deck, and fallen instantly to sleep. Huddled over the rudder wheel, Linc sat, his forehead on its upper rim, eyes closed, motionless; his shirt was ripped down the back, a long bloody gash on his dark skin. Lauffnauer was forward at the pumps, and Moreno stood at the Kingston levers, a thumb slowly rubbing the polished surface of one of the grips, the left side of his face raw and bruised. Vic sat on the deck under the depth gauge, forearms on his knees, head cradled on them. In the aft compartment Rosa moaned, and I made my head turn by an effort of will, and saw her sitting up on the deck, a hand swiping at her forehead. Then I was kneeling beside her and supporting her. "How are you?" I said, my voice tight in my throat.

"I am all right," she mumbled. "Where are we?"

"On the surface; we're out of it."

Moreno raised his head to look across at us, and a corner of his mouth lifted in a little grin. "Yeah," he said wonderingly, "we got through at that, didn't we? And he didn't depth-charge."

I nodded, helping Rosa to her feet, then I stood supporting her, dully thinking about it, and I knew what had happened. Passing over the boiling turbulence of the *Mary*'s beginning wake, the destroyer captain had dropped no charges, not directly downward, at least—because he couldn't. Until the *Mary* picked up speed, distributing the turbulence of her wake over a little distance, he could not count on the action of his depth-charge pressure settings. They could have exploded instantly in the complexities of pressure just below the surface of the massive whirlpool of the *Mary's* beginning motion—lifting the destroyer's own stern from the water. And it was in those first moments—the *Mary* barely under way, the giant propellers thrashing almost in one spot—that we had passed under them. Nor could his asdic detect us in those moments, through that incredible roaring boil of water.

Rosa gestured wearily, indicating that she was all right, and that I was to leave her alone, and I stepped forward into the control room.

"What's he doing now, Moreno?" I said, and he shrugged; he hardly cared just now, and neither did I, but he pushed himself forward and began climbing tiredly to the deck, and I followed. The circle of sky overhead was still blue, but on the surface it was dusk; on the far-off shore ahead, already invisible, I saw the first pinpricks of light. Then I turned and saw the *Mary*, still high on the sea, her stern broad and huge still, but already a mile or more off. There was no sign of the destroyer, and I said it again: "What's he doing, Moreno?"

"Figures we're a fast modern sub, maybe," he answered, his shoulder moving in a little shrug. "Able to keep up with the *Mary* for a while, and hanging under her as long as we can. Probably figures we can dive six or eight hundred feet—" he grinned, and shook his head at the idea—"and that we're diving at the same time. I don't know—" he shrugged again—"but he sure as hell wouldn't figure us to do what we did; he'd never figure we'd pop up far to the rear. He had to guess, that's all; he couldn't detect us under the *Mary,* he just knew we were there somewhere. He had to guess where we were, and what we were doing, and he guessed wrong. That happens; more often than not." We stood staring at the *Mary* then, shrinking steadily and rapidly, her hull dropping now, on the darkening horizon. "He could still get us," Moreno murmured. "Just turn around, and come back; we're a sitting duck." I nodded. It was true; there'd been a full twenty minutes, nearly ended now, in which the destroyer could have swung about, and found us easily, wallowing nearly helpless astern of the *Mary*. His radar might not have picked us up too easily, the sub just barely awash on the surface, our tower only a yard high. But it might have, too; radar can pick up a gasoline tin bobbing on the surface, under optimum conditions. I just didn't know. Nor did I know the effective range of a destroyer's radar, which is classified information; by the time we'd surfaced, the destroyer may have been too far away. But even without radar, he could have turned around and very soon seen us with his own eyes, and easily.

He didn't though. Lost somewhere in the small silhouette of that great stern far to the north and east now—or perhaps ripping through the water around the huge liner, guarding the ship and hunting us with her asdic—was the destroyer; we couldn't even see her. Undoubtedly her captain felt that his primary duty was to protect the *Mary;* in any case he stayed with her. We heard search planes, presently, but they'd arrived too late; it was full dark.

Steps sounded slowly on the iron rungs just below us, then Rosa's head appeared at our feet. Moreno stooped to help her up, and I climbed out of the tower onto the deck to make room for her.

Linc stayed at his wheel, and Moreno remained in the tower with Rosa; I was quite certain neither Vic nor Lauffnauer would join us on deck. The deck was almost awash, just barely over the surface, and wet, and I stood there beside the tower staring ahead. It was very dark now, with no moon, and I couldn't tell, not certainly, whether we were gradually sinking lower in the water. I felt sure we were, though; the sub was leaking in a score or more of places. But the pumps were working, too, the water gaining only slowly, and I knew we were going to make it. With no moon, the search planes didn't worry us, and while I didn't know how soon Navy and Coast Guard ships could reach this particular area to join the search for us, I didn't think it could be any sooner than we could leave it. For the time being, at least, we were safe, though somehow I hardly cared; the enormous sense of relief that washed through me suddenly, was about something else entirely. We did not have the money we'd set out to steal, and now standing in the darkness beside the little conning tower, staring silently ahead, as were Rosa and Moreno, I knew I'd escaped something dirty that would have spoiled and corrupted my life forever.

The big adventure had turned into something rotten, and I turned to glance at Moreno in the darkness beside me; would he actually have fired those torpedoes at the *Mary,* if it came right down to it? Maybe not, I thought, looking at his tough bearded face. Maybe he wouldn't have, no matter what he thinks himself. I'm going to decide that he wouldn't have, I told myself; but I knew that Lauffnauer and Vic believed that he would. And telling myself now that Linc, Rosa, and I didn't know the torpedoes were live only made it worse for me. I'd been right along with the others, and if those torpedoes had been fired, I'd have been as dirty and smeared and guilty as they'd have been— without even the sense to know it. I shook my head slowly in the darkness. That's what I'd escaped from, and the enormous sense of relief was still with me; but I'd been in this right up to my neck with people like Lauffnauer and Vic, and I didn't like thinking about it.

Then I smiled. The things I'd once talked and worried about—freedom, living my own life—suddenly seemed a little unreal now. Or at least incomplete. Rebellion, resistance, not accepting everything that's set before you—they're fine, they're okay, I thought. But there had to be something more in back of them than simple selfishness, and now I knew it, and began to feel a little peace, and at some sort of reasonable terms with life. Then I climbed below, squeezing past Rosa and Moreno, to check my engines.

Watching the lights of the Inn at Point O' Woods, ahead to the east and well to the south, occasionally calling a command down to Linc at the wheel, Moreno brought us in, a mile off shore opposite the little rented house on the beach at Fire Island. I was on deck again, and as Moreno climbed out of the tower then to begin untying our raft, I climbed down inside. "We're here," I said to Linc at the rudder wheel, and he nodded and stood up. Lauffnauer and Vic standing near the periscope said nothing, and I didn't even glance at them; but as I walked aft toward the engine, I heard steps climbing the ladder. I shut down the engine then, and ran back toward the control room. The pumps stopped, I was in a hurry now, and I saw that Linc and Vic were gone. But Lauffnauer sat on the little padded seat before the periscope, and for an instant I thought he meant to stay there as his captain once had. Then I saw that he was writing—a large book, the ship's log, open on his knees. As I reached the ladder, he looked up, not at me, but staring off at nothing.

"*Kaput,*" he said softly, then closed the log and tossed it to the deck. I climbed up then, and out of the tower onto the deck, Lauffnauer following. Then, once more, just as he had forty years before, Lauffnauer slammed the hatch shut behind him.

Moreno had the raft inflated and waiting, and Linc had brought up the paddles. Now we crowded into it, Moreno steering in the stern, Linc forward with the other paddle, and moved carefully away, the sides of the overloaded raft only an inch or so above surface. We didn't bother anchoring the little sub; her engine off, her pumps stopped, she was dead and sinking, and we wanted to be well away when she went under. A good fifty feet off we stopped, and sat watching her. Already her deck was two feet under, only the tiny conning tower above the surface. I saw that a swatch of the new paint had been scraped from it when she'd nudged the underside of the *Mary;* and in the faint beginning starlight a part of the old paint underneath it was visible again. I couldn't see all of it, or even actually read it in that light, but I knew what it said: *U-19*. Then, the last remnant of the little ship's diminishing buoyancy abruptly going, the faded white letters slipped down into the sea, and we left the *U-19*—to rest there forever now—where her first crew had left her half a lifetime before.

Fifteen

WE DIDN'T EVEN SAY GOODBYE—not all of us, anyway. In the little house behind the beach, I walked directly to the bathroom, and—first trimming my beard as closely as possible with scissors—I shaved as quickly as I could. Watching my face in the mirror, I smiled a little. We'd been going to divide perhaps a million and a half dollars here, Linc taking his share in English pound notes, the rest of us taking ours in American and whatever English was left; Lauffnauer was to take the French currency, if it amounted to ten thousand dollars or more; if not, we'd have jettisoned it. We'd have stayed hidden here in the house for a week, only Rosa and Moreno showing themselves on the beach. Then, shaved and wearing the city clothes Moreno had brought here over a week before, we'd have left with our money one or two at a time, after dark, and on a crowded weekend. Instead, I stood here, back where it had all started, and I was very nearly broke; to be caught soon, perhaps, and imprisoned, maybe even hanged. Yet I knew now that I preferred it this way.

I wasn't staying now, either. In the bathroom I changed into my blue suit, a tie, white shirt, low shoes, and a felt hat, and when I came out Linc was sitting on the old davenport, forearms on his knees, hands clasped before him, staring down at the floor. Vic sat bent over the dining-room table, forehead cradled on his folded arms, and Lauffnauer stood at a front window staring out to sea. I didn't see Rosa or Moreno. "So long, Linc," I said, and he glanced up to smile wanly. "So long, Hugh," he said, and I walked out then, without a word or glance for Lauffnauer or Vic.

As I stepped onto the porch, Rosa stood on the sand at the foot of the front steps, Moreno on his knees beside her at the deflated raft, rolling it up, and they looked up at me. For a moment, pausing at the head of the stairs, I stood looking down at them in the yellow light from the front windows—looking at the handsome woman in the black slacks and sweater whom I knew I was in love with. Then I walked down the stairs. "Rosa," I said, "I want to see you again. I want to see you a very great deal."

For a moment she stared at me, then looked down at Moreno beside her; Moreno knelt there motionless, staring up at me. "Maybe," Rosa said then, turning to look at me, then once more she looked down at Moreno. "I don't know," she said then. "Right now, I just don't know, but . . . perhaps."

Moreno was getting to his feet, his eyes never leaving my face, and his lips were drawing back from his teeth in the beginning of a snarl. "I'm going to get her, Moreno, if I can," I said, staring into his eyes; then I smiled suddenly, and held out my hand. "So long, Ed," I said gently.

He glanced at my hand, glanced up at my face, then took my hand. "So long, Lieutenant," he said, mockingly as always, but his voice, now, was affectionate, and he grinned at me.

I was maybe a quarter mile up the beach walking toward the ferry in silence, except for the regular slow crash of the surf on the beach beside me, and the crunch of my footsteps in between—when I heard the sound. It was far off, far to the north and east, and only just barely audible: the deep-chested, rumbling, foghorn growl of an enormous ship. It might not have been the *Queen Mary*'s; it could have been another ship, I suppose. But the horn of a ship like the *Mary* can be heard for miles at sea, and it could have been hers; it just might have been. I think that it was.